I'm Back!

By

John Bobin

It is 2094. A genetically
modified robot falls in love
with an artificially reincarnated man.
What could possibly go wrong?

Copyright © 2020 John Bobin.

All rights reserved.

This book is a work of fiction. Names, characters, places, and incidents are products of the writer's imagination or have been used fictitiously and are not to be construed as real. Any resemblance to persons, living or dead, actual events, locales or organisations is entirely coincidental.

ISBN: 9798679126428

Imprint: Independently published

Dramatis Personae (and more)

6D: The best way to enjoy films, TV, and virtual reality in 2094

Adam Thurley: A specialist at the World Reincarnation Organisation (WRO)

Adam Vincent: The man who invented a Teleportation filter which detects flies

Aerobus: A much more modern version of a helicopter

Agneta Abramsen: The first COO of the WRO

Alec I. Lykit: A vital signs inspector at the WRO

Alice Springs: The first love of Ian Tudeep (AKA Alice Nuisance)

Anne Telope: A friend at Ian's primary school (later Sister Angelina the Jolly)

aPad: A landing place for an aerobus

AR: Artificial reincarnation

A. Scapegoat: A man who takes the blame for a WRO problem

ASP: A top secret government committee (Absolutely Secret Projects)

Beryl Henderson: Ian Tudeep's first wife

Billy Turnbull: A spirit extraction operator at the WRO

Bob Zyaruncle: The man who discovered the emotion genome

Brando Marlon: Ian Tudeep' ex-wife's new toy boy

Breastomatic Astrosponge: The material of which Susie Q's breasts are made

Brenda Thackary: Bruce Thackeray's wife

Bret Allover-Oncemore: Health and Safety and Compliance Director (WRO)

Bruce Thackary: A DCI in the East Anglian Police Force

Chopperator: A household refuse disposal system

Christalee-Petal: Brando Marlon's new girlfriend

Condenselow: A compact, one storey living space similar to a bungalow

Dean James: A library assistant

Dogbots: Realistic robotic canine friends

Eddie Biggs: Rita Loza's larger than life friend

Eeeny, Meeny, Miny and Moe: Eddie Biggs' four dogs

Electrajot: A much more modern version of a Smart Phone

Eleversor: A high speed lift with a force field instead of walls

Emma Bobby: A DCI in the East Anglian Police Force

Emily Nice-To-Meet-You: A WRO nurse

Enid Brighton: The alias of Susie OAT236

Frank Pilgrim (Mr. and Mrs.): Guest house owners in the Gower

Freda Springs: Alice Springs' mother

Gerald Hoffer: The Prime Minister of the UK

Hiram Prendergast: The new CEO of the WRO

Holovision: A much more modern version of TV, incorporating holograms

Honey Blonde: A bosomy newscaster

Ian Tudeep: The first Artificial Reincarnation patient

Ida Tudeep: Ian's deceased sister

I. M. A. Nosey-Parker: An inquisitive neighbour of Alice Nuisance's

Immersephone: Like a landline but with inbuilt 'being there'

Ivy Creeping: Another inquisitive neighbour of Alice Nuisance's

Jess Honly-Temporary: The interim CEO of the WRO

Jim Sutcliffe: Rita Loza's first husband

Julie Noted: A WRO Nurse

Karl Yoder: A WRO specialist

Kursaal Jones: A property developer from Southend

Leif Aggen: The first CEO of the WRO

May Brian: An astrophysicist

Mechanical Amygdala (MA): An artificial amygdala

Mirabelle Hoffer: Gerald Hoffer's wife

Mitch Springs: Alice Springs' father

Molly John: A Police Constable in the East Anglian Police Force

National Deselection Force (NDF): 'Deselects' people at the age of 50

Paul Somebody: A popular newscaster

Population Police (PP): The PP collect people for 'deselection' by the NDF

Ralph (Tosser) Pancake: A former WRO robotics technician

Richard Small: The previous owner of the body used for Ian Tudeep's AR

Rita Loza: A friend of Eddie Biggs and Alice Springs (AKA Alice Nuisance)

Sally Forth: Eddie Biggs' girlfriend (later Sally Biggs)

Sheepbots: Realistic robotic sheep

Sister Angelina the Jolly: A nun in The Order of Murphy (AKA Anne Telope)

Sister Beverley: Another nun in The Order of Murphy

Sister Matic: Yet another nun in The Order of Murphy

Stacked Condenselows: Several condenselows snapped one on top of another

Susie AI10009: One of the Susie robots used by the WRO

Susie AI10039: Another one of the Susie robots used by the WRO

Susie OAT236: An earlier Susie now owned by One Amour Time

Susie Q: Our heroine, who is also a robot

Ted Springs: Alice Springs' father

Tim Tiny: A WBC newscaster

Tom Anick: Mike Anick's brother, a Cabinet Minister of the UK government

Walter Nuisance: Alice Springs' first husband

Wilbur Tudeep: Ian Tudeep's father

Willy Waving: A WBC local correspondent

Worldwide Alcoholics Anonymous charity: (WAA)

World Broadcasting Corporation (WBC): The only official broadcasting service

World Reincarnation Organisation (WRO):The organisation which conducted Ian Tudeep's AR

Solar System Web: A galactic version of the World Wide Web

Dedications and Acknowledgements

This book was written during the Covid-19 pandemic, which horrified us all in 2020. A lot of the effort put into this offering was made during lock-down, as I was being shielded. I thought it would be good to keep myself busy, and so I determined to write this, my fifth book.

All my books have been written to raise money for charity, and this one is no exception. Every penny I receive will be donated to NHS Charities Together. 'I'm Back!' is dedicated to my wonderful wife, Pauline. Without her encouragement and her loving kindness, I would be lost. She is a real diamond. I am pleased to thank her for the artwork on the front cover of this book.

I would also like to dedicate this book to The Bobin Pack. We have had many terrific canine pals, and the trio of four legged friends who make up our latest set of doggy companions are loyal, affectionate, and funny. They all have their own personalities. Monty is my biggest fan, and he has been with me with every word I type. He is highly intelligent and knows many words. He constantly amazes me with his linguistic talent. Woody is our smallest, bravest, and most independent dog, He is a huge dog in a small body. Fifi is our Diva Dog. She is our controller. She likes to organise the others, and she is the one who leads the pigeon patrol whenever one of these birds dares to land on our conservatory roof.

I had invaluable help from my friends Helen Beard and Eric Boulter who did a sterling job on the final proof checking of *I'm Back!*

Finally, I must say that without my father, I may never have set pen to paper (or rather fingers to keyboard.) He was a real writer, but I believe I am just an accidental author. When I was a truculent teenager, he would tell me that he would give me advice, even though he knew that I wouldn't pay attention to his guidance. He maintained that you only learn by the mistakes you make. How right he was. I wish I had realised how wise he was when I was young. This book is for you too Dad.

Chapter 1

Ian Tudeep knew that artificial reincarnation had been tested by the World Reincarnation Organisation (WRO), for many years on rats, mice, and chimpanzees. These poor creatures had been bred by the WRO and kept in cages before being used for their experiments. They had found it hard to come by enough animals to use for their many tests. After a while they bought a stock of small mammals, to use as luckless parents for the progeny which became casually used, and then discarded, creatures.

Wildlife in the world was diminishing at a rapid rate especially for larger beasts, such as elephants, lions, and tigers. By sacrificing the smaller home-grown animals, the WRO had come a long way from its inception. They said that they would eventually hope to offer a whole raft of attractive options to its potential customers.

For quite some time, Ian had been interested in reincarnation, as a most fascinating concept. He knew that it was also called transmigration or metempsychosis. He was astounded that so many people believed in rebirth, especially in Asian traditions, but that it also featured in the religious and philosophical thoughts of some religions.

Some people apparently viewed the soul as being capable of leaving the body through the mouth or the nostrils and of being reborn, as an animal. He had also heard that other religions believed that when a person dies, the soul stays near the grave for a short time and then seeks a new body. That might be human, mammalian, or reptilian.

Ian had suffered a long run of appallingly bad luck, which led him to take a closer look at his future. He was utterly despondent. He felt that he had no way out of his sad, miserable existence. He had always had very few close friends, and several of these had

I'm Back!

died naturally over the years, or they had been mercilessly carted off by the Population Police, because they had reached the age of fifty. Their future was to be handed over to the National Deselection Facility (NDF), to be put down humanely.

This was the age when the government considered that people were of no further use to the country. Ian was only five years short of the age at which mandatory euthanasia was inevitable. The powers that be allowed absolutely no exceptions. The deselection was cruel but apparently necessary.

Ian had also lost his job as a librarian. Libraries had evolved from the old musty places with many shelves of books, DVDs, and related materials. They were now remotely curated, virtual places of learning and cultural enjoyment. These were tended to by modern-day librarians working from home. It was Ian's job to make it easier for people to find cookie driven suggestions. This helped them to choose their favourites and to download or stream literature, academic tomes, music, audio books, and many other items which were freely available to members of the public.

Ian had been asked to make a physical visit to the head office of the library for which he toiled. He got up early, showered and shaved. He made the mistake of looking at himself for some time in the virtual mirror, which was projected onto the shower room's one vacant wall. He couldn't believe how old he looked. He noticed that his mousy, brown hair was wispy and that he had bloodshot eyes. His eyes had always been the colour of dirty water. He thought that at least the pretty shade of red in his eyeballs gave him a touch of colour. Ian was unremarkable in the looks department. He was medium in height and weight and his features were also ordinary. He wasn't a snappy dresser, and he merged into the background at parties and other gatherings.

Ian wondered why the East Anglian Library had asked him to make this visit to their head office in Bury St. Edmunds. He announced himself at the reception desk when he arrived. The youth who took his details was obviously an expert at showing how bored he found his mundane job. Ian saw that he wore a name badge and that his full name was Dean James. To Ian's mind, this name was the only remarkable thing about a perpetually yawning and blinking teenager, with about three thousand spots on his face. It was only remarkable if one had an interest in old films, as did Ian.

After a tedious wait of twenty-eight minutes (carefully timed by Ian), he was asked to go to an office on the third floor. It was easy to find, and Ian knocked on the door and entered as directed to by its only occupant. A disagreeably over-jovial and much too confident young man stood up and shook Ian's hand. He didn't beat about the bush.

In just five minutes, Ian was told by this arrogant and super smooth consultant, who looked about twelve, that he had been given a wonderful opportunity to find new horizons. The consultant said this was part of what he called the company's exciting downsizing project. Ian resisted the even more wonderful opportunity to punch the pompous, little tyke on his greasy, sweaty nose. He gave Ian a pile of what he called exit material and a letter confirming what his redundancy package would be. Ian briefly considered arguing with this upstart, but he realised that this would make no odds. He was out, and whatever was in the letter was not likely to be changed.

'That's it, the final straw,' thought Ian. 'I've had enough.'

Ian's callous wife had left him recently for a much newer model. Although Ian was careful with his money, his spendthrift spouse had run up huge debts before she left. Just after she went, she drained their joint bank account. To make matters worse, she ran away with a juvenile person, whom she called the love of her life. She conveniently forgot the fact that she had also called Ian just that. This was when they had been married fifteen years previously. To cap it all, Ian found out that her new beau was good looking, extremely rich and sick-makingly talented. He was also twenty-five years younger than Ian. Ian took to the alcohol pills in a big way. These pills had been designed to replace beer, wine, and spirits. Ian's liberal use of the pills lasted for some while, but he was saved by The Worldwide Alcoholics Anonymous charity. The WAA people had been a great help temporarily, but Ian had soon backed out of regular meetings. He hated the whole 'Hallo I'm Ian, and I'm an alcoholic,' nonsense. One day at a time, he managed to get off the alcohol pills, in true cold turkey fashion.

Ian was at his lowest ebb when he decided to investigate the possibility of rebirth. He knew that the WRO had been formed to do experimental research into the possibilities of what they had termed artificial reincarnation or AR. He found that the organisation was mentioned many times on the Solar System Web, and with his previous experience as a virtual librarian he was able to get a better feel for what they had achieved. He spent several weeks poring over the information that was freely available.

Dr. Leif Aggen was the original Chief Executive Officer of the WRO, and he oversaw their pioneering experiments. At first, they had lofty ideas and ambitions but no clear direction or structured policies. They tried many times to extract the spirit (or soul), of the poor defenceless animal being used in their tests and to insert it into freshly thawed, 'taking' bodies. They also wanted to transfer memories from the 'giving' brain to the taking one, but this proved to be exceedingly difficult.

Leif wondered if it might be possible to store the soul and memories in another astral plane temporarily, until they were ready to reuse them. Astral travel had been immensely popular for some years before the establishment of the WRO. Many people loved the multiple choices it gave them for unusual holidays. The people who took holidays became smaller in number as the years passed, and holovision holidays became more available and amazingly realistic.

The WRO tried out Leif's idea of using another astral plane as a temporary home for the soul and memories of their 'patients.' It seemed to work quite well for the poor defenceless animals on which the idea was tested. However, it was not easy to tell if mice remembered anything from their previous incarnation. Even if they could, they were unable to explain exactly what they recalled to their torturers. Leif was itching to do some pilot trials with humans, but he was conscious of the moral difficulties he would encounter. Being a highly principled man, he knew that the WRO had to be confident that their activities would be safe, before letting loose his reincarnation specialists on men or women.

Leif was a true gentleman, and he was an inspiring mentor to his staff. His angular form and high forehead lent him a scholarly aspect, and he had indeed written many medical books, when he was acting as a well-paid consultant specialising in the neurological aspects of his chosen branch of medicine. He had a habit of constantly pushing his greying, floppy fringe off his face. However, he was not vain or over proud. He was friendly and courteous and was always willing to listen to his employees. He stooped a little and walked with an uneven gait, due to an old cycling injury to his left ankle. His face was unremarkable, but his deep brown eyes were alert and bright. He had a real thirst for knowledge and was, at heart, a kindly man.

On the other hand, his Chief Operating Officer, a Swedish ice maiden, was totally different. She had startlingly beautiful, pale blue eyes, and her irises were surrounded by dark blue outer rings. She was slim and lissome. She had corn blonde hair, but despite her undoubted attractiveness, she was another stinking kettle of fish. Agneta Abramsen was a magnificent specimen of womanhood. It was said more than once in the press that she was considered, by many people, to be the best-looking lady in the whole world. She was a statuesque stunner, but she was as hard as nails and an absolute, poisonous bitch. All the early WRO staff hated her with a venom. She thus proved the saying that beauty is only skin deep.

When Leif's early experiments went badly astray, she had no sympathy for the poor animals that were used in the WRO's clumsy testing. She said that as they had been bred especially for scientific experiments, they were lucky to have been alive at all. She averred that as there were hardly any large animals in the wild at all, and not that many smaller animals, their short lives were a bonus. The near extinction of wildlife had upset most of the general public, but you had to be a caring person to be concerned about animals. Agneta was anything but.

She was wooed by many lovelorn men, but although she had several short relationships, none of them amounted to anything permanent. She positively scorned the idea of marriage. She discarded her men friends like yesterday's newspapers (when the world still had real newspapers), after she had decided that she was no longer interested in them.

It was Agneta who came up with various potential, artificial reincarnation options, which had not at that time been visualised by any other person. The range of possibilities was an ambitious wish list. Leif was concerned that they included outrageous choices, for what he considered to be obscene manipulation of AR. He thought that Agneta was a dangerous visionary. He worried that if these selections ever came about people might opt for them casually, not recognising that they were more prone to give rise to accidents than standard AR.

Agneta's list included backwards reincarnation (for people who regretted their original AR), double reincarnation (for devoted partners), placed reincarnation (for people who wanted to come back in a favourite location), cloned reincarnation (for those who were vain enough to want to look like their old cast-off self), timed reincarnation (for history fans), and reincarnation as a fictional character (too stupid to even think about.)

She and Leif argued many times about her risky objectives.

In the end Leif said:

"Please be more patient, my dear. We must take one small step at a time, Agneta. AR is still in its infancy. We've had some tiny successes, but you of all people must know that we've also had lots of big disappointments. Many of our early experiments failed abysmally. Some of the AR taking bodies only lasted a few hours, before the patient died. Also, what about the strange outcome, when one of the new bodies started to fade in and out of the other astral plane? You must know that the taking body just unaccountably disappeared."

"Leif, you're the biggest disappointment in the WRO. In fact, you're probably the biggest disappointment in the entire world. We need younger people, with more wide-ranging ideas. When we do perfect standard AR, we can exploit the commercial opportunities to the maximum by offering a menu of choices. If we do that, we will all be rich."

"Agneta, although the board members of the WRO each own equal shares of the organisation, I don't believe that the other executives share your rather greedy view of what we are doing. We want to help people who think they have no future, and who are brave enough to step outside their own bodies and to be reborn in a new body. The important thing to bear in mind is that, in most cases, the new body will be healthier and more robust than their original corporeal vessel."

"Bugger that Leif, I want to go further than anything envisaged in your namby pamby vista. And I want to be extraordinarily rich."

Agneta started to evangelise, craftily and sneakily, about her way of looking at the future for the WRO on the quiet. One by one, she persuaded the other executives that her view was the one that should be adopted, and that she should run the WRO. She also lied and told the other board members personally, that Leif had sexually harassed her. She maintained that she was psychologically damaged as a result of his constant attempts to kiss her and cuddle her. Worse than that, she alleged that he had groped her and tried to force himself on her. She had perfected the art of weeping copiously when she said this. She also batted her eyelashes at these gullible men, who were flattered that she had confided in them.

At a special EGM, she finally managed to get her own way. She pushed through her outrageous plans for what she described 'as a thrilling future for the WRO.' She also openly challenged Leif by calling for an immediate vote of no confidence in his

I'm Back!

leadership. Sadly, the board all agreed with her. Of course, they also thought that this would solve the problem of his unwanted sexual attentions to Agneta.

Leif resigned, with quiet dignity, before he could be ejected. He lived the rest of a happy life in rural surroundings, in a seaside cottage in Northumberland. He died at the age of 76. (The Population Police seemed to have left him off their death list by accident.) He enjoyed a peaceful retirement, and he kept an extremely low profile, in case the PP did ever come knocking. He thought that they might find out that he had missed being deselected.

He was unable to cycle due to his ankle problem, but he had three dogs. There were two mongrels, called Tom and Dick, and a rescued Saluki which he had named Agneta. He reasoned that although she was a bitch, she was lovable, unlike Agneta Abramsen. They had all delighted in the long walks on which they had been with their master, along several windswept, sandy beaches near his cottage. His favourite was Bamburgh beach, which wasn't far from his home.

The WRO continued to grow and to work with other organisations who were interested in their fascinating research. They had by now been re-funded by large global conglomerates and several governments. They could envisage a time when they could capitalise on their investments in the organisation. Agneta became CEO when Leif resigned. Thankfully, she was eventually fired, after the board members in whom she had confided came to learn that she had used them. She had told each of them that she was only sharing her problems with them. She had said she admired them and knew that they were kind people who would not reveal her secret despair, caused by Leif's (totally imaginary), unwanted advances. They found out in conversation with each other that she had told the same story to all of the board members.

In 2094 Ian Tudeep finally decided to volunteer to be the very first human to be artificially reincarnated. He knew that all his memories and his spirit would be downloaded from his giving body and pumped into another astral plane, before being retrieved and inserted into a taking body. He had found out, from his careful research, that the WRO had been experimenting on small animals for some time, and that part of their tests involved the complicated task of transferring memories from the giving to the taking body. He fully understood why they believed that memories had been transferred successfully, but that it was difficult to find proof. The animals certainly seemed to remember food, drink, and copulation.

'I remember copulation,' thought Ian, 'but not lately.'

These animals' memories seemed to be of basic needs. It was not totally clear if this wasn't just instinctive behaviour. The animals seemed to be scared of the technical people who had performed the actual AR processes. However, they appeared to be fond of the nurses who gently pre-assessed and prepared them before their procedures. It was as if they knew that the nurses were there to care for them when they woke up in their new bodies, whilst the technical people were known to be cruel.

The WRO had concluded that they desperately needed humans to volunteer to undergo AR. They had mounted a world-wide advertising campaign to find suitable people to be invited to be AR patients. Ian had seen many posts on social media, on the holovision and in the digital press. Most of these contained appeals for volunteers, which were made by the new CEO of the WRO. His name was Hiram Prendergast.

Hiram had joined the WRO after Agneta Abramsen had been ousted and had proved his worth quickly. He had impressed all and sundry, because of his zeal, ambition, and technical talent. He had previously worked as a senior consultant in the field of organ transplants. He had also been employed by several huge pharmaceutical companies in executive posts. He had made reincarnation his hobby horse. When he joined the WRO, Leif Aggen had already gone, and so had Agneta Abramsen. There was an interim CEO named Jess Honly-Temporary. It was immediately apparent that Hiram was a major force to contend with. He worked under, then alongside Jess before being appointed to the post of CEO.

I'm Back!

Ian made his approach to the WRO using their Solar System website, the link for which had appeared in various articles. He filled in a preliminary digital submission form, which asked tricky questions like 'Is there anybody who will miss you, if things go wrong?'

He was soon contacted by one of the WRO's robots, using his immersephone number, which he had given to them when he was using the WRO's site.

"Hallo is that Mr. Ian Tudeep?" the robot asked. (She had seen his name displayed, as he had been added to their contacts.)

"Yes, who am I talking to?"

'Bugger,' he thought. 'I should have said to whom am I talking.'

He fully recognised that he was a pedant, but he glorified in endeavouring to speak what used to be called The Queen's English. He wondered what it should be called now that England had no monarch.

"This is Susie AI10009. I'm your electronic guide to the WRO registration system. I understand that you wish to volunteer for our pilot artificial reincarnation programme. Is that so?"

"Yes, please. I think I am a good candidate. I have hardly any friends and no relatives. If anything went awry, I wouldn't be missed. I know that this is an important criterion in your procedures."

"That's right. I've been instructed that we must be extremely strict about that for human AR."

Susie AI10009 then took Ian through the potential problems, like losing consciousness in his present body and never regaining awareness in a new vessel, being reincarnated in a body with serious health issues and even waking up speaking a different language.

"I'm definitely still interested. I really want to help the WRO. I know I could have problems, but I don't care."

"We'll send you the registration papers by rMail, as they must be signed and witnessed. When you've completed them, you may return them by teleportation, or you can scan them and use rMail. We'll also need DNA and blood samples. I'll give you a code to be used at a pop-up reincarnation depot locally. The nurses are all robots like me."

'...robots like I,' thought Ian.

"They'll take samples from you. They will also arrange for them to be sent to us."

The conversation finished abruptly, and Ian leant back in his well-worn but comfortable armchair. He sighed heavily. He fervently hoped he was doing the right thing. During the next few days, he completed the registration forms which had arrived safely. They were accompanied by what were described as 'standard disclaimer documents.' He visited the reincarnation depot as arranged, and they gave him some vile tasting liquid to drink, before setting in motion various pre-assessment tests.

"What's this awful drink?"

"That's reincarnation milk," said the robot nurse, "it enhances various bodily markers, so we can judge whether or not you are suitable for artificial reincarnation."

"Do I really have to drink this?"

She nodded. She was very pretty. Ian wondered what he would think of her if he had met her in an alcohol pod. (These had replaced pubs long since, and alcohol pills were served there, together with crisps and nuts. They were also in pill form.) He would never have guessed that she was not a human. She even smelt like a woman. It was not like perfume, nor cosmetics of any kind.

She exuded a distinct animal muskiness. It was that particularly feminine aroma which had grown more and more prevalent in humans as genetically modified embryos had been used, instead of the natural ones. The normal embryos often had faults. The rules now precluded the use of any embryos with known weaknesses. It seemed that

I'm Back!

this robot had been programmed to somehow mimic that extraordinary, but wonderful, lady smell.

She promised him that the test results would be sent to the WRO, within the next day few days. She finished by telling Ian he would hear more in two weeks. He could hardly wait. On the fourteenth day, as he paced up and down in his shabby condenselow, he felt more and more restricted by the tiny one-floored home. His immersephone notification sounded, and Ian was pleased to hear the same mellifluous voice of the WRO robot to whom he had been talking during the first contact.

"Hallo Susie, it's lovely to hear from you again," Ian said politely.

"I'm one of the many Susies. I am SusieAI10039. We all have the same voice. It was computer generated, but it was modelled on the popular voice of a woman who used it with her natural body many years ago. She was apparently an actress; her name was Joanna Lumley."

"I wanted to tell you that your formal application for artificial reincarnation has been officially approved. We'll send you teleportation tickets by rMail. You can go to the nearest public terminal. When you've entered the booth, the tickets will automatically be recognised, and you'll be beamed to the WRO's headquarters. You will materialise in our reception area, and one of our robot Susies will guide you to the preparation area. You'll have some further tests. You will live in a one bedroomed pod, with suitable bodily function evacuation tubes. There will also be an adjustomatic autocleaner, which will envelop your entire body, to your exact dimensions. It will wash, dry and powder you, whenever you say the world 'cleanse.'

You'll be required to be totally naked in the pod for seven days. Once all this has been done, one of our consultants will go through our disclaimer forms with you in greater detail. You must realise that this procedure is experimental. You will be the first human to undergo this process."

Ian nodded, and the Susie at the other end of the conversation smiled. He was pleased with his new immersephone. Susie seemed to be sitting right next to him.

That night he had nightmares about his reincarnation. It wasn't surprising. His application to pioneer AR in humans would lead to an experience which was quite different to natural reincarnation. When it all happened in the ordinary way, people didn't always know that they had lived before. They also didn't know what they might become. In their new natural incarnation they might be a shepherd in a far-flung land, tending sheepbots, a clown or an atomic scientist. They might be a midget, a giant of a person, or even a different colour.

The old normal reincarnations came about using human embryos in mothers' wombs. They received DNA and genetic instructions partly from their mothers and fathers (and brain cells from who knew where.) Artificial reincarnation would allegedly enable the person being reincarnated to be brought back as a baby, or at a selected preferred age.

The tickets, and other papers, came into his rMail in box ten days later, after the WRO had restudied his registration form. The next day, Ian left his condenselow and travelled on an aerobus, high up in the sky, hovering to the teleportation terminal. This was still called Heathrow, even though the antiquated airport had long since gone.

He showed his papers to a smiling faced, robot assistant by using his electrajot. The barrier was lifted automatically, and he walked a few steps to the booth to which he had been directed. This would enable him to be sent to Switzerland, where one of the WRO's Susies would greet him. The doors slid shut and a sepulchral voice said:

"Sit in the curvochair and wait for the safety web to envelop you."

Ian did as he was told. The safety web fell over him smoothly, and it started to mould itself around him and the curvochair. The thermo-dynamic engines thrummed, and Ian felt himself disintegrating. He had been told, by a friend, that people used to drink lots of beer, to get much the same woozy effect.

"We're here darling," said a Susie voice.

I'm Back!

His body reassembled itself, thankfully with his limbs in the right places and joined to the correct things. The safety web disappeared. The door of the teleportation booth opened with a loud swooshing sound. Ian stepped out gingerly, and a Susie greeted him. It was eerie to note that whilst the glamourous robot looked just like a real woman, her face and body were exactly like the Susies he had seen when using his immersephone and the robot nurse who forced him to drink reincarnation milk.

"If you sit here in our reception area, you will be called when the consultant is free. There are food and drink pills in the dispenser over there. If you still prefer old-fashioned, real food you can order something from this menu, which has been specially prepared for us. We are one of the few public places in Switzerland officially offering real food."

Ian glanced idly at the limited menu:

Swiss Fried Chicken – Tempting morsels of herb encrusted, dead bird.

McFisher Burger – Ground dead fish patties.

Beef stew – Dead cow in a greasy sauce.

Liver and Onions – Animal organs garnished with strong onions to mask the over-rich flavour of offal.

He decided to opt for the usual food and drink pills. He swallowed the pills and waited patiently. After a short while, a tall, gaunt, and prematurely silver-haired man of about forty, opened a door to the side of the Susie's desk.

"Good morning, Mr. Tudeep. Please come this way," said the specialist, in a dark brown voice, only slightly affected by a Scandinavian accent.

'Norwegian maybe,' thought Ian.

Ian walked into the consultant's office, which was furnished with glass and chrome furniture (or what passed for glass and chrome in 2094.) There was a bookcase behind the consultant's desk, fully stocked with nicely bound tomes. All of them were entitled in gold lettered Universito, the worldwide language which had replaced

Esperanto a good few years ago.

The bookcase and its contents might have been a hologram, but they looked real to Ian. Ian had never learned Universito, and he still spoke English. There wasn't much call for Universito in Southwold, which was where Ian had lived ever since he was born. The town was much bigger than it had been. There were now over three and a half million people living in condenselows and larger blocks of stacked condenselows in Southwold. These stacks were remarkably like what used to be called flats in the olden days. However, they were easier to assemble than traditional buildings (and they were simple to disassemble when they had outlived their purpose.)

"I'm Karl Yoder, and I am your AR specialist. I understand that you've been accepted by us, to become our first artificial reincarnation client. AR has been used in experiments with rats, mice, and chimpanzees, but the results have in some cases been surprising. We need to take you through some examples of potential mishaps which might occur. We're in a position now to tell you that these are unlikely, but we must make you aware that side effects, or even secondary benefits, can occur.

I'll list them for you:

One: You may not experience any change at all. This happens when we cannot extract your spirit and your memories from your current body. If this happens, we will close off the AR process quickly, before any real damage is done. This is usually achievable, but in some cases the giving body may reject the reparation process.

Two: We may successfully perform the extraction but find that some, or even all, of the insertion into a new bodily receptacle goes wrong. You may be reincarnated as a mutant or with no (or few), memories.

Three: The AR may be successful, but you might find that you accidentally become a vastly different age when you come back to life.

Four: There may be unexpected benefits. It could be that you may find that you have new skills, like being able to play piano or being a gifted artist.

I'm Back!

These are just a few examples. This process is very new, and we just want you to be aware of these potential issues. Here is a complete list of the problems that have been experienced in the early experiments."

He handed Ian a folder, in which there was a closely printed 74-paged double-sided document. Ian flicked through it, and he couldn't believe how awful the accidents must have been. He sighed and considered what his future might be if he abandoned his brave project. He had in mind that he had lost his wife (to the younger and fitter man who was her personal trainer), and he had been downsized from his job as a virtual librarian. Worse than that, his dogbot had broken down and was beyond repair. Many of his friends had reached the national euthanasia age, and they had been whisked away, one by one, to the NDF.

The government had explained that they had to do this, as there were far too many people in the country. It was impossible to get away from this dismal prospect, as all countries had signed a worldwide Population Thinning Pact. Ian was only just forty-five. He hated the thought that on his fiftieth birthday, he would be collected by two beefy Population Policemen, who would take him to the place where he would be summarily dealt with.

"I'm certain I want to go ahead."

Karl Yoder smiled a thin, watery sort of smile. It was the kind that started quickly, stayed visible for a mere two or three seconds and disappeared just as quickly. It never even reached his eyes, which were cold and fish-like. Yoder stood up, clicked his heels, and nodded his head. He gave Ian the kind of handshake which sought to prove that Yoder was stronger than Ian was. It was as if he wanted to be dominant. Ian tried to grip Yoder's hand more firmly than his was entrapped, but in the end, he gave up the ridiculous pissing contest.

"I'm so pleased that you wish to continue. If you wait in reception, you'll be escorted to the pod which will house you for the next seven days. One of our Susies will show you the ropes."

Yoder sat down at his desk and picked up a file casually. He seemed surprised that Ian was still there when he glanced up a few seconds later. Ian took the hint and left the specialist's office. The receptionist Susie gave him a warm smile. It was better than Yoder's feeble attempt at showing pleasure, even though the Susie was not human.

Ian was beginning to warm to the robots. He had considered getting a female robot when his wife had ditched him, but the cost of even a half-way decent looking one was way beyond his means. He knew that the first-class models were fantastic. Some of them had switchable modes, like happy, sad, loving or 'I am having a monthly period.' He couldn't imagine who would want to select that mode, or even the ominous preceding one. This was the 'PMS: Be careful what you say and do,' mode.

Yet another Susie entered the reception area and beamed at him. She touched his left shoulder, gave him a smouldering, come-hither look and led him to his pod. Ian wondered what life would be like, with an expensive Susie switched to an 'I'm up for it,' mode. A friend of Ian's had tried a robot lover in what used to be called Thailand. He had told Ian that he had the most wonderful time for five days. He said the four nights of his rental period, before he had a massive heart attack, were even better.

Ian's chum was whisked off to a local hospital and treated well. However, he only lasted a short time after he came back to England. The funeral director had a lot of difficulty getting his face to look peaceful. He was very skilled, and he didn't think it was appropriate for Ian's friend to be buried with a wide grin on his phizzog. Ian had received some most unnecessarily detailed immersephone calls from his chum, about how wonderful the robot had been, during his stay in the Far East.

The Susie who was leading Ian, encouraged him to enter the pod, and she said:

"This button activates your bodily function evacuation tubes. A sliding panel will open. You can use the seat which will be revealed. If you prefer, or if your needs are more simple, you can place your member in the tube to the side, and you may pass

I'm Back!

water like that.

"The adjustomatic autocleaner can't be used with your clothes on. I'll help you to undress. You'll have to be naked for seven days in the pod, as we told you previously."

(Ian quite liked that idea of her stripping him.)

"When you use the autocleaner you must stand on this raised dais. The cleaner will mould itself to your body, and it will wrap itself round your entire body. It will wash, dry and powder you, whenever you say the world 'cleanse.' You won't need to adjust the temperature or water pressure. The cleaner will do that automatically.

There is an immersephone, or you can put the supersound buds in your ears. You can also use the special 6D spectacles. There are films, news and other programmes in a huge holovision library of 247,000,000 titles.

The bed rises from the floor when it senses that you're tired. You can use artificial blankets, which will feel, and seem to weigh, much like real old-fashioned bed coverings. They won't actually be there. Can I do anything else for you? I'll do anything, anything at all in my power to make you happy."

Susie gave Ian a radiant smile. He wondered if you could fall in love with a robot.

"Are you allowed to make love to me?"

"I'm so sorry, but I don't have a suitable receptacle for sex. I can ask for a special Susie to visit you if that's your wish."

Ian was now rather embarrassed.

"No that's OK. I was just joking," he lied.

The Susie left, and the pod door closed.

Ian quite enjoyed his stay in the pre-AR pod. It was small, but amazingly comfortable. He had found that the ear buds could produce very realistic sounds and the specs delivered fantastic 6D quality pictures, which seemed to surround him in a virtual reality world. He enjoyed the nature films of almost extinct animals like horses and rhinos.

Each morning, he was woken up by a Susie alarm call speaking to him in that wonderful Joanna Lumley voice. He didn't know what Joanna had looked like, so he tried to find some films of her. There were a few on the Solar System Web, but the quality of the old films was awful compared to the modern ones. He had to admit that she was classy.

"Good morning Ian. It's time to get up. Your autocleaner awaits you, or would you like breakfast first? The food and drink pills are in the dispenser, which has been re-filled overnight. You can have real food delivered to you, but the pills will give you adequate nourishment, based on your height and weight. We believe you are slightly too heavy, so the pills have been adjusted in strength accordingly."

"Thank you, Susie. I'd like the full English breakfast."

"I'm so sorry, but that wouldn't be allowed. It's far too fatty and is unbelievably bad for you."

"OK. The pills will do. Are there any games in the pod? I couldn't find any?"

"What would you like to play, Ian?"

"How about Ludo? I used to enjoy that."

"Ludo is regarded as a silly game for children. Why not try Mah Jong, or we could play Who wants to be a Trillionaire?"

"No thanks. I haven't got many friends to phone, and there's no audience to ask."

"All the Susies, including me, are your friends, and as everything you do in the pod is observed by our scientific and medical experts you do have quite an audience."

Ian was a little embarrassed to remember that he had done some things in the pod which he would not have wished to be observed. The days went by more quickly than Ian had expected. He was becoming increasingly nervous about his forthcoming AR experience, but he had mentally resigned himself to his fate, whatever that may be.

I'm Back!

On the morning of the eighth day he was autocleaned as usual. He ate his boring breakfast pills and then waited for the time he would be called to be reincarnated. He had been told that his appointment would be at eleven o'clock that morning. Precisely on the dot the pod doors opened, and a Susie entered. She gave him an open backed gown, like they used to have in hospitals.

Hospitals had long since all been closed. As there were so many people in the world, it was easier to let people either recover from their illnesses at home, or to let them expire naturally. This helped the Population Police who would have less people to deal with on their fiftieth birthday.

"Are you one of the Susies whom I have met already, or are you another one who is new to me?"

"It's not that easy to tell. The Susies here are automatically synchronised on a constant push basis. We therefore all think we've met you, even if we haven't done so. It's a little confusing, but for example I know that you asked one of us for sex. It might have been me, but I could never know that for certain."

Ian shrugged on his natty little gown, and the ever-helpful Susie fixed the back, so his hairy arse was no longer hanging out. She led him down the same corridor along which he had walked on the way to the pod, but just before the doors to the reception area she turned left.

They stood on an eleversor, which glided up twelve storeys. Ian was never happy in eleversors. There were no walls. Although he had been assured that the surrounding force field would prevent him from falling, he didn't like the sensation of seeing nothing which looked like a positive barrier. The eleversor came to a smooth halt. Susie took him by the hand.

"You must be nervous. I can tell you that I do have a nice artificial vagina. Would you like to use me for a while before you are reincarnated? I'm one of only a few Susies who have the necessary receptacle."

Ian felt himself blushing, and even though the prospect was tempting he politely turned her down.

Susie didn't appear to be offended. Ian was glad she was still holding his hand, as he was now terrified by the thought of his AR appointment. He had admitted to himself that whilst he would have loved to have had sex with this Susie, he didn't think he would have risen to the occasion.

Chapter 2

Susie took Ian to what looked like an old-fashioned operating theatre. The walls were white. The window frames of the control and viewing room were white. The instruments were white. Poor Ian was also white with fright. He was trembling so hard; he could hardly stand up straight.

A masked and gowned figure led him to the operating table. Ian had seen operating theatres in ancient photos. He was encouraged to lie down on the table by a nurse. Electrodes were then connected to his head, his chest, and his ears. He was handed ear defenders (which were also white), and the masked man spoke for the first time.

"I'm your personal AR specialist. My name is Adam Thurley. This is a pilot project. As you are aware, you're the world's first person to undergo Artificial Reincarnation. In order to satisfy our Health and Safety procedures, I'm obliged to read to you the disclaimer documents which you've already seen, and which you have signed."

This took some time, as he read all of the pages slowly and carefully. When this boring exercise was complete, he said:

"Please say your full name, your home address, and also let me have your rMail address."

"I'm Ian Wilbur Tudeep. My address is Condenselow 786, Happy Condenselow Park, Blueberry Hill, Southwold. My rMail address, which you allocated to me, is iantudeep@rmail.world."

"Thank you. That's exactly what we have in our records. How old are you Mr. Tudeep?"

"I'm forty-five."

"Please state your date of birth."

"21/04/2049."

"Do you understand that you're going to be artificially reincarnated?"

"Yes."

"For the record, please say that you understand that you are going to be artificially reincarnated."

Ian just couldn't help himself. (He was wearing his pedant's hat again.) He knew that the specialist should have said:

"For the record, please say 'I understand that I am going to be artificially reincarnated.'"

He thought better of so saying, and instead he just replied:

"I understand that I am going to be artificially reincarnated."

"Excellent, we can now proceed. Are your bowels empty?"

Luckily for Ian, he had used the bodily function evacuation tube in his pod earlier. If he had not done so, he feared that he would have been unable to keep his waste products inside!

Mr. Thurley left the room. Ian was now able to see that there were four people in the AR theatre.

A lady in a white uniform said:

"I'm Emily Nice-To-Meet-You."

"It's nice to meet you too."

"No, you misunderstand me. My surname is Nice-To-Meet-You, with three hyphens. It's nice to meet you too, but with no hyphens. My colleagues are Billy Turnbull, who is a spirit extraction operator, Alec I. Lykit (who is a vital signs inspector),

I'm Back!

and Julie Noted. She'll be your brow mopper and general soother."

They all nodded. Ian thought that they were probably smiling under their masks.

Emily continued to instruct Ian as to what would be happening to him.

"We'll begin the procedure in ten minutes. You'll be anesthetised, and the injection which I'll give you will make you very drowsy almost immediately. I'll count to 27, and you'll be fast asleep. When you wake up, you'll be hosted by a new and younger body. It'll be in rather better condition. As you wake up, you must say, 'I'm back!' You'll need to tell me your full name, home address and rMail address again."

Emily reached over to a trolley by her side, and she picked up an enormous hypodermic syringe, with bright green liquid inside.

"This will be slightly painful. The prick will be small, and the fluid which I'll inject may feel rather cold. Are you ready?"

Ian nodded.

"You must say that you're ready. My questions and your responses are being recorded, for training and health and safety purposes."

"I'm ready."

She must have been an expert because he hardly felt the injection. The fluid was not that cold, and Ian started to yawn once the full contents of the syringe had been injected into his body.

"1, 2, 3, 4, 5,6, 7, 8, 9, 10, 11, 12 ,13, 14, 15, 16, 17, 18, 19, 20, 21…"

Ian was now well under. The four other people in the room busied themselves with complicated tubes, electronic monitors, syringe drivers, additional electrodes and all manner of clamps, lights and breathing apparatus.

Adam Thurley was manipulating robotic hands from the control room and viewing what he was doing on a large screen. The other functionaries were assisting him by looking after Ian, and they were watching his vital signs.

Chapter 3

Ian woke up with a start. It was better than waking up with an end, he supposed. He dutifully followed orders and said to Adam Thurley:

"I'm back!"

"What is your full name and your home address? Also, please let me have your rMail address."

Ian reiterated the required details. He was surprised to feel so small, and he couldn't believe his voice was so high.

"Mr. Tudeep, we've had had a slight problem. The taking body we'd planned to use totally rejected your spirit and memories. This was even though we utilised specially tailored immunosuppressant drugs. Rather than lose you completely, we used a standby body. You're now inside that body, which used to house a young lad, who was eighteen months old when he died."

Ian was completely dumbfounded. In fact, his flabber was well and truly gasted.

"Mr. Yoder will explain what we'll have to do, to encourage your body to grow naturally but at a vastly increased pace."

Ian felt like crying, but he just sucked his thumb. He was forced to lie on the bed for some considerable time before they allowed him to get up. Ian tried to do this himself, but Emily picked him up like a mother hen, and she put him down gently on the floor. Everything seemed so huge to him, but he was reassured when she took his hand and led him to Yoder's consulting room. She smiled at Ian and lifted him onto the chair. It was much too high for him to get on it by himself.

I'm Back!

Yoder goose-stepped into the room.

"Mr. Tudeep, I know this setback must be disappointing for you, but we have in mind a special power diet. This will be supplemented by human growth hormones, daily injections, and electronic stimulation processes. They'll make you seem to be twenty-five years old, within just six months. Would that be acceptable to you?"

Ian squeaked:

"Yes."

"You'd be obliged to stay here in Geneva, during that entire period, so we can keep a close watch on your progress. You'll be allocated your very own special Susie, and she'll attend to your every need."

Ian remembered, with sadness, the enticing offer which he had turned down, from the Susie with a special receptacle.

Yoder smiled a grim sort of smile, clicked his heels, and he nodded as he left the room. Very shortly after that a Susie entered.

"Have I met you before?"

"Yes, I've been told that I offered you a special treat, but you turned it down."

She was making a sobbing noise.

"I didn't mean to upset you, but I was very embarrassed."

"Can I stop crying now?"

"Yes, I was hoping to show you that I care about you. I'd like you to be happy."

Susie opened her blouse and slid open a cover, under which there were four buttons. They first three were labelled as Sounds, Fake Emotions and System Update. The last one said Hot Love.

"You can choose any one you like."

Ian couldn't help himself. He pressed the Hot Love button. To his surprise, he suddenly heard a rock band from many decades back. He recognised T Rex, but although he quite liked the song, it was no substitute for real Hot Love, or even Hot

Love with a robot.

Susie laughed.

"Sorry, that was my idea of a joke. I created some virtual buttons with comic labels. Robots can be programmed to make jokes, but I've been told that our attempts at humour are not always deemed to be funny by humans. According to the records which were uploaded into my memory bank, it won't be that long before you can attempt Hot Love in the flesh. Well, in the flesh for you, and in the silicon pouch for me."

Susie picked him up, and Ian felt like crying.

"Don't be sad, little one. Soon you will be like a twelve-year-old, and you'll be able to learn again how to enjoy yourself (with yourself), if you see what I mean?

"I can't wait," muttered Ian, who was still thoroughly dispirited.

"Do you remember signing all those papers?"

"How could I forget?"

"One of them was a Non-Disclosure Agreement. It states that if you talk to the press, social media or any third parties about what happened, you agree to be given to the Population Police. In that event you would be no more, in a flash."

Ian was even glummer if there is such a word. Glum, glummer and glummest, does that work, he wondered?

"Cheer up! Let's go and play in your pod. We could do some drawing, or we've got colouring books."

"I'm not eighteen months old. I may have an eighteen-month-old body, but I've got the intellect of a forty-five-year-old man."

"Come on then big boy, let's go to the pod."

Once they were in the pod, Ian almost began to see the funny side of things. Susie was chatty, bright, and funny. She was a real head-turner, especially considering she was just a robot. She had the most beautiful pale blue eyes. The lovely Joanna

I'm Back!

Lumley voice was a bonus, and she gave great cuddles. He was sad that he was unable, as a pseudo toddler, to really appreciate her remarkably realistic breasts. He could also see that she had shapely limbs and a surprisingly natural smile.

She told him that if he didn't want to press her buttons, he could control her by using just his voice. He said he had already tried to control his ex-wife by just using his voice, but that hadn't worked. He was looking forward to seeing how things turned out, with his very own Susie.

Susie explained that she had a special brain which learned all the time, when she was partnered with a special friend.

"It's like pairing Bluetooth devices, if you can remember those very old-fashioned things."

"Am I really your special friend?"

"Of course, you're definitely my extra special friend. I've had an overview of all your memories copied onto my memory banks. Try talking to me about a memory we might now both share."

"Wasn't it lovely, when we walked along the beach at sunrise in Skopelos?"

"Oh yes, and we'd just eaten kleftiko, followed by baklava. The little goats were in the field at the top of the cliff, weren't they?"

Ian was delighted until she said:

"What is kleftiko exactly?"

Chapter 4

Susie said that Ian could either live by himself for the period in which he would be forced to stay with the WRO or, if he wanted, she would be allowed to stay with him.

"But there's only one bed, Susie."

"I don't need a bed. I just plug myself in for a recharge, put myself on standby, and then I stay still until you wake me up. All you have to say is, 'Wake up Little Susie, Wake up!'"

That sounded easy enough to remember, but Ian asked if he could have a notebook to use. He thought that there would be many things he would have to bear in mind. Susie went out for a short while, and she came back quickly with a high powered electrajot. The digital pen used with these devices never ran out of ink, and the on-board memory was phenomenal.

"Thanks, sweetie."

"What does sweetie mean?"

"It's a term of endearment."

"Do you mean like darling, baby and treasure?"

"Yes, sweetie pie."

"If sweetie is a term of endearment, why would you want to make an antiquated food item out of me?"

Susie looked worried. Ian started to explain, but she said:

"That was another joke. I told you that we can all make up funny jokes. Some of

I'm Back!

us were used as what they called standup comedians in the olden days."

Ian told her that his favourite old time comedian was Freddie Starr. He had only seen him on very aged TV shows, which had been hologrammatically recreated to mimic today's standards of reproduction. Ian thought he was hilarious, even though his humour was sometimes cruel. Ian believed that Freddie had been rather dangerous, even though he was funny.

Susie said:

"Did you know that he was an early robotic experiment? He wasn't even a real person."

"You're pulling my leg, aren't you?"

"No. I'm only having a joke. I haven't touched you."

Ian laughed. Susie needed some of the finer details about humans to be explained to her.

Susie smiled and said:

"What would you like to do, sweetie pie?"

Ian chuckled. He was beginning to see that she would be great fun.

"When I'm bigger, I'd very much like to go to bed with you."

"I told you that I don't use a bed."

Susie opened her big blue eyes wide, and then she winked.

"You'll find that I'm more clever than I look."

Ian ate some food pills and tablets that were supposed to be like fine wine, but they weren't very convincing. They tasted more like chalky, indigestion tablets. However, they had the desired effect, and Ian realised although he was only a toddler, he wanted to be cuddled by Susie.

"Why don't you sit on my lap?"

"Ian, I weigh much more than you. Sit on my lap, and you can put your head in between my fake breasts."

Ian did as he was told and said:

"Mermpellypdasmlftnefrplstcbrstsangag."

"Ian, if you want to talk to me, you'll have to take your head away from my breasts."

"I said, many people paid a small fortune for plastic breasts not that long ago." Susie faked outrage very successfully.

"I challenge you to tell the difference between my synthetic specials and the real deal. Mine are finest breastomatic astrosponge, and I've got realistic breathing effects to make them jiggle."

Ian tried to feel the magnificent fake appendages. He was hampered by Susie's tight-fitting blouse. It had buttons down the front, but Ian was finding it difficult to undo them. Susie gave a secret, whispered command, and they all popped open.

"Is that better? I can use verbal opening instructions, or there's a button on my neck."

Her desirable objects were exposed. Ian soon found that they really did feel genuine. He was amazed to feel a strong sense of déjà vu. Although he was trapped in a toddler's body, he still had the remnants of the expected reaction to such fine feminine bazookas.

Susie reminded Ian that, in the morning, he would be starting a strictly enforced growth programme which would include the special diet, injections and electronic stimulation processes. She said that the diet would be maintained by unusual food and drink pills which also contained growth hormones. These would replace the ordinary food and drink tablets which he had been using since he came to Geneva.

The injections would be used to boost his metabolism and to aid rapid digestion, so that he could have up to six 'meals' a day, every day, for the next six months. At the end of that time he would be to all intents and purposes, just like a normal man of twenty-five. She reminded him that he would still have all the experiences which he had

I'm Back!

gathered during his real forty-five years of living in his previous normal incarnation.

"Won't I be normal anymore?"

"No, babykins, you'll be my special cutie pie."

Ian could see that Susie had a good sense of fun. There was indeed more to her than met the eye.

'Mind you,' he mused, 'what meets the eye is wonderful.'

He hoped he would be able to sample forbidden delights well before he reached an artificial age of twenty-five.

"Time for bed," said Ian as he scrambled off Susie's lap.

She got up, walked into the corner of the pod opposite his bed and stood up straight. After plugging herself into a concealed charger which had rolled out of the wall of the pod, she said:

"No bed for me. Standby now starting."

Ian saw her close her eyes. Her head drooped, and her blouse buttons did themselves up at lightning fast speed. Ian wished he were tall enough to kiss her. It was very frustrating, being only about thirty inches tall.

Chapter 5

When Ian woke up, he looked at the hologram digiclock, and he saw that it was already seven thirty in the morning. He remembered all that had happened the day before, but he could hardly believe that he wasn't dreaming. During the night, he had experienced another nightmare. He was on the table in the WRO operating theatre, and Karl Yoder was leaning over him. Yoder gave an especially wide (and almost convincing), grin and said:

"Sorry old boy, but it's gone very wrong. We put you into a replacement body, but we need to use that now. We can pickle your memories in a jar, or we can mix them with some pre-prepared memories from an assortment of our previous, failed experiments. We told you that you were the first AR patient, but we lied a teeny, tiny bit.

We've tried hundreds of times, to do this with humans. Extracting memories, the spirit and other bits and pieces was quite successful. The trouble was, that when we wanted to insert them into a new body, even if the corpse had been preserved well in our cryogenic laboratories, the body often liquified into a stinking mess on the floor of the theatre.

We now have millions of memories packed tightly into a condensed storage medium. This is used to create a homogeneous memory, which is the same for all taking bodies. We call it 'Memories are Made of This.' We'll use your body for another session, or if that doesn't work, we'll make some tasty sweetie pies with condensed brain gravy and crushed bones."

I'm Back!

Thankfully, Ian had woken up, but he had gone back to sleep immediately. The rest of his night was dreamless. He was pleased to see Susie standing in the corner.

He said:

"Wake up, Little Susie, Wake up."

She opened her eyes, licked her luscious lips, and unplugged herself from the charger, which obediently retracted itself into the wall. The cover of the charging cupboard slid shut. Susie yawned and turned to Ian with a fabulous, dazzling smile.

"Good morning, Ian."

"Hallo Susie. I've met several Susies at the WRO. The others were apparently all called Susie and then a number. Do you have a number?"

"No, I was one of 26 first issue Susies. At that time, we all had an alphabetical suffix. I was the seventeenth one of the first batch. I'm therefore Susie Q."

"Oh, Susie Q, baby I love you."

She surprised him by reciprocating. He knew that he should be pleased. He was amazed and could hardly believe his ears. However, Ian wondered if Susie Q had just been programmed to respond in that manner, or if she really loved him. Then he realised that he was being silly. She was a machine and could have no real feelings. He felt disappointed by that cold hard fact, but then she reached down and pinched his bum.

"Oh, Susie Q, I can hardly wait until I'm a specially aged twenty-five, or maybe younger if I can still remember how to make love."

Susie Q busied herself in preparing his morning pills and his injection. The extremely large food and growth hormone pills and a huge syringe were soon on the table, which had been automatically lowered from the ceiling of the pod. He tried to swallow the pills, but it was hard to do so. They were so big, and his mouth and throat were both only toddler sized. Susie Q found a sachet of special pill lubricant in the pod's delivery tube, and she squirted some onto the massive pills. This helped, and very soon he had forced them down his throat.

"And now for your first injection of the growth programme. This'll be easier than you think."

Ian turned his head away, and he felt a small twinge in his upper arm.

"Nearly done, darling!"

Susie Q strapped some cuffs over his wrists, which were attached to a small socket in the wall of the pod by thin wires ending in a flattish, oval plug. He was worried. He knew that he would need to have six sets of pills and daily sets of injections for a whole six months. He also had to have the electronic stimulation, and the thought concerned him. Supposing Susie Q had a mechanical breakdown, or her memory banks failed. What if she became tired of pretend flirting with an eighteen-month-old toddler?

"Susie Q, do you have to go in for a periodical service, or a regular check on your memory banks?"

"Oh no, that happens every time I'm on standby. If I need an update to my operating system, or if previous updates have introduced a glitch, that's all taken care of in the charging period."

Ian was very worried about this.

"I know you have a lovely soft outer shell, but do you have a metal frame, cogs and wheels and all sorts of machine-like parts?"

"Bless you Ian, how little you know about robots of today. The best models have real bones made from deselected people. There are some parts of me which are like you described, but we also have naturally evolving parts, like nails and hair. Our memories are contained on small chips that are as powerful as three million old main frame computers. We can answer difficult questions at lighting speed, and we have access to cloud based additional computing and memory backup if required."

"Let me ask you an extremely hard question. Can a robot ever really love a human?"

I'm Back!

"I can try, or better still it may happen naturally."

"You did tell me that you loved me too, just now."

"Yes I did say that. It's been programmed as the correct response, as we robots are only allowed to say nice things. It would be much better if humans had that same restriction, don't you think?"

The days went by slowly. Ian could hardly bear to tot up how long he had to go before he was (sort of), twenty-five. He remembered old stories about prisoners who were kept in cells, who painstakingly scratched a mark on the cell wall for every day of their incarceration. Now that the prison service had been disbanded, all prisons had been converted into high class accommodation.

The inmates had been handed over to the Population Police when the buildings had been decommissioned. They were all humanely deselected. There was much less crime now as many misdemeanours, such as rape, murder and other serious crimes were treated as a one-way ticket to an NDF depot. Minor crimes were dealt with very simply. One crime meant you had to do community service for five years. The second crime rated a physical mutilation (although you could choose what would be chopped off), and the third guaranteed that the miscreant would be dealt with by the NDF.

"Susie Q, how can I know what age I am during different parts of the growth programme?"

"Tests are done every two months. After these tests, we can tell you how old you now seem to be. You'll also be measured every day, without you even being aware of it. Gentle laser beams surround you every five minutes, and the data is fed directly into our massive main frame computers, which are housed in a huge complex in the Sahara Desert.

The big computers are called ETHEL and WARREN. ETHEL stands for Extended Transient Hosting Etherweb Logarithmic processing, and WARREN stands for Watchable and Auditory Reincarnation Reproduction Editable Nano computing.

They're careful to make sure that when they replace parts for ETHEL or WARREN, they use the right pieces for the specific machine. It would be terrible if they used a WARREN piece for ETHEL."

"Wow! Is that all true?"

"Some of it, kiddio. I made the rest up for a laugh."

Susie Q giggled. Ian had to laugh too.

After two months, Ian was told that he was now the size of a ten-year-old. After four months he was similar to an eighteen-year-old. By the end of the six months he was indeed looking like a person of twenty-five. Way before that, when he was an artificial sixteen, he had felt the sap beginning to rise, and he was looking forward to asking Susie Q if he could have a kiss and a cuddle. He had very much hoped that something else could be requested. He dithered somewhat, but he had finally taken the plunge.

"Susie Q, my dearest, would I now be allowed to kiss you, and can we just see where that leads us?"

"Are you sure Ian? I wouldn't want you to be disappointed if things didn't go to plan."

Ian thought about this very carefully for at least ten seconds, and then he said:

"Let's go for it!"

"Ian, please be very careful with me, because I'm worth ten million pounds."

"I'm afraid I can't afford that much, darling, but you can share some of my pills!"

Ian moved gingerly towards Susie Q, and he brushed his pursed lips very gently across hers. Her lips felt lush and moist and not at all like a machine's extremities. He smelt again that inexplicable feminine scent, coupled with the faintest hint of lily of the valley.

"Are you wearing perfume?"

"My artificial pores have exuded that for you, as it seemed the right thing to do."

I'm Back!

Ian didn't want to be reminded that Susie Q was just a machine, even if she was worth a fortune.

He leaned in for another gentle kiss, and he was surprised when she moved towards him and returned his kiss with ardour. The pleasant interlude was brief, but it was most promising. He felt like a real teenager, tiptoeing towards the precarious ravine of adolescence. He had just reached the edge of that yawning chasm in his current incarnation, and he had fallen head over heels into the most satisfying experience of his life. They kissed and cuddled for some while, and they finally made love, at first cautiously but then with unrestrained enthusiasm.

Susie Q and Ian were now lying in each other's arms on his pod bed. Luckily, he had the stature of a normal sixteen-year-old, and Susie Q was petite. He cuddled her and kissed her smiling face repeatedly. Suddenly, he sensed that she was crying.

"My love, my angel, why are you weeping?"

"Ian, what is weeping?"

"Those drops of water falling from your eyes are tears. We humans call that crying, sobbing, or weeping."

"My lamb, I don't think that has ever happened to me before. Perhaps something is amiss inside. I'll ask for an emergency service today, to make sure that nothing is leaking in my tubes and pipes."

Ian sighed. For a tiny, sublime moment he had forgotten that Susie Q was not a perfect, loveable human. He sat up, blinked, and cried like a baby.

"Ian, why are you crying, sobbing, or weeping?"

Chapter 6

Susie Q had contacted the WRO robot maintenance service, and she had been thoroughly inspected. They had found nothing amiss at all with her internal workings. The robotic brain technicians had also been consulted. After giving her various tests, they had concluded that she might be suffering from a cyborg infection called humanitis. Humanitis was rare, and it was regarded as being a true sign of vulnerability. Because it was rarer than a beard on a eunuch, many technicians didn't believe it existed.

Robots had always been built to be impervious to any emotions. Happiness, sadness, joy, laughter, jealousy, love, tenderness et al had been eradicated from their mental programmes as far as possible, in order to stop robots becoming too attached to humans, or to each other.

The experts decided that as Ian was the very first AR subject, that it would be imprudent (and perhaps over hasty), to remove Susie Q from his presence. She was vital to the success of his progress. More to the point, she was automatically relaying everything that was happening to Ian to the WRO databases, all the while she was with him. Even when she was on standby, she was his own personal monitor. In this way, the technical people, medics, and nurses were receiving constant updates, that were discussed every morning at the multi-disciplinary meetings held by Yoder and the other specialists.

They all had mixed feelings about humans and robots coupling, especially as Susie Q was so valuable. It wasn't totally unheard of, although previous episodes had been very brief and without emotion. They had also been with early robots who were

I'm Back!

not much better than inflatable dolls. Susie Q was a more complicated thing, and although Ian had been acting with her as if she were a woman, she was after all just a superior technical machine, not a warm-blooded human being.

After a heated discussion, they had decided to let this ridiculous 'romance' run its course. What could be the worst that could happen? Susie Q might be accidentally contaminated or broken by undue contact with an excitable human. They could always take her to bits and use the parts for new robots. Automaton progress had been amazing, and they believed that soon they could make vast armies of robots, so that the human population could be further still (and very usefully), reduced.

Although Susie Q continued to spy on Ian and to send details to the powers that be in the WRO, she didn't sense that this was happening. She did know that she was monitoring him, but as it was all automatic, she had no need to concentrate on the process. Therefore, she didn't feel guilty. In fact, as emotions were foreign to robots, it was very doubtful if she would have felt any regret, even had she been fully aware of snitching on Ian. The only reservations that the multi-disciplinary team had concerned her apparent tears. Humanitis was the only possible explanation (if it was a real phenomenon.) They concluded in the end that it was more likely that it was just due to a faulty piece of wiring, or a pipe that had kinked when she and Ian were canoodling.

Day by day, Ian and Susie Q became even closer. Ian looked forward to bringing her out of standby by every morning, and she felt a strange sort of glow when she was in his presence.

The daily half a dozen pills, and multiple injections, had a marked effect on Ian, who had become more muscular and toned than he ever was in his old body. The electronic stimulation used cuffs like a blood pressure machine, and the current being fed onto his wrists wasn't unpleasant; it just felt rather strange. He had been doing simple exercises every day, and Susie thought he looked peculiar doing star jumps and squats.

"Ian, do you realise that when you squat, you sometimes make a growling noise from your bottom?"

Ian had to laugh. He had always been inclined to fart a lot, and several of his girlfriends, and his disloyal wife, had remarked that farting was not funny. Ian had retorted that all his male friends thought doing so was hilarious. It seemed that this was a marked divide between men and women. It was great that Susie Q was not worried about the occasional bottom burp.

He was finally allowed to leave the pod every two or three days, provided he had Susie Q with him. This was fine by him, as he realised that he was even more in love with her than ever. He had to constantly tell himself to remember that she was only a machine. She was so funny, witty, and loving. As their relationship developed, he had found her to be more and more touchy feely, and that suited him perfectly.

It was now four months into his growth programme, and he had reached the age of twenty-two according to his structured development chart. He was delighted, and he had even grown a stylish beard. Susie Q knew what a beard was, but unlike all his previous female partners, she never complained. Also, she didn't ask him to 'shave that bloody thing off.'

When they left the pod, they often visited the multi-sensory hologram room. They could use different experience modes, such as fields, lakes and mountains, beaches, and zoos. Ian's favourite was the beaches setting. You could even choose which beach the room should become, or just let the equipment do its own thing.

Susie Q asked him one day what a zoo was.

"Oh, have you never heard of, or seen a zoo?"

"No, Ian but let's try it!"

In a flash, the zoos mode was implemented, and it was lovely wandering round the paths, and even inside the cages. The animals weren't real, and therefore Ian and Susie Q could come to no harm. Susie Q had never seen gorillas, elephants, lions, tigers

I'm Back!

and many other of the virtual, penned animals.

"Why haven't I seen these animals before, sweetikins?"

"Because they are all very nearly extinct."

Susie looked baffled.

"What happened to them?"

"Some of them were hunted, and people shot them."

"Were they hungry?"

"No, they were just cruel and nasty people."

"Did these awful people get executed or imprisoned?"

"No, I'm afraid not. Though a lot of people hated the hunters, they got away with it."

Susie Q burst into tears.

"Look Ian, I'm crying, sobbing or weeping, and I feel sad."

Ian put his arms round his precious Susie Q, and he knew that he had never felt a greater love for anybody, than that he felt for his beautiful treasure.

Chapter 7

The next day, Ian woke early, and he was worried when he saw that Susie Q was no longer in the pod. He pressed the emergency button of the pod's immersephone and his call was answered immediately.

"Emergency, which service do you require: pod, pills or robot companion?"

"Robot companion please, this is very urgent."

Yoder was suddenly on the line, but to Ian it looked and felt as if he was standing right next to him.

"Where's my Susie Q? I'm worried that something has happened to her."

Yoder gave his usual half-hearted smile and said:

"She's cried again, and we're trying to desensitise her, so that these unnecessary feelings don't cause her to overheat."

"Mr. Yoder, you really are a heartless person. I love her dearly, and she's my soul mate."

"That is a fallacy, my dear Tudeep. You think you love her, but humans shouldn't have deep relationships with robots. We know that you have had artificial sex with her. Some of my team thought that this was inadvisable, but others thought that it would help you get through the six months of the growth programme. I personally, do not favour sex at all. It's unbelievably messy, and I think it's much over-rated. Strangely, some of the younger members of WRO quite like it."

"When is Susie Q coming back?"

"When you wake up in the morning, she'll be there, plugged in as usual..."

I'm Back!

Ian pressed the end call button whilst Yoder was still speaking. Our hero couldn't be bothered to talk to him any longer. Ian couldn't think of anything else but his dear Susie Q all day, and he was desperately worried that whatever they had done to her would change their relationship. He took his pills at the right times, and he gave himself the injections the way that Susie Q had shown him. He also administered the electronic stimulation to himself. If he forgot his pills, his injections, or the stimulation, a voice which seemed to be inside his head reminded him that he had omitted parts of his growth programme.

He tried to be a part of a 6D film sensation, which promised ultra-lifelike enjoyment, but he was unable to amuse himself with anything at all, in the absence of Susie Q. He went to bed early, and he had more nightmares. In one of them, Susie Q had returned as an aggressive and domineering woman, who nagged him incessantly.

She told him that sex was messy and over-rated, and then she metamorphosed into the dreaded Yoder. He twitched the corners of his thin-lipped mouth and told Ian tersely that he was a naughty boy. He said that Ian was going to be put on an anti-growth programme to return him to his earlier eighteen-month-old toddler state. Ian woke up shivering and shaking. He looked over to the corner, and thankfully Susie Q was back.

"Wake up, Little Susie, Wake up."

She opened her eyes.

"What did they do to you, my sweet little love?"

Susie unplugged herself and then walked over to Ian. She kissed him and then tapped on his hands in morse code. It was one of Ian's strange hobbies, and he had offered to show her how it worked during a short power cut in the pod, just for fun. She had been an exemplary pupil. Learning and remembering the whole morse code alphabet in just under four minutes had seemed easy for her. He had offered to inspect her morse, but she said she would always remember the letters and how to use them.

"What are you doing? Is that mor…"

Susie Q silenced him with a kiss.

She resumed her tapping. She told him that she knew that they had tried to desensitise her. She also explained that she had somehow managed to roll herself back to a previous version of her operating system, so that their desensitisation update had not taken effect. She morse tapped that Ian should be careful what he said to her out loud.

He tapped on the back of her hand, that he thought they should run away. She said she was scared to do so. She told him that she would be worried about what would happen if she needed technical attention. She was frightened that she might break down and become little more than an expensive heap of wires, pipes, and microchips. Even the naturally evolving parts would deteriorate rapidly in that event.

Ian cuddled his darling girl and thought hard. Thinking hard didn't do any good at all. He was perplexed. He tapped, 'let's wait until I am twenty-five, and then we can think again. We're caught in a trap.'

Chapter 8

The days seemed to go by quickly, and the growth programme wasn't as hard to bear as Ian had thought it would be. The drudgery of six over large pills, injections and electronic stimulation was leavened by the exciting robotic company he kept.

Susie Q seemed to learn more and more about how to please Ian every day, and she was affectionate, kind, and attentive. Ian was still worried that she was only a machine. Nonetheless, he was instantly charmed out of his doldrums, every time she spoke to him. She was funny and inquisitive. She said she was interested to learn what Southwold was like, as she knew that was where Ian lived.

"There used to be a big brewery there in the olden days. It was popular, and they even took visitors round the brewing and fermentation rooms on regular tours. Sometimes, they couldn't go to the fermentation room, as there was a high CO_2 level, and a red light warned people not to enter."

"I could've gone in there at any time, as I don't breathe."

"But I've seen you breathe Susie Q."

"It's just an automatic thing that serves no purpose. If you look at me when I'm breathing, you'll see that I don't actually inhale and exhale."

"Every breath you take, I'll be watching you in future, to see if I can tell that you're just mimicking us humans."

"Tosh, Ian. I think you know I'm worth £10,000,000."

"To me, my precious, you are priceless."

"That always seems to me to be a funny word. If it means that something is so precious that its value cannot be determined, it should be pricemore."

Ian had to laugh. Susie Q looked at him archly, raised her eyebrows and giggled. He couldn't always tell when she was joking.

"Can I ask you a serious question?"

"Of course, but you may not get a serious answer."

"My wife always used to tell me that I was boring. She said I was old before my time and I was already in what she called 'the pipe and slippers brigade,' when I was a teenager. Am I that boring?"

Susie Q lifted her head, gave a short snort, and she said:

"Sorry. I fell asleep, did you say something?"

Ian was dismayed. In a few short seconds he was undismayed, when he realised that Susie Q was just joshing, yet again.

"My wife also used to say she hoped I died before I got even older. I thought that was cruel. Do you think I'm too serious?"

"How can anybody be too serious? Or too anything? They are what they are, and that can't be changed. I'd like to be a real girl but look what happened to Pinocchio!"

Ian wasn't sure he fully followed her reasoning. He was also surprised she even knew who Pinocchio was.

"How do you know who Pinocchio was?"

"Sometimes I know things, but I don't know why. I think I told you about the universal knowledge that we all have, us Susies."

Ian was suddenly worried. He had forgotten about her shared knowledge, and he was very conscious that all the other Susies would know that he and his dearly beloved robot girlfriend had been kissing and much more, in the comfort of his recovery pod.

Susie Q seemed to read his thoughts.

"Some of the other robots have asked me what making love is like. I'm one of

I'm Back!

the few Susies with that special receptacle that you seem to like so much. It's difficult for me to tell them how nice it is, and the ones without that receptacle could never experience it without being modified."

"Do you really like it?"

"I like it. I like the way you run your fingers through my hair."

Ian had a vague memory of an old song, and he wondered again if Susie Q was teasing him. She looked at him with those big blue eyes and said:

"You'll never walk alone."

"Are you joking again?"

"If I am, does that mean that I'm becoming more human?"

"I just wondered if you had any special training in old music?"

"I don't need any training; I've got instant access to twenty billion songs. I know that poor music fans normally have only a tiny fraction of those at their disposal. I must say though, that a large proportion of the songs are not my cup of coffee."

"Don't you mean not my cup of tea?"

"I may do, but don't you think it would've been more polite to ignore my little mistake?"

"It's important to get things right."

"Balderdash and fiddlesticks! And bumholes. If you don't stop being mean to me I'll turn on my angry mode, and I'll shout at you."

Ian was sad when he realised that Susie Q and he had just had their very first quarrel. He wondered if he ought to tell her that the word bumholes was not generally used as a swear word. He decided that this would not be very tactful.

"Susie Q, do you know that real women often take ages to forget things said in the heat of the moment? Some of them never ever forgive their husbands or boyfriends for minor infringements or hasty words."

"Ian, robots never forget anything. However, we do know that forgiveness is a pretty good thing, and it's programmed into our behavioural processes. It's impossible for us not to forgive."

"What a fantastic notion!"

Chapter 9

As the end of the growth programme drew near, Ian and Susie Q had many morse code conversations. They knew that Ian would be discharged very shortly, but they didn't yet know how they were going to manage to run away together. There were several problems. The most major one was that Ian could hardly just walk out with Susie Q, without being caught. The tapping session went like this:

"What if I asked for a friend to come here, to help me on my journey?"

"They might allow that, but who could you ask? And how would that help?"

"I've got no real friends that would be suitable, but maybe I could hire a robot escort from a dating site? I could ask her to pretend to be you as we leave the WRO complex together."

"She'd have to look like me."

"All the other Susies look like you."

She pulled a face, as if she could smell something rank.

"Poo! You might be able to hire an inferior robot who just looked like me. But she wouldn't be in the same class!"

Ian was surprised that Susie Q could feel pride. Ian decided to try to find a supplier for robot girl friends on the Solar System Web. He hoped his electrajot was not being monitored. He set to immediately, and he quickly found an interesting site. Fortunately, it guaranteed that it was securely encrypted, and it promised that no users could be spied upon as they were choosing new partners to be hired. Ian looked at their services, and he was pleased to see that robot escorts were offered, as well as humans.

He spent a long time looking at these 'ladies,' and he was delighted when he came upon a Susie section. He found out that they were refurbished robots which used to belong to the WRO. They had discarded the old robots when they built more sophisticated models, like the Susies that they now used. None of the earlier robots had artificial receptacles like Susie Q. Ian laughed. Even he thought of her silicon pouch as an artificial receptacle. He was pleased, but rather disturbed, to see that they all did look exactly like Susie Q. Fortunately, that suited his plan down to the ground.

In the special delivery instructions, Ian asked for the lady robot to be sent to the WRO complex perimeter on a certain date at a particular time, and he selected the Joanna Lumley voice option. He also wanted her to wear an outfit that would be a good likeness to the outfits which Susie Q customarily wore. He entered those details too. Finally, he gave instructions that she should wear a face mask, and that when she arrived she should explain that she was Ian Tudeep's friend, Enid Brighton.

He completed his delivery instructions by saying that Enid would need to explain that she had come to keep him company on his way home. If questioned further she should say that once she was at his home, she would help him to get used to his new incarnation. If asked why she was wearing a mask, she was to say that she had an accident with boiling water, when she was a small child, and that she was nervous when people looked at her scars.

He pressed the 'buy now' button and started to plan how they would inveigle the Enid robot into staying behind, when Susie Q and he left the WRO.

I'm Back!

Chapter 10

On the day that Ian and Susie Q planned to depart from the WRO, he was on tenter-hooks. He wondered what nineterhooks might be, and he even looked up the derivation of the word tenterhooks. Yes, Ian was that sad. His ambitious (and probably flawed), plan was that he should go to the room that housed the WRO's teleportation booths early that day. He would have to be there before Susie Q arrived. (If challenged when she was on the way, Susie Q was to say that she wanted to make sure that Ian left Geneva in good spirits, and to ensure that he followed all the discharge procedures properly.)

The robot escort (hopefully as good a fake Susie Q as she looked on the website), would have to come by long-distance aerobus rather than teleportation, and she should be told to go to the reception area. She should announce who she was and explain the ostensible reason for her visit. Susie Q would collect her double and bring her to the teleportation room. Once in the room, she would tell the robot escort that she should wait there, while she and Ian entered two of the booths to do some technical checks. Susie Q was hoping, like Ian, that Enid would be a comparatively old model. These would always have been programmed to follow orders, even if they emanated from another robot.

Everything went surprisingly well. The escort turned up on time wearing a mask, and she checked in with the receptionist Susie, who had no reason to doubt her story. Enid sat patiently waiting for Ian's helper, as she had been asked to do. Susie Q arrived and told the receptionist that she would deal with the visitor. She took Enid to the teleportation room. Ian asked if all was well.

"Oh yes. Enid was waiting for me. There were no problems."

Ian smiled at Enid, and he said:

"Enid, I'm Ian Tudeep. I want you to wait here while we just check these two booths. When we come out again, I'll show you round. If you take your mask off when we go into the booths, you'll find it more comfortable."

He didn't know if that would make sense to a robot, who probably didn't care if she had a mask on or not, but Enid nodded. She took her mask off and gave it to Ian. Ian hid it in his trouser pocket. He was most gratified to see that his choice of escort had been justified. She was genuinely like Susie Q. Even he had to admit he would have been fooled, if she had told him that she was his own beloved robot.

The teleportation booths were all ready for action, and Ian and Susie Q knew that they would already have Heathrow in their stored destinations. (When people were teleported to the WRO these were created by automatic storage of the locations from whence people had come.) Susie Q, as a senior robot, had full authority to be in the room if other people turned up. As she was also responsible for Ian, she could probably bluff her way out of any tight spots, if they were disturbed. They were in luck, as nobody came there while they were implementing their hare-brained escape plan.

"Wait there, Enid. We just want to check some settings in these booths."

"OK, Mr. Tudeep. I'll sit here and read something on my memory banks. They uploaded some incredibly old magazines for me, and they look quite interesting. I'd never heard of Readers' Digest before, but these periodicals seem to have some funny stories in them."

Ian couldn't help being a little startled by Enid's Joanna Lumley voice. Joanna was the preferred and default voice for all of the Susies, but it still seemed strange to him, hearing all of them using one voice. He and Susie Q entered the booths, and they set the controls to speed them on their way to the Heathrow terminal. Ian wondered

I'm Back!

how he would feel when he got back home, with a very glamourous girlfriend. The doors of the booths shut (more silently than the one he had used on the way to Geneva.) They were on their way!

Chapter 11

Their teleportation was completed easily. The booths no longer had accidents with flies, like they used to do in the olden days. It had been inordinately expensive to upgrade all the old terminals and to ensure that new ones had the same degree of protection. The man who had designed the scanners which detected the presence of foreign bodies in the booths, was Adam Vincent. The costs were phenomenal, but Vincent said they were justified, and he had written a scholarly article for the medical journals, which he had called The Vincent Price.

Susie Q seemed genuinely interested in the reason why they would need to use an aerobus to get to Southwold from Heathrow. She was confused as Enid had used a long-distance aerobus to get to Geneva from England.

"Aerobuses are generally used for shorter voyages. Teleportation seems ideal for people who want to go from one country to another. We wanted Enid to use a special long-distance aerobus to get to Geneva. That was because we wanted to meet her before she went to the teleportation room. The way we did it, we were able to make sure that nobody else was in the room before we went into the booths.

You may not know this, but not all places have ready access to teleportation. As it happens, Southwold has always been a place where old-fashioned things have been prized. Way back in the dim and distant past, people used to go there because it seemed to them to be like time-travelling. Even in the 1990's it was likened to going back to a town in the 1950's. The local council refused to have chains of shops represented in Southwold for a long while."

I'm Back!

Ian was quite pleased to show off his historical knowledge. His ex-wife, Beryl, had always said it was one of his most boring traits.

"What are shops, Ian?"

"They used to be places where people went to buy things. There are still a few scattered here and there, but most people prefer to buy everything online."

"What kind of things did they used to buy in shops?"

"All kinds of everything. At one time they had to close on Sundays, and most of them also closed on one weekday for the whole afternoon. On the other days they were usually open from about nine in the morning until five o'clock, or so, in the afternoon."

"Why didn't they open all the time?"

"Some shops tried to be open 24/7. That's 24 hours a day and seven days a week, but that didn't seem to work out."

"I thought people always bought everything on the Solar System Web."

"Oh no. The start of online shopping was when people used the World Wide Web. That was a long time before the Solar System Web was invented. After the Solar System Web was deployed, our technical experts started to collaborate with aliens from Mars, so we could all buy things from huge warehouses situated on their planet. They managed to speak to us, after quickly learning Universito. Massive depots could be rented cheaply there. They used huge robots to build them. The move to place them elsewhere in the solar system was first mooted by a guy called Archie Kevin. He talked about space so often they used to call him Kevin spacey. In our early dealings with Martians we never saw them. Everything was discussed and agreed remotely."

"If he was a Guy, why was he also called Archie?"

"Was that a robot joke?"

"Could be, my lovely!"

"Be quiet, sweetie, and listen. It was also before we fell out with the Martians, who didn't like the way humans treated each other. They also abhorred the way we were so cruel to animals. They said that although they'd studied our seven deadly sins before they came to visit us, they couldn't understand how humans could be so nasty. They knew about The Ten Commandments too, and they thought those rules were very sound. They couldn't understand why people didn't live by them. Anyway, I'm getting ahead of myself.

We had sent several spaceships to Mars much earlier, but our astronauts didn't encounter the Martians when they were there. We thought, incorrectly as it turned out, that the Red Planet was uninhabited. Mars used to have water on its surface, and it was thought that it might be capable of supporting life. Mars is smaller than Earth."

"What is Earth, Ian?"

"That's where we all live, Susie Q dearest."

"But that's crazy. Humans don't live in the soil. They live on top of it."

"No, dear. That's just what our own planet is called. I don't know why. Mars is the seventh largest plant in our Solar System, and I don't know why that's called Mars either. I do know that the length of a day on Mars is only slightly longer than ours. It's also colder than it is on Earth."

"If we didn't encounter the Martians when we sent space craft there, why did they want to meet us? I can understand us asking 'Is there Life on Mars?' But did they already know that our planet was inhabited?"

"Apparently they did. They managed to learn other languages of ours, including English. They were very clever, and they even listened to, and understood, snippets of our old TV programmes. Their favourite was Inauguration Street. That's been running since the 1960s. The original actors are now dead, so they use holograms now. After listening to Inauguration Street, the Martians thought that all humans normally talked with a Northern accent. They even tried to imitate that accent. Some of the Martians also tried to use Lancashire slang. They had quite some difficulty understanding various words and phrases. Apparently one of the eminent alien scholars thought that a hotpot

I'm Back!

was a form of torture.

We were negotiating with them, in English by then, so that we would be allowed to have those huge warehouses on their planet, and we paid them in Japanese Knotweed plants. They love these because they taste like Rhubarb. It's their all-time favourite taste. They weeds were sent to Mars on several further missions and unloaded by robots, so that they could take them to their nurseries. They always thanked us for such huge quantities of the weeds. They seemed very surprised that we had sent such large plants and in vast quantities.

Anyway, back to my explanation about the Martians and their experiences of dealing with humans. Our dealings with the Martians came about because, after our early Mars missions, we heard a few bars of music coming from the Red Planet, with a regularly repeated passage. The music was short; it was just a few bars. A prominent astrophysicist called May Brian wrote an important paper, called The Mars Bars. She also sent back a variation of The Mars Bars, and they responded. They re-transmitted The Mars Bars to us, this time in a different key.

We had been communicating with them for quite a few years before they arrived. When they finally landed on Earth, they were surprised that we were so enormous. That was when they twigged why the Japanese Knotweed deliveries were much larger than they thought they would be. We were convinced that they would be vaguely humanoid, and we thought they would be of a similar size to us. We were wrong in both cases.

When they did come, we didn't even see them at first. They saw us though and were amazed at how gigantic we were. We realised that a lot of places had infestations of tiny creatures, which looked like disfigured crustaceans. It turned out that they were the small Martians. That was when we finally realised that these small creatures were members of vast armies of highly intelligent Martians. We took advantage of their size and bullied them. We treated them very badly. They all left one morning, using their invisible spaceships. Since then they've not talked to us. They also convinced all the aliens on other planets to have nothing to do with us."

Susie Q totally ignored Ian's Martian digression and said:

"Wow! It must have been most inconvenient having to go to shops."

"Men always thought the same, but women seemed to love going shopping. There used to be large complexes, called shopping malls, which ladies loved. Men hated them. One shop even had a way of forcing you to go round very single aisle, even if you only wanted one thing and knew where it was. They also used to sell furniture which you had to assemble yourself. The parts were badly labelled, and they often didn't fit together well.

Another one of men's most hated shops, was one which sold things with labels that showed expensive recommended retail prices. The labels were marked with massive, but probably false, reductions in the prices. The shops were very untidy, and often there were things lying all over the floor. It was almost impossible to find anything."

"Sounds horrid to me. But what was Southwold like, when people came to see the town at its most popular in the past?"

"It was busy in the summer, but almost deserted in the winter. There were a lot of places that were rented out for holidays, or which were second homes."

"Were people allowed to have more than one home, Ian? How wasteful. And what were holidays?"

"Lots of people had second homes, and some of them had many. Nowadays, we are encouraged to have only one home. Holidays were taken when people left their places to go somewhere else. They used to spend a week or two on breaks away, just for a change. Holidays don't happen nearly so much now though."

"Why didn't they use technology to give them the same kind of experience we had with the zoos mode?"

"They just didn't have that kind of reality-based technology. They even thought there were only three dimensions."

"How primitive!"

Chapter 12

After an uneventful trip to Southwold from Heathrow on the aerobus, Ian and Susie Q arrived at Blueberry Hill, and Ian showed her his condenselow. He had used his eWallet to pay for the aerobus, as he had no other option. He wondered how long it would be before the WRO found out where they had gone, after leaving Heathrow.

"It's not much, but it's mine."

"Ian, robots don't care where they are situated. That means we don't therefore have a liking for any particular buildings."

"That's a shame. In the past men built some fantastic edifices. There were some fantastically creative craftsmen, and they built cathedrals, castles, and wonderful palaces. Some of them took hundreds of years to build."

"What a waste of time and money. All that's needed is something purely functional, like your condenselow. I just need to plug myself in every night, to recharge myself. I'm still a little concerned because I won't get my regular system updates and fixes. If I start to do anything strange, will you be patient with me?"

Susie Q started to sing a doleful song and hopped up and down in front of Ian.

"My heart is like a buffalo,

My love is like a deer,

My sweet is like a truffalo,

Tra, la, la, I have no fear."

Ian was alarmed at this absurd behaviour, but he didn't know what to say.

Fooled you! I've been trying to learn how to play spanks."

I'm Back!

Ian was considerably bucked up by this idea.

"Sorry darling, my predictive toxt has gone rang."

"Oh no my love, what can we do to get it fixed?"

"Fear not, my stewed plum, I'm now on tip of thongs."

Ian was aghast. (Not a ghast, you understand but aghast. Sorry, but this sort of nonsense is catching.)

"Oh Ian, my poor little lamb. That fooled you. I was just tricking you. Perhaps I'll do some more comedy routines for you.

Knock, knock.

Who's there?

Susie.

Susie Who?

No, Susie Q!

All joking aside, there's a distinct chance that my innards will give up or start to malfunction. Who's Mal Function anyway?"

"Susie Q, I must admit that although you are very clever and good at most things, comedy isn't your strong point."

In spite of his breezy reply, Ian had made a mental note that they would need to find a robot technician to keep Susie Q serviced and updated regularly. He wondered if that could be done remotely, like it was when she was at the WRO..

"What shall we do, my darling?"

"Why don't you show me your diginews machine. Have you got a nice modern one?"

Ian groaned; he knew that a lot of his household appliances were very dated. His diginews machine received regular feeds for his delectation, but the screen was small. It was only 75 inches, and the picture was not even 6 dimensional. He turned the machine on by using a wake word, and the World Broadcasting Corporation news started to play.

There were the usual things about slippery American presidents and well-known soap stars. (Nothing had changed in many years.) The newscaster, Tim Tiny, said he had some breaking news. He tried to seem masterful (without much visible success), before he said:

"We now go to Geneva, in Switzerland, where our local correspondent Willy Waving will be interviewing the Chief Executive Officer of the World Reincarnation organisation. Hallo, Willy."

There was an instantaneous reply from Willy. The problems of audio latency had long since been fixed. There was no gap between Tim's salutation and Willy's response.

"Good morning Tim. It's a sunny day here in Geneva, and I'm in the office of Hiram Prendergast, who's the CEO of the World Reincarnation Organisation. The WRO is very well known to our viewers and, despite a slow start in 2067, they've been making steady progress in what they call AR. The full name is Artificial Reincarnation. Initial research, using small animals, attracted violent protests from people who disapproved of vivisection, in all its forms. Their work has continued to create a lot of interest and discussion, regarding the morality, technical feasibility, and efficacy of AR.

Hallo, Mr. Prendergast. Thanks for making me welcome today. I know that you've got an important message to give us, but will you allow me to set out more of the background to our news item first?"

Hiram nodded his approval. He didn't have much choice. Ian found it difficult to take him seriously because he was the spitting image of Mr. Magoo. Ian knew that this fictional cartoon character was created in 1949.

"I understand that a little while ago the WRO was seeking a volunteer to become the first human patient to undergo AR. Forgive me, but I must tell our viewers that when you first started to try to find this human guinea pig, you had some strange requests. For example, who can forget the transgender man who was worried that he might be reincarnated as the original woman he used to be?"

I'm Back!

"Mr. Waving, it was understandable that people should be concerned, but our Health and Safety and Compliance Director, Bret Allover-Oncemore, has brought in tough new policies and procedures which have weeded out frivolous requests, and which would help us to police any human AR trials with great precision. We had one lady applicant who wanted to be reincarnated as Jennifer Lopez or Brad Pitt. (She'd become enchanted by both of them, when she viewed old TV programmes and films.) Her request was turned down because we were not entirely certain that she'd be a serious candidate, who'd carefully considered the gravity of the ground-breaking AR trial.

We had another communication from a man who was called Wilfred, but wanted to be a woman after his AR. He said he'd only consider AR if he could be called Milfred. We turned him down as we thought it was a prank call. The very next day a man called who said he was a stevedore. He told us he would only submit to AR if he could be a woman called Dora Steve. We think it may have been the same fellow, or maybe it was a friend of his. We rejected his application too.

As you are probably aware, when the WRO started to make these experiments, everything was done very much under wraps. We set up a small laboratory in Geneva, and began tests using small animals. Things went badly at first, and because we couldn't talk to our early patients, it wasn't possible to find out if cognitive and behavioural processes had been affected by AR.

We wanted to use humans to get over that difficulty. We were extremely conscious of the fact that even when human experiments started, the first few attempts might be viewed, by people who had a limited knowledge of AR, with derision and horror. We knew that some people would think that our experiments were little more than replications of the famous (but thankfully fictional), Dr. Frankenstein's efforts to create a new human being.

We knew that we were working on real (if artificial), reincarnation. We're pleased to say that our taking bodies are sourced legally from the deselection facilities of several major countries These cadavers are deemed to be in the absolute best condition, having been carefully preserved in our cryogenic facilities in Zurich.

We were approached by a serious candidate called Ian Tudeep, who met all of our requirements, and he fully understood the risks. He signed the relevant disclaimer papers, and he was artificially reincarnated six months ago. He's been well looked after. As well as the technical specialists keeping an eye on him at all times, he was tended to by one of our fabulous robot nurses, whom we call Susie Q. Ian absconded from our premises, without going through the proper discharge requirements, which would have given him very strict instructions about post AR checkups, including where and how these would be made. He also ran away with Susie Q. He thinks he is in love with her.

To make matters even worse, Susie Q may have developed an exceedingly rare robotic illness called humanitis. This is so uncommon that some technicians even deny its existence. This possible condition may have led to a mistaken belief by Susie Q that she has real feelings for him too. We tried to desensitise her when we noted that she used words of endearment to him. She also appeared to cry.

From a human point of view, Mr. Tudeep's going to be very disconcerted when he realises that his current relationship with Susie Q will never last. Financially, her loss would be a big blow to the WRO, as she's worth ten million pounds sterling. We need to speak to Ian Tudeep immediately, and very soon one of our top people will be on the way to Southwold, where we believe they are at present, in order to remonstrate with him. Our man's name is Mike Anick and he will be leading our search for Mr. Tudeep and Susie Q."

Ian turned the diginews holovision off. He needed to think. He was very confused, and worried about Prendergast's prediction that his relationship with Susie Q was doomed. Susie Q held his hand and gazed up at him. She'd been lying in his lap when they watched the news flash.

I'm Back!

She licked her lovely lips and said:

"I think we have a problem, sweetie pie!"

Ian tried to think of a place where they might hide. Try as he might, he couldn't envisage anywhere that might be safe from the WRO. He tentatively wondered if they might be able to get into the ruins of the old lighthouse. The landmark building had been condemned many years previously. It was boarded up, awaiting demolition. It had been bought by an historical society. They had also bought bits of the derelict pier, including the remains of the artwork showing George Orwell, and the water clock. These things were in storage awaiting renovation. The pier had been bombed by the World Royal Air Force, in order to make sure that it was destroyed properly. Their mission was only partially successful. The foreshore end was still in place.

The society had been particularly pleased to snap up some relics from the old brewery, which had been closed following the official banning of all alcoholic drinks. Ian knew that some people still brewed their own beer and made wine. The more adventurous people even distilled spirits. This was all done secretly. There were also some shops that still sold alcohol, but whenever the authorities found out that they were doing so, they took swift steps to close them down.

The Ministry of Health had decided that there was no longer any need for beer and spirits, as artificial alcohol pills had the same effect. Furthermore, they didn't cause the associated health problems and the consequent risk of anti-social behaviour. The alcohol pills, allegedly tasting like beer, were sold in pods designed for social gathering and pill popping, and they also had six-dimensional pub games like shove ha'penny and darts. The real ale enthusiasts had been very disgruntled, until the scientists who designed the alcohol pills had brought in new flavourings which they said successfully mimicked the old beers. Pills that were promised to taste just like various spirits were also introduced.

Ian reluctantly decided that the remains of the lighthouse were not suitable as a hiding place. He used his electrajot to go through his contacts, to see who might house them temporarily. One by one he disregarded them, as he decided that they were unsuitable or remembered that they were no longer alive. The ones who were no longer around had either died naturally, or they had been dealt with by the NDF. Some of the others were friends of his ex-wife. Ian ignored them as they might have been disinclined to help him, in view of their presumed loyalty to his former spouse.

There was one glimmer of hope. He came across an entry for an old school-friend of his, a lady with whom he had had a brief but memorable adolescent intrigue. This only lasted a matter of weeks, before she had been grounded by her father. He had come to see Ian's parents in a towering rage. He deprecated their relationship, as he said that they were far too young to be in love.

Luckily, Mitch Springs wasn't aware that Ian had deflowered his pretty daughter, Alice. Had he known that he would have been even more purple in the face, and his rage would have been skyscraping instead of just towering. Alice and Ian had been forewarned by her mother, Freda, when Mitch had been on the way to tackle Ian's parents about the danger of him leading his beloved daughter astray. Alice's mother was some twenty years younger than Mitch. She liked Ian, and she had admitted to herself that if Alice tired of him, she wouldn't mind being the cougar that helped him to regain his confidence. Ian was happily unaware of this, which was just as well, as Alice's mother was not bad looking at all. In fact, she could have made a young man a happy boy.

Freda had found out that Ian and Alice had been sleeping together, and she had told Ian that he might just get away with a telling off, if he and Alice denied that they had been making love for all of that summer, in the small but pleasant church yard just behind the high street. This was where Freda had spotted them late one night, as she was on the way home from visiting one of her friends. She thought it best not to tell Ian's father.

Mitch had banged on the door and Ian's Dad, Wilbur, had let him in. After a real

I'm Back!

argy-bargy, they had both decided that Alice and Ian should be permanently banned from seeing each other. The young ones were both fifteen, and they considered that they had been lucky to get away with it. More by chance than design, Alice wasn't pregnant, and although they were sad at being kept away from each other, they soon seemed to recover. When they had last met, Alice had snuggled up to Ian who had said:

"Dear Alice, I will always love you!"

"Darling Ian, I know that we've got to part. Please remember this vow. If ever you want me to help you with anything, and I mean anything, just call out my name and I'll come running, to see you again!"

They had both wept buckets of tears. They had never seen each other properly during the intervening thirty years. Ian had noticed her a couple of times, from afar, in the High Street, and each time it had an enormous effect upon him. His heart had leapt when he saw her. The Springs moved to Southend on Sea later, but Ian thought of Alice from time to time with great affection and sadness for what might have been. The address in his electrajot was where she used to live with her parents.

Ian relayed this story to Susie Q. He thought that they should go to Southend to try to enlist Alice's help. He had no immersephone or electrajot number for Alice, but he decided to ask their old school association if they could help. Whilst waiting for their help, he found out, by using the Solar System Web, that Alice had been working in the Multiple Resources department of an insurance company in Chelmsford, until she had married a man called Walter Nuisance. He wondered what on earth a Multiple Resources department was.

He found the answer on the company's official website. They said that Human Resources was a term they no longer used, as it might be thought to be demeaning to those animals that were still not yet extinct. It might also offend robot owners, as these machines were being used on a much wider basis, due to a lack of human applications for jobs. The company said they preferred to use the new term Multiple Resources. Ian thought this was complete hogwash. Or was that demeaning to hogs?

After a few electrajot calls, the school secretary (who also ran the association for ex-pupils), said that she would ask Alice if she minded her giving her current address to Ian. He was extremely nervous. He wondered if the representative of the WRO might turn up before they could get away. They therefore decided to travel to Southend immediately, on the off chance that Alice would have given the secretary permission to release her new contact details to Ian by the time they got there.

Chapter 13

Their journey to Southend was filled with many questions from Susie Q, who was fascinated about all manner of things. As she had only ever been in the WRO complex in Geneva, there were plenty of new sights to catch her attention. The aerobus to Essex was on time. The weather was fine, and they could see for miles. As they came near to the aPad in Southend, they saw the remains of what used to be the longest pleasure pier in the world.

Ian knew that at one time Southend had been a popular destination for day trippers. He had found out that many of them came from the East End of London. The East End was now an upmarket area, and old houses there were worth a fortune. Ian had looked at the ups and downs of various towns and cities over a period of many years. He thought that it was fascinating to see how some areas could become fashionable, with corresponding increases in the value of property, for no particular reason. The reverse also happened.

Ian had even seen digitally restored films of the beaches in Southend jam packed with tourists, enjoying Sunday outings to their favourite place. Southend had deteriorated badly in the latter part of the 20th century. It had been plagued with drug dealers and addicts, alcoholics, and aggressive beggars. The old independent shops had all closed, and with the burgeoning sales being made online, most of the chain stores had also been forced out of business. The main street was now half full of residential properties, and the other half was all comprised of food pill restaurants and alcohol pods.

Southend's decline and fall had been made even worse when the bombs on the SS Richard Montgomery had exploded, out of the blue, in August 2048. Ian had always been fascinated by the past, and his research into various historical events had been one of his favourite hobbies. His domineering ex-wife had scoffed at his interest in the past. She used to say that he would be better off paying more attention to the here and now, and then maybe his future wouldn't be so dull. Ian wondered what she would have made of his recent unwanted publicity.

The Richard Montgomery was carrying more than 1,000 tonnes of bombs to France in 1944. The ship sank in the Thames estuary, near Sheerness, when it was carrying its dangerous cargo to Cherbourg. The resultant tsunami, when the bombs eventually exploded, was much worse than had been expected, even though residents in both Southend and Sheerness all knew about the unstable nature of the explosives. Sheerness was not too severely affected. Southend took the brunt of the huge waves, which effectively destroyed its tatty area of amusement arcades, which was laughingly called the golden mile.

The mayor of Southend at the time was Kursaal Jones, who had been named thus by his parents. Jones' grandparents used to go to The Kursaal amusement park. It was one of the early purpose-built parks of this nature at the time it was opened. Ian had seen old photos of the Wall of Death, the Water Splash, and other attractions. He had also heard of a family who had found a dog swimming in the pool at the end of the Water Splash slide. They had taken him home, and they called him Splash. Ian also knew that there had once been an elegant ballroom in the Kursaal, where young couples could dance the night away.

At the time of the explosion and the resultant tidal onslaught, the amusement park was long gone, but the Kursaal building was still there. It had been disused for many years, and it was crumbling away, like an aged pensioner in the corner of a care home. Jones had taken a flyer and bought it very cheaply. It became a stacked

I'm Back!

condenselow plot, where one storey condenselows were slotted together to provide housing. The Kursaal was at the end of the old golden mile. However, the real end of the golden mile was when the waters ripped through the whole area and flattened everything in sight.

After that event, many building firms expressed an interest in developing the land where the arcades has been. Finally, a consortium headed by Jones' company, including various other opportunist contractors, redeveloped both ends of the promenade. This took in land from where the Kursaal building used to be, to just below where there had once been a theatre. It was called The Cliffs Pavilion. The operation included rebuilding the cliffs on the Western Esplanade, after removing the remains of the Cliff Lift. The locals used to joke about a singer who was called Cliff Richard. They said the Cliff Lift was actually a facial improvement operation.

The land behind the Eastern Esplanade was turned into a residential area with large fashionable houses. They named it Cornucopia Place. It was named after a tiny public house which had been the smallest place to buy alcoholic drinks on the golden mile, back in the day. Ian had been surprised to learn that the pub sometimes had naked female dancers. He had wondered what the punters thought about having such distractions so close to the bar. A large and beautifully landscaped park was originally planned for the area behind the new buildings, but in the end that also became housing.

The aerobus landed gently, after hovering over the aPad. Ian and Susie Q climbed down the steps which had been lowered automatically, and they headed towards the town centre using a shuttle bus. There had once been a reality celebrity from Southend, who was called Victoria Plaza. She was blonde, bouncy, and dim. She had a TV show called, 'It's Victoria – Innit?'

Her fame didn't last long. Ian wondered if her stage name had been a joke. He knew that there used to be a shopping complex at the top of the high street that had borne the same name. He had also discovered that even before that, there was a roundabout in the same place, which was called Victoria Circus. He had laughed when he found out that gents' and ladies' lavatories had been installed on the roundabout. It was called Bog Island by the locals.

Ian knew where Alice's parents used to live, and he had decided that if he heard nothing soon from Alice or the school secretary, they should go there, to see if Mr. and Mrs. Springs would give him her new address.

Susie Q was looking a little puzzled.

"If this is Southend, where's Northend?"

"This town was originally the south end of a place called Prittlewell. Prittlewell is in The Doomsday Book."

"The Doomsday Book, what's that? And why was Prittlewell called by that name?"

"William the Conqueror ordered that The Doomsday Book should be written to show who owed what in England. And as for Prittlewell, it's likely that there was a well in a place called Prittle."

Susie Q said that all sounded very uninteresting. Ian cuddled Susie Q and said:

"I know somebody who can prattle well."

"I hope you're not referring to me, you cheeky monkey. And you can take that look off your face!"

As they were walking up the street where Alice used to live with her parents, Ian's electrajot pinged. There was a welcome new message, which was from Alice's old school. It said that she had given permission for her address to be released to Ian and showed her contact details. It turned out that she was still living in the same house. Quite by chance, Ian and Susie Q were already headed the right way.

"Here we are Susie Q. This is where Alice lives now. It belonged to her mother and father. I hope she'll help us."

He pressed the intercom buzzer, and Alice's face appeared on the screen.

I'm Back!

"Hallo, do I know you?"

"Alice, you won't recognise me as I've got a new face, and a new body, but I'm Ian, and this is my lady friend Susie Q."

"Be quick. Come in now, as there will be people looking for you."

Ian was relieved that she seemed to want to help. The door clicked open and he and Susie Q went inside. Alice was in fine fettle. She had always been a naturally good-looking person, and she had matured into a lady-like and still attractive woman. Ian remembered that she must now be forty-five, like Ian used to be before his AR. Her violet eyes and brunette hair (with just a few hints of grey), made her a rather glamorous, middle-aged woman.

Susie Q saw Ian giving her the once over and felt rather strange. She wondered what jealousy felt like. She had an anxious, nagging feeling, which she had never experienced before. Susie Q didn't like it at all when Alice hugged Ian. She was a little relieved when Alice did the same to her.

She thought:

'Perhaps Alice is just a friendly person?'

An unpleasant looking and burly man, of about the same age as Alice, had entered the room into which Alice had ushered them. He was short and heavy. His close-cropped hair had balding spots here and there, and he had ugly warts on his head. He had a steely look about him, and Ian took an instant dislike to him.

"What've we got here, Alice? I suppose this is your old lover and his rusty machine?"

Ian's first reaction was to punch this man on his red-veined nose, but he managed to keep his temper.

Alice said:

"This is Walter Nuisance, my husband. Walter, this is Ian and his lady friend Susie Q."

Walter shook hands with Ian. He had a limp handshake, like a cold, wet kipper and eyebrows like fat, hairy caterpillars. He stared at Susie Q, obviously very much liking what he saw, even though she was a mere machine. He put his plump, sweaty arms round her, and he cuddled her tightly and for much too long. He then kissed both of her cheeks. Susie Q wondered what hate felt like. She felt revulsion, jealousy, and anxiety, in a triple whammy. It wasn't surprising that she didn't understand her feelings.

Walter had just been looking at a detailed news item on his electrajot, about Ian and his valuable robot companion. A reward of £1,000,000 had been offered for information leading to her return to the WRO. He wondered how he would spend the reward.

Chapter 14

Lovely Alice brought some tea pills for their visitors and her vile husband. Ian couldn't believe that a kind, gentle person like Alice had been saddled with a repulsive husband like Walter. They also nibbled some biscuit pills, thoughtfully provided by Alice. She said:

"It's so nice to be with you again, Ian. I've often thought of you. But more to the point how can we help you now that you're on the run?"

"I really don't know what to do, Alice. We had to get away though. I'm so pleased that Susie Q agreed to come with me. I was afraid that she'd want to stay at the WRO."

Susie Q said nothing, but she took Ian's hands in hers and gave him a soft and warm smile.

Walter shrugged and said:

"I don't know why you're making such a fuss. She's just a bloody machine."

Ian bit his tongue and resisted the impulse to hit Walter, again. He only just managed not to rise to the bait.

"Come now, Walter, it seems that Ian's very fond of Susie Q. Who wouldn't be, as she's absolutely delightful?"

Ian stood up and paced round the room nervously. He started to say something but then stopped. He looked thoughtful, but he was silent for a while.

At last, he said:

"We need to lie low for a few days at least. We can then make better plans about what to do, where to go and how to evade our pursuers. Walter, it seems you have mixed feelings about us, but I love Susie Q, and she loves me. Robots aren't normally able to feel real love, but she may have something called humanitis and is able to love, laugh, and to experience all the normal human emotions."

'…unlike you,' he nearly added.

"Please may we stay here, while we decide how to avoid being caught? The WRO probably don't care that much about me, but Susie Q is worth an awful lot of money, and they won't want to lose her."

Walter's piggy little eyes gleamed when Ian said those words. He was trying to decide when and how to shop their visitors. Alice said nothing, but she was aware that her husband was up to no good.

"You must be tired after your journey. I'll make up the bed in our spare room."

Alice left the room and Walter tried (not very successfully), to turn on the charm with Susie Q.

"I must admit I've never seen such a pretty robot, Susie Q. How comes you've fallen for this scallywag?"

Susie Q flushed. She hid her revulsion well and smiled in sweet deception.

"I love Ian."

She turned to Ian and said:

"I'm hopelessly devoted to you."

Walter sniffed, and walked out of the room, scratching his plump behind. Susie Q whispered:

"Ian, I don't trust that man. We must get out of here as soon as possible."

Alice returned and asked Ian and Susie Q if they wanted to retire to their room for some shuteye before dinner. They went with her to the room she had prepared. It was delightfully old fashioned, with a double bed covered with an antique candlewick counterpane and old photos of Southend on the walls.

They undressed quickly. Susie Q was very speedy as she used her automatic

I'm Back!

unbuttoning thingy. Ian could never believe how well made she was. To all intents and purposes, she looked and felt just like a real woman. She was so beautiful, and he could hardly believe that she loved him so much.

As she got into bed she said:

"Ian, what's an orgasm?"

He did his best to explain. He said that when a woman became sexually excited, she felt a huge warm feeling and was overwhelmingly breathless with passion. He realised that his explanation was poor.

"It's as if a huge mountain has been moved, and the sensation is of happy relief."

"Do they call it coming?"

"Yes, my darling."

Susie started to hum thoughtfully to herself. Ian recognised an old tune. He had to laugh when he realised it was 'She'll be Coming Round the Mountain, When She Comes.'

"Have you been playing a joke on me, Susie Q my dear?"

"It's not unusual!"

They had a happy and energetic time in their bedroom. Susie Q hummed that same song from time to time.

Chapter 15

They heard a discreet knocking on the door. Ian thought that it must be Alice.

"Come in Alice. I hear you knocking," said Ian.

He was right, it was Alice. She entered the room and she sat on the chair next to the bed, while Ian and Susie Q still lay there. They had pulled the ruched counterpane up to their chins.

"Shush, I want to help you both, but I suspect that Walter has got other plans. Be careful what you tell him. I've got a good friend who lives in Broadstairs, and I'll speak to her to see if you can stay there until the coast is clear. I've been with Walter all afternoon and I know he hasn't contacted the WRO yet. He's been popping beer pills one after the other and is now sleeping. He's snoring like a slumbering whale. I've got something to show you."

She pulled up the long sleeves of her dress, and she showed them her arms. They were badly bruised. She lifted her sweater at the back, and they could see that she was equally marked there.

"He hits me all the time. He pinches me and bites me too. He tries not to wound my face, although that has been known. He's a typical, cowardly bully. He usually strikes me or squeezes me where it doesn't show. I'm so scared of him. He weighs much more than me. Sometimes he pushes me up against the wall and just leans on me, with his hot nasty breath stinking right at my face. I've wanted to get away from him for years."

Ian and Susie Q were horrified that a compassionate person like Alice had been suffering from such domestic abuse for a long time, without being able to summon up the courage to report him to the police. Despite the fact that the police tried to help victims of domestic abuse, it was well known that many victims still suffered in silence. Domestic abuse was now punishable by leaving the abuser in a locked hall with fifty battered wives. It was indeed a punishment to fit the crime. The batterers always made the most of this time. Those abusers rarely made it out alive.

"Don't say anything to Walter about how he treats me. It would only make him angry. And you mustn't tell him where you are going. I'll speak to my chum now, while you get dressed. I hope you had a lovely afternoon."

Ian hardly knew what to say.

"We certainly did; we were tired out after our journey," said Ian.

"Speak for yourself, Ian. We robots never get tired! And you didn't seem that weary to me."

Ian wondered whether he should explain how to be discreet to Susie Q. Alice went out of the room in a state of some embarrassment. Susie Q looked at Ian. Ian looked at Susie Q. They both tried hard not to laugh. It was impossible. They were soon tittering. It wasn't long before Alice returned. She'd called her chum on her immersephone.

"I've spoken to my friend, who's called Rita Loza. She knew all about you two and your fun and games with the WRO. She said she's more than happy to shelter you, until it's safe to leave. Here's her address. Why don't you pack your things quickly and get out, so you can be safer? I wouldn't want revolting Walter to report you to the police."

She turned towards the door, and she was mortified to see that her dreadful husband was standing in the hall, just outside their living room. He shifted his feet as he almost over-balanced, and he leaned against the door jamb. He had obviously heard what Alice said. He looked very red in the face and the ugly veins on his equally repugnant nose stood out like small worms. They could see by the state of him that he hadn't stopped taking alcohol pills. He staggered into the room and put his arms round dear Alice. He moved his face close to hers.

"You bloody bitch! These people are in our home, and we can hold them until the police come. That reward is virtually mine. I can then get away from you, you insipid weakling. I want a real sensual woman, who'll do what I want. You're an excuse for a female. You're a parasite who's been bleeding me dry, with your whining and begging. 'Please don't hit me. Leave me alone. You've been at those drink pills again.' Your constant, irritating drivel makes me sick to my stomach. Here's a little lesson for you."

With that threat he punched her savagely on the nose, and hot wet blood covered his hand; her poor broken nose had erupted. He put his gnarled hands round her throat and pushed her violently against the wall. Alice was petrified. Ian went towards Walter and was trying to pull him away from his wife. He was suddenly aware of a terrible screaming noise as Susie Q pushed past him, swinging a heavy stone statue, which had been standing on the floor near the door. She swung the statue with all her surprising force at Walter's head, three times. Not content with that, she repeated the procedure, just to make sure that she had finished the job in hand.

"Take that, you filthy bastard. And again, and again for Alice, and three more times to be certain that you'll never do this again!"

Walter collapsed on the floor. His head looked as if it was cracked open, like a walnut hit by a sledgehammer, and something pink and awful seeped from his terrible head wounds. There was blood here, there, and everywhere. Susie Q dropped the statue and put her arms round Alice, who was hysterical. She was in a state of shock, and Ian also put his arms round Alice and his sweetie pie. Susie Q started gasping, with relief, terror, or guilt…who could tell? There was a long interval during which none of them could talk.

They knew that Susie Q had probably saved Alice's life, but all of them were certain that when this became public, the police would redouble their efforts to trace them and to bring them to justice. Ian could argue that Susie Q was trying to help Alice, but it would be hard to convince the authorities that such a terrible death was justified.

Alice was the first to speak, in a soft but determined tone. She was by now calmer than the other two, and she said:

"Thank you, thank you, thank you. Without you, I would have been dead, instead of this vicious, malevolent man. He's made my life a complete misery for many years. We must leave right now, and we should all go to Broadstairs. I need to clean my nose up and change out of these bloody clothes."

She marched out of the room. Ian was at a loss what to say. He was even more staggered when he saw that Susie Q was using her incredible strength in a ferocious way. She had started ripping Walter's corpse to bits.

"What on earth are you doing?"

"It's quite simple. We must get rid of this body. Once these pieces are small enough, we can mince him up in the household chopperator. I saw it when I was having a nose around earlier. (You were still asleep.) It's in an outhouse. He'll be sucked away into the refuse tubes, and when his remains get to the central incinerator, he'll soon be just ashes and puffs of smoke. That'll serve him right!"

By this time, Alice was back in the room. She hadn't changed her clothes yet, but her nose, although bent, was no longer bloody. She saw what Susie Q was doing, and without a word she turned on her heel. She came back with some of those illegal plastic sacks that were still quite easy to come by, even though the authorities had banned them many years ago.

She and Alice started stuffing bits of Walter into the bags. Alice and Ian couldn't believe how energetic Susie Q was. They soon had ten bags full of Walter, after pushing and prodding the surprisingly small pieces of his body into the sacks. They carried some each into the outhouse in the garden, where the gaping maw of the chopperator was situated. They stuffed the sacks into the machine, closed the lid and pushed the start button. There was an awful grinding sound, and Walter went away in the underground refuse pipes. They hosed down the chopperator and bleached the machine. They also tidied and cleaned the outhouse. Soon it was if Walter's mangled body had never been there.

Alice and Susie returned to the living room, ripping up floor coverings, scrubbing walls and cleaning with Gusto, the world's top selling domestic cleaning product. Anything that was beyond redemption was also decimated and stuffed into the chopperator. Ian felt out of place. He could understand how Alice might have been able to recover her composure so quickly. She must have felt an immediate sense of relief that Walter was out of her life. However, he had been astounded by Susie Q's actions and the cold, merciless way that she had got rid of Walter. He made his mind up never to have a serious argument with Susie.

Under cover of darkness, they left Alice's house, and they travelled to the aerobus station. They asked for passage to Ramsgate. They had decided to go there and to walk to Broadstairs, just in case the pilot was questioned, and he remembered where they were heading.

On the aerobus, Alice whispered to Susie Q:

"I can never thank you enough. You saved my life. It was instant karma. I hope you feel OK."

"Don't worry about me. For me it was a thing that had to be done. I felt peace straight away. It was instant calmer!"

Ian was chilled when he heard them both snickering, like naughty schoolgirls.

Chapter 16

It didn't take long to get to Ramsgate, and once they had walked down the retractable stairs of the aerobus, the triumvirate were pleased to see the sea. Ian had always liked living near the beach in Southwold. He had observed the murky waters in Southend and been surprised that the town dared to call itself Southend-on-Sea. Southend was perched on the edge of the Thames estuary, and although it had quite a pleasant outlook, it definitely didn't have a real sea view.

Alice led the way along the prom and headed towards Broadstairs. The five-mile walk would take them about three hours. She had contacted her friend Rita again, using her electrajot, as soon as they were off the aerobus. Rita said she would be at home, as she had recently been made redundant from her job as a parking attendant. Rita had known that Alice's marriage had been unhappy, but she had not been told about Walter's abusive treatment. Alice had decided to keep that to herself. She shared her thoughts with Ian and Susie Q.

"For the time being, we need to keep the lid on the problems I had with Walter and the way he used to treat me. If we let that out, it could complicate matters still further. I'm going to tell Rita that Walter left me for another woman, and that he refused to tell me where he was going. I'll have to confide in her about you two, but we must act as if there was no connection between you coming and me leaving Walter. I'll tell her that Ian looked me up because we were old friends."

Susie Q and Alice were both flushed. Susie Q was again experiencing what she thought might be jealousy, whilst Alice was remembering that Ian and she had both had their first sexual encounter, together, at the much too young age of fifteen.

"I'm sure that Rita will keep shtum about you two, as she's always had a thing about protecting the underdog."

Susie Q asked Ian what an underdog was, and she wondered aloud if there was such a thing as an overdog. Ian had to laugh, but he still wasn't always sure if Susie Q was joking. Maybe her extensive shared, robotic, universal knowledge had never come across that word. He made his mind up to look it up on the Solar System Web when they were less encumbered by their hastily packed bags, to see where it had been derived from. He explained the meaning of the word underdog, and Susie Q just smiled without pursuing her question about overdogs.

The walk was pleasant. The sun was shining, and the temperature was warm. There was a gentle sea breeze coming from the coast of France, which was thirty-five miles away. (That was much further than the Kent coast was from Southend-not-on-Sea across the Thames estuary.)

Susie Q had been rather quiet since the Walter episode. She was worried that her excessively violent attack on him, and the subsequent tearing apart of his limbs and his body might have revealed a serious fault in her programming. She had heard that robots were always set up so that they could do no harm. She was concerned that she had broken what was probably a basic robot rule.

Worse than that, she thought that Ian (and Alice) might regret becoming saddled with a machine which had a nasty, quick temper. Even though she was disquieted, she knew that if she had been in that position once more, she would act in the same way. Despite her certainty that she would do it again, she was surprised to feel unsettled when she thought about what she had done. She searched her memory banks and discovered that she might be feeling guilty.

"Ian, do you still love me, even though I murdered Walter and tore his body to bits?"

I'm Back!

"Darling Susie Q, if I'd been nearer to Walter, I might've even done the same thing with that statue. And I wouldn't have been strong enough to rip him to bits, so it was just as well you did that. We would've found it difficult to dismember him, ready for the chopperator, without you."

Alice put her free arm through Susie Q's equivalent. (They were each carrying a bag.) She squeezed Susie Q's arm and smiled at her.

"My dear girl, there have been many times when I've thought about getting rid of Walter. Every time he beat me, I had thoughts of revenge. He often carried on taking alcohol pills, after he'd taken his ill temper out on me. I only weigh about eight stones and he was fifteen and a half stones, so his treatment of me was not only cruel, it was brutal. He was a big bully.

When he collapsed in a heap into his armchair, each night, he was often snoring, belching, and farting in his drunken stupor. I often dreamed of using a cushion to bring an end to his miserably wasteful existence. I'm glad you saved my life and finished him off."

She was solemn for a while after her outspoken admission, but she soon recovered her composure. They had reached Broadstairs and walked down the cliff path to Viking Bay. The sea looked choppy, but the view was amazing. She had been to Broadstairs before to see Rita, and they had walked from Viking Bay through several other bays, which were all guarded by white chalk cliffs. They had trudged along the beach when the tide was out. Alice and Rita had talked cheerfully for some time, sitting on a small wall at Dumpton Gap. They had been eating ice cream pills. They returned the way that they had come, but by then the tide had turned, and they used the concrete path next to the cliffs.

"Rita's got a condenselow in a stack, where the pubs and restaurants used to be some years ago. Her place is in Morelli Heights."

Ian knew that there had been an Art Deco ice cream parlour where Rita's abode was now. It was called Morelli's. They climbed the few steps to the front entrance of Morelli Heights. Alice pressed the buzzer for the holovision intercom, and a vivacious, auburn-haired woman with green eyes smiled at them cheerily.

"Welcome to you all. I'll click open the door. I'm on the third floor, and my number is 3:25."

The door opened, and they all walked up the stairs inside to Rita's condenselow. The condenselow stacks were snapped together like huge Lego bricks. Each condenselow was lowered carefully into place by huge cranes, and the workmanship was so exact that they always snapped into place easily. Some of the condenselows had automatic house cleaning facilities.

The walls, fixtures and fittings, the furniture and everything in these auto-flush condenselows was made of heavy-duty plastic. All you had to do was to press a button and water impregnated with liquid soap and disinfectant ran down the walls and across the slightly sloping floors, to the central drain. This was uncovered when the button was pressed. After the flushing was finished, hot air was then blown through the heating vents and the whole condenselow was dried very quickly. Ian couldn't afford a condenselow like that, so he still used old fashioned mops and buckets. Rita's non-flushing condenselow was similar to Ian's, except for being on the third floor.

She had opened her front door before they reached her, and she hugged all of them in turn.

"I'm so pleased to meet you, Ian and Susie Q. I know that you must be good people – well Ian is a good person, and Susie Q must be a good robot. I'm sorry, I'm making a bit of a hash of my welcome, but you know what I mean. In future Susie Q, I'll treat you like a real woman, and I won't even mention anything that implies that you are anything else."

Alice spun her the yarn about her leaving Walter, and Rita said:

"It's about time. I never liked him, and you're far too good for him. I'm so glad

I'm Back!

you've come to your senses."

Susie Q felt charmed by this bubbly woman's good natured, but rather rambling, greeting and her ability to make them feel at ease. She had also been thinking that it would be easier if they all looked upon her as a human. That would be so much simpler for them. She was wondering when she should tell Ian that she would have to change her face, so that she was not so easily recognised. She knew that robots could have new faces quite easily, if the old ones wore out or if they were damaged in any way.

The official supply channels were all controlled strictly by the government. There had been a small number of cases when rogue robots had mutinied and ran away. They had sometimes tried to get new faces, but it had proved hard for them to do so, as the rules governing face replacements for automatons were strict.

Susie Q knew that there were black market faces that sometimes became available. She wondered how she could source a new (and hopefully equally acceptable), face. She was also concerned about how this could be fitted before she was spotted.

Chapter 17

When Ian and Susie Q left Enid Brighton in the waiting area just outside the teleportation booths, they couldn't possibly have anticipated that her cover would be blown as quickly as it had transpired. The WRO twigged almost immediately that the alleged Susie Q robot, left by Ian and the real Susie Q, wasn't her. It so happened that a senior WRO technician, named Mike Anick, came to inspect the teleportation facilities as part of a routine check. As he entered the room outside the booths, he nodded politely to Enid.

"Hi. Have we met before? I know that I've come into contact with lots of Susies, but I'm not sure if we do know each other."

"I'm not a Susie anymore. I was told to call myself Enid Brighton. I used to be a Susie though. I'm still a robot, but I work for a dating agency."

Mike was baffled by this convoluted answer. He put his toolbox down and asked her to unbutton her blouse. She pressed something on her neck, and all her buttons popped open, but not as quickly as Susie Q's did. (Enid was an older model.) The technician found her serial number by using a special digipen, which highlighted the normally invisible number on her left breast.

After checking this, he scanned the number into the search field on a special instrument, and he was staggered to find that this robot used to be owned by the WRO. She had been sold in a job lot, to a firm called One Amour Time. He wondered why she was back in the WRO's premises.

"Why are you here, when you were sold to a company in England?"

I'm Back!

"I was programmed to come here by the company which I work for, and I was instructed to wear a mask. I was told to call myself Enid Brighton and to say that I was a friend of Ian Tudeep's. I was asked to say that I'd come to take him to Southwold, after his artificial reincarnation. When I got here, another female robot met me and there was also a man with her. He said he was Ian Tudeep, and I think I heard him call her Susie Q.

They told me that they were just going to check these booths, and they'd be back out very quickly. They must've both pressed the send buttons after calling up a recent destination by mistake. The next thing I heard was the noise that the teleportation booths make when they're working. I was beginning to wonder what to do."

"Don't worry. I'll find out what's going on."

Mike went to the two booths which had been used recently and checked the last destination fields. He noted that Ian Tudeep and Susie Q had both been teleported to Heathrow. After doing so, he told Enid to stay where she was and went back out to the reception area. He looked up Susie Q on a schedule of robot values, and he discovered that she was worth £10,000,000.

He asked the receptionist Susie to call Hiram Prendergast, as he had realised by now that Susie Q had run away with Ian Tudeep. He told the receptionist robot that he needed to speak to Prendergast very urgently, as a valuable robot had gone missing. She spoke to the CEO's secretary, who put the call through to him immediately.

"Mr. Prendergast, I'm deeply sorry to tell you that an expensive robot of ours, called Susie Q, has eloped with Ian Tudeep. I know that he is the man who was our first human AR candidate. I looked at their destinations as shown in the teleportation booths and they've gone to Heathrow. I will check where Ian Tudeep lives, as I suspect that he and Susie Q will go there as their first port of call after leaving the terminal at Heathrow. Susie Q could eventually suffer from a catastrophic mechanical breakdown, as she won't be getting her regular monitoring and operating system updates.

We need somebody to go to England as quickly as possible to get her back. If it would help, I'll go. I could also check Susie Q, to see if any software patches need to be applied to bring her up to date."

"My goodness Mr. Anick, this is profoundly serious. She is our most costly robot. We can't afford to throw away £10,000,000. Also, Ian Tudeep needs regular follow up health checks, to make sure his AR is not causing any untoward issues. I'll authorise the teleportation return tickets to Heathrow. You'll need to catch an aerobus from the terminal to take you to Suffolk. I'll also have some money for expenses transferred to your eWallet. Come to my office so we can have a private chat about the limits of your authority and the measures which I want you to take."

Mike hurried to the CEO's office. Hiram Prendergast shook him by the hand and asked him to sit down.

"Would you like some coffee and biscuit pills?"

Mike shook his head.

"I'm going to tell you something that only three people know. I want you to sign the non-disclosure agreement document that my secretary sent to you by rMail, as you were coming to see me. Please read it now and use your digipen and your fingerprint to confirm that you will abide by this NDA. It applies now and always in the future, especially if you ever leave the WRO.

You'll receive a handsome bonus immediately (in fact it's about to hit your bank account any minute now.) That'll be followed by the same amount once you bring Susie Q, and hopefully Ian Tudeep, back here to Geneva. Once you've done that your salary will be doubled."

Mike reviewed the NDA, which also mentioned the bonuses and the salary increase. These inducements were subject to 'this, that and the other' and more 'this, that and the other.' He knew that NDAs were always over cautious, intricately worded, and subject to 'if this' and 'but that' terms and conditions. The bonuses would be very

I'm Back!

handy, and the salary increase was the icing on the cake. He signed the document, pressed his finger on the sensor and sent it back to Prendergast's secretary.

"What I'm about to tell you will amaze you. You may even disapprove of what's been done by the WRO, but you won't be able to talk to anybody, nor to the press about our actions. Similarly, posts on social media will be banned. I noticed that you didn't read the full terms and conditions of the NDA. One of the sections makes it clear that if you break the NDA requirements, the Population Police will come to collect you, by force if need be, to take you to the NDF once you return to the UK.

We really don't want to have to do this, but that serves to underline how serious this situation is. The people that know what I'm going to tell you are myself, Karl Yoder and Gerald Hoffer, the Prime Minister of the UK. When Susie Q was created, we were working out how to make robots more life-like. We'd already been doing experimental genetic modification of DNA as part of our early AR trials on animals. After many false starts we managed to inject GM human DNA into a part of Susie Q's brain. The experiment was funded by the UK government, under a 'need to know' protocol. They hoped that in the future robots with feelings could be used to care for young children, so that young mothers could all be forced to go out to work to boost their economy. They believed that women staying at home to bring up children was economically wasteful.

The aim was to make Susie Q able to feel real emotions, such as love and tenderness. The plan went awry, and we think that she may also be able to feel the more negative and destructive emotions. These could include anger, jealousy, and depression. Lately she's been observed crying. Some WRO technicians (not as senior, nor as experienced as you), have concluded that she may be suffering from humanitis.

The two of us at the WRO who were in the know did nothing to persuade them otherwise. I expect you know that humanitis may not even exist. The technicians who examined her also said that perhaps a lubrication pipe may have become blocked or kinked, thus causing the alleged tear drops to spill from her eyes. The lubrication also supplies moisture to her artificial vagina, which is made of silicone.

By the way, we thought that if this special receptacle worked well, it might give us another good revenue stream when we did the same thing for a production run of a new breed of robots. We knew that Ian Tudeep and Susie Q had been making love. We had some long discussions about that, but in the end, we decided not to interfere. At least it proved that there might be a future for that kind of requirement. However, if our genetic fumbling ever came out, we'd be subject to a massive outcry from the press and the licensing authorities which have hitherto approved our more general work with robots and reincarnation.

We may even be forced to shut down the WRO. I'm sorry to repeat myself, but Susie cost us £10,000,000 to produce. When we re-examined the test results, we decided that it would be far too expensive to continue making these special, feeling robots. We also had some more technical problems which affected her behaviour. We tinkered with her internal workings, and we thought that we'd fixed the problem regarding her emotional control. I must be honest. To coin a phrase, it ain't necessarily so. We're going to authorise a reward of £1,000,000 for the safe return of Susie Q to the WRO.

If you're the man who returns her to us, you'll be paid that reward, as well as the amounts of which we spoke and your doubled salary. I've got to tell you that Gerald Hoffer is aware that Susie Q is at large, and that she's the first emotional robot we made using their funds. Are you fully in agreement with our plan to get her back, and the conditions which apply?"

Mike wasn't happy that he could potentially be deselected by the NDF, but the money situation was a huge attraction to his involvement in the scheme.

"Yes, Mr. Prendergast. I'm ready to follow your orders. I'll leave for Southwold as soon as possible."

Mike was surprised that the CEO had taken up his offer of trying to track down

I'm Back!

Ian Tudeep and Susie Q so quickly. Furthermore, the offers of substantial incentives had been made too swiftly. He felt that if everything went badly, he stood a good chance of being dragged down with the senior WRO officials. Mike was no fool. He had previously been a successful owner of a business which offered customised household robots. His partner was his sister, Penny. They had always got on well, and he had thought that she would be a good co-director. She was shrewd, quick-thinking, and efficient. Sadly, she was also untrustworthy. Although she looked as if butter wouldn't melt in her mouth, it would probably would have done so immediately.

The butter reference was apt for her though because she always knew which side her bread was buttered. She had worked in various commercial jobs and owned her own companies for many years. She had dipped her fingers into the coffers of all her previous employers and every one of her own companies. Some of her companies were run into the ground deliberately and sold for £1 each, to other companies who wanted to use their debts to reduce their tax liabilities. Mike was blissfully unaware of her long history of double-dealing. He thought his cute little sister, with her curly blonde hair and sparkling hazel eyes, was a dainty dish to set before the king.

They formed a jointly owned company, to enlist customers who would purchase bog-standard, assembly line produced robots for after sales customisation. The robots in question were sourced quite easily, as there were always new developments and fads which made slightly older robots an unattractive proposition. Mike and Penny's company would give their customers many options for tailoring the robots which they sold. For example, they could have different faces, new voices, or they could speak multiple languages. The usage of new faces for robots was conducted under strict regulations, but their company bent the rules willfully. They also created dog-bots in all shapes and sizes, and they offered ones that looked and sounded just like real four-footed friends who had crossed the rainbow bridge. Everything went swimmingly until the admin manager of their business, Jerry Bilt, ran off with both the firm's cash and

Penny. This left Mike holding the baby, and he had to come to an arrangement with the firm's creditors. In the meantime Jerry and Penny re-surfaced in Chile, where they set up another robot related business. Jerry lived there with Mike's sister for ten years on the outskirts of Santiago.

He was involved in an unfortunate skirmish with local bandits. They wanted him to allow them to use robots supplied by Jerry and Penny's organisation, to deliver arms to terrorists. Jerry had refused. They had warned him that this was a refusal that could not be accepted. The argument escalated and became out of control. A shot rang out and Jerry collapsed in a bloody heap on the ground. The man who was 'negotiating' on behalf of the people who wanted to use robots for arms deliveries was most surprised. He was Cisco Pancho, also known as El Malvado: The Evil One. It wasn't El Malvado, nor any of his bunch of scoundrels, who had killed Jerry.

Penny had come into the room just in time to hear what was going on. It was she who had shot Jerry. She thought he had long since outlived his usefulness. She had been planning to take over their company for some time. She was the secretary, financial director, and operational manager of the company. She had already taken Jerry off the board of directors secretly, milked the company bank accounts dry and transferred the funds to a private bank account in Switzerland. It seemed that poor Jerry had never heard of segregation of duties.

She had planned to kill him somehow, and the situation with El Malvado's men was fortuitous. Even as she pulled the trigger, she was working out how to blame the Evil One. Cisco made that unnecessary. He said he knew where there was an old disused mine. The main shaft had been covered over in a make-shift way, and he gave orders for two of his men to take Jerry's body to the site. He asked them to dump the body down the shaft, after saying a few respectful words. (He was a Catholic, after all).

The robots were used for the nefarious purpose required by the dodgy customer. Penny made even more money, and after a while she shut up shop. She disappeared

I'm Back!

from public view and moved to Switzerland. She had already persuaded her customers, including Cisco Pancho, to pay large sums in advance for robotic services. After she took off, El Malvado found an empty office. There was no way of contacting Penny to persuade her to cough up. He was furious and put his best man onto the job of finding her. His mission was to get close to her, to gain access to her bank account(s), to liquidate her and to transfer the cash to a Swiss bank account in the name of Mr. E. Odavlam.

To cut a long story short, Penny was traced, wooed, and tricked into revealing her bank account details to Cisco's man, who promised to love her forever. Once he had access to the cash, he smothered her with a hotel pillow. He then disappeared and took the cash with him, by transferring it many times, to try to hide its provenance. He was found later, splattered all over the pavement, after toppling off the roof garden of an expensive hotel in Oslo. Falling twenty-eight storeys had not done much to improve his appearance. The money still languishes in one, several or maybe many Swiss banks, but not the one in the name of The Evil One, as planned. It has been unclaimed to date.

When Mike was at school, he had always been fascinated by robots. He read everything he could about the subject, some of which was lurid pulp fiction, but he also found learned articles which described the history of robotics, the way that they had been used in the past, and the way that they might be used in the future. How was he to know what a key figure he was to be when the Ian Tudeep and Susie Q story unfolded in such a dramatic way?

Before he had his own firm with Penny, which was known as 'Your Robot: Your Way,' he had worked his way through several technical and then managerial posts in robot related firms. He worked in the USA for a while in Massachusetts, in the San Francisco Bay area and in Phoenix. By the time he got to Phoenix he was a rising star within his profession. His application to join the WRO had been accepted with alacrity.

John Bobin

Mike wasn't able to leave as quickly as he had hoped, but the following day he was teleported to Heathrow.

Chapter 18

Susie Q, Ian, Rita, and Alice spent many hours talking about the situation in which Ian and Susie Q now found themselves. Lots of ideas about how to evade the police, some simple and some more complicated, were mooted. Susie Q had already had a notion which she thought might work. She knew that her face was detachable. This could only be done by a skilled robot technician, but she thought it was just possible that the same man might be able to give her a new face. She told Ian about her idea. He was not happy as he loved Susie Q's existing face. He said he was against that plan.

"But sweetie pie, it would still be me. You might find that my new face was even prettier."

"I very much doubt that, and how on earth are we going to persuade a robot technician to do the necessary face removal and replacement? We're not rich, so we'd have to appeal to his better nature."

Rita came to the rescue. By sheer coincidence, she knew a geeky man who had been studying and working in robotics for years. He was also sweet on her. He wanted her to marry him, but she was still trying to decide how to tell him that she would not want to take his surname, which was Pancake. Her friend was called Ralph, but everybody called him Tosser.

"I know that Tosser would do anything for me. He knows more about robots than he's forgotten. He's always worked as a consultant, and he's done work for lots of high-class robotics companies. He even worked for a time for the WRO."

A sudden thought occurred to her.

"Susie Q, do you know when and where you were made?"

"Just a minute, and I'll look at my internal specification. Here it is, I was created in 2092, and it was at the WRO. The names of all the technicians who worked on me are listed. Wow, this is a spooky coincidence! Ralph Pancake was part of the team, and he completed my safety certification on 01/05/2092. If anybody could take my face off and give me a new one, he's the man."

Ian was feeling a little more comfortable about Susie's new face idea.

Rita said:

"Tosser's generally recognised as an excellent robotics technician. If anybody can give Susie Q a nice new face, it's Mr. Pancake!"

Ian said:

"But I've grown accustomed to her face!"

Chapter 19

That night, they celebrated with special food pills. These were supposed to replicate the flavour of a nice roast pork dinner, but they decided that the attempt to do so was a huge flop. Rita went into her tiny kitchen. (Large kitchens were no longer needed, now that most people used food pills.) She came back with some alcohol pills which were branded as being 'Just Like Merlot.' These didn't hit the spot as far as the flavour, bouquet and nose were concerned, but after ingesting a few each they were all merry, nay sozzled.

Alice put her arms round Ian and mumbled something he didn't quite catch.

"What did you say, dear Alice?"

Alice started to cry, and blubbed for a few minutes, before saying:

"Maybe I shouldn't have said that."

Susie Q told her that she should feel free to say anything to her dearest pals.

Alice looked at Rita, Susie Q, and Ian blearily.

"Ian, I just wanted to say that I've always loved you, ever since I was fifteen. I wanted to contact you many times, but I didn't know how my approach would be received. I saw that you'd married Beryl Henderson, who was also at our school, and I gave up all hope of us getting together. There you are. I've said it now, and I hope we can still be good friends, even if I will never be your wife. I can see that you love your Susie Q, and who wouldn't; she's dazzling."

Susie Q looked at Alice, and she held out both of her hands. She clasped Alice's in hers and said:

"If anything ever happens to me, I sincerely want you and Ian to be together forever. I may be recaptured and reprogrammed, or even disassembled to be used as parts for other robots. I may break down irretrievably, as I'm not being maintained properly. Perhaps Tosser Pancake can keep me going by checking my set up, but it's unlikely that he'll have the very latest system patches.

I may do unexpected things, like I did to Walter. I may start to speak gobbledygook. And what would you do if I just stopped working completely? Ian, promise me that you'll look after Alice, if I'm no longer around."

Susie Q sensed that her announcement had been rather grave, and she worried that she might have shaken her friends. She felt she should lighten the mood a little.

"But you're not allowed to make love to Alice, until I'm gone!"

They couldn't help laughing. Alice gave a little secret smile, inwardly. She made herself promise not to wish that Susie Q was removed from Ian's presence, nor that she experienced technical problems.

"Maybe I can just have a little token kiss and cuddle, sometimes?"

Ian looked at Susie Q. Susie Q arched her eyebrows.

"Go for it Ian. But not too much, and not too often."

Ian hugged Alice and planted a kiss on her lips. Alice raised a tearful face and held his cheeks.

"That's enough, Ian. You've got to save your kisses for me!"

They all laughed. They continued talking about Tosser, and Rita offered to contact him in the morning.

Chapter 20

Following their intake of breakfast pills, Rita said she would speak to Tosser. She left the room, and she came back after ten minutes or so on the immersephone.

"I've got two bits of news."

They all looked at her expectantly.

"Tosser said he'd be delighted to help. He maintains that the WRO treated him very badly when they cancelled his contractor's agreement without notice. Before he left the building, he tried to delete his NDA on their database. He wanted to do that so he could use his inside knowledge of their dealings without risking the consequences. The NDA wouldn't open at all, and he suspected that the file had been corrupted. He took the precaution of deleting his footprint in the system's audit trail, so nobody would know that he'd been trying to do things to the NDA.

He says he took some robot parts when he left. He only took small items, and he never told the WRO how angry he was with them. They didn't search his bag when he was shown out by his boss. He'd always liked Ralph, and he trusted him implicitly, so there was no problem when he went to the teleportation area. Tosser said goodbye to his line manager, went into the booth and left very quickly. He says he's got some half-built robot faces, and he's also got the tools and the know-how to make a very acceptable face for Susie Q."

Ian asked what the other news was.

"Tosser's asked me to marry him soon, and he says he'll happily change his surname to Loza, when we tie the knot. I've said yes!"

They gathered round Rita and cuddled each other, like the proverbial bunch of grapes.

"Tosser's coming here in about half an hour. He only lives round the corner. He says he'll look at Susie Q's face, and after that he'll have a better idea of how he can detach it and replace it with another one. He says he may be able to fashion some faces that are based on actresses who were famous in the past.

He asked if Susie Q would like a face looking like Michelle Keegan, Diana Dors or Meryl Streep. I've never heard of any of them, but apparently it was quite fashionable a few months ago to use replicas of these old faces. He says we can decide what to do when he's with us, and he'll bring his tools and faces with him."

Ian suggested that they should use his electrajot to search the Solar System Web.

"We might be able to call up old images of these actresses. It'll be interesting to see if we can all agree on the best replacement face. I do hope we can store Susie Q's current face, so we can replace it, when all this fuss has died down."

Ian activated his electrajot with his fingerprint and began searching for pictures of these ladies. The first one he found was Michelle Keegan. (He made a mental note that it would be difficult to choose a better face.) He found the others just as quickly. Once he'd saved all the images, he pointed the electrajot at his three companions.

"OK. Choose the one you like best, but don't say who it is out loud. When we've all made a choice, lets reveal our individual preferred new faces and see if there's a measure of agreement."

The others scrolled up and down and from side to side. They nodded, one by one, when they had made their choice. Susie Q had chosen Meryl Streep. The picture looked as if it was a photo taken when she was quite young. Rita had chosen Michelle Keegan. Alice had chosen a young Diana Dors. Susie Q looked at Ian and said:

"Come on then. Who have you chosen?"

"It was very difficult, because you are so lovely, and any new face wouldn't be as pretty as yours."

Susie Q pinched his arm and said:

"Flattery will get you nowhere. Stop prevaricating and let us know who you want me to look like."

"Very well. My choice is Michelle Keegan."

Susie Q asked if Ian could call up a holovision version of Michelle Keegan.

He did so and projected it on the wall. He tried to reassure Susie Q:

"She's very pretty, sweetie pie, but she's not in your league."

He was lying through his teeth. Alice closed the subject by saying that they had two votes for Michelle. It seemed to her to be a final answer. She put her cards on the table by saying:

"We could ask a friend, but that would risk us being discovered by the WRO. Let's plump for Michelle Keegan."

Susie Q felt a strange, anxious feeling again. She had heard about resentment, but surely robots shouldn't feel that destructive emotion?

"Ian, when I have a new face, will you still love me?"

"Susie Q, my darling, I'll love you forever. Come here and be my baby!"

The intercom buzzer sounded, and Rita looked at the screen. She could see that it was Tosser waiting in the street, and she buzzed him in. He didn't take long to walk up the stairs, and he came bounding in like a happy bunny.

"Hallo everybody. I'm Ralph. I always say that, but nobody ever calls me by my real name. I'm also known as Tosser, and some people say that I am a right Tosser too. I'll leave you to make that judgement when you know me better. Before I do anything else there's something I must do."

He turned to face Rita and kneeled on the floor.

"I know you've already said yes, but will you be my wife if I promise to change my surname to Loza? To be frank, it's a better name than Pancake anyway. And it's a better name than Frank too."

He was still down on one knee. Tosser was a chubby bear of a man with ginger hair, masses of freckles and a wide smile. He radiated good humour, and Ian, Susie Q and Alice liked him instantly.

"Yes and yes again, you big lummox. Come here and give me a sloppy kiss!"

They embraced, and the others all gathered round, congratulating the newly engaged couple. Tosser seemed to want to prove that he had the right credentials to remove Susie Q's face and to replace it.

"I've been interested in robots ever since I came across an old story called 'I Robot' by Isaac Asimov. That changed my whole life. There was also a play written by a Czech playwright even before 'I Robot,' which featured mechanical men. There are quite a few different definitions of the word robot.

Susie Q is a very advanced and special machine. Back in the olden days, there were simple machines that might be regarded as the forefathers of today's sophisticated robots. However, the closest thing to a robot, as we know it today, was one from the nineteen fifties. That was made by George C. Devol, who was an inventor from Kentucky. I could rabbit on about robots and robotics for hours, but I can see your eyes glazing over already, so I'll shut up."

Tosser asked Susie Q if he could study her face. She concurred, and he pressed a hidden button under her chin. Her face slid upwards, and this revealed the mechanism by which her face had been fitted to her head.

"Hmm, that's a good fitting. It's deep enough to anchor the face, and yet flexible enough to allow smiling and other facial movements. I'm sure I could fit a replacement face quite easily. It does take some time though. Why don't you all go into another room, leaving me with Susie, so I can spread out my tools and do the best I can."

Ian thought this sounded ominous.

"Is this very difficult?"

I'm Back!

"It's easy to fit a new face if it's a permanent replacement. However, I think that we need to keep the option of giving Susie Q her old face back at some stage. We may even need to fit another different new one, if there are any problems with this one. You'll just have to trust me. I assure you that I'll do my absolute best. After I fit the new face, I'll use some elastaskin to make the joins invisible and to soften the face itself."

Susie Q and Tosser were left on their own, and Tosser gently unfastened her old face. This sounds easy, but it took two hours before he could remove it completely.

"Which face was chosen?"

Susie Q found it difficult to talk without a face. She picked up Ian's electrajot and pointed to Michelle Keegan.

"My favourite too. But not nearly as lovely as your old face."

Susie Q tried to say something. She gave up and used Ian's digipen to write:

"Bullshit. Even I have to admit that she's stunning."

Chapter 21

Three hours after removing Susie Q's old face, Tosser called them back in. He was pleased with his handy work.

"Susie Q has a new face. It looks great to me. I hope you like it. She's tried talking, facial expressions and moving her head around. She did that gently at first, but then she shook her head violently. There were no signs of looseness, nor of the face becoming detached. She says it's just as flexible as her old face. I've packed the old face in a special container, which will keep it safe. It'll also keep it flexible. We may want to use it again. Come on Susie Q, tell us what you think of the new face."

Susie Q had been looking in a virtual mirror that the electrajot had created above the virtual fireplace. This seemed quite appropriate as Susie Q was only a virtual woman.

"My goodness. I'm really beautiful, aren't I?"

"That's our girl," said Alice.

Rita asked what the plan was, especially now that Susie Q had a Michelle Keegan face. Ian said he would shave his beard off, as the photos which had been shown during the WBC broadcasts showed him with his post-op beard.

Susie Q took up the thread:

"That's good, so we'll both have new faces."

They continued to admire Susie Q's new face. Rita kicked Tosser in the shin.

"Don't you have something to do this afternoon?

"What did you have in mind?"

"Tosser, why don't you come out with your brand-new fiancée. You need to buy

I'm Back!

me a real ring. Let's see if that old-fashioned jewellers is still open at the end of the High Street. I don't want one of those horrid rings that look like they have come out of a Christmas Cracker."

Tosser smiled broadly, and Alice laughed.

"Tosser, you really do have the grinniest face I've ever seen. Anybody would think you were in love!"

Susie Q was still glued to the virtual mirror.

"Ian, I think I may like me as Michelle Keegan even better than with my old face. Let's hope there are no problems. Ralph said that he believes it should be OK. I'm a little nervous, as he said the basic part of the face which he used was quite old. It was one he took from the WRO store cupboard a few years ago. Let's keep our fingers crossed that everything stays in place and it doesn't seize up or anything. Ian, am I still attractive?"

"Susie Q, I thought you were perfect before, but you're even more perfect now."

The inner pedant groaned.

'You can't be more perfect. You are either perfect or not. It's the same with pregnancy,' thought Ian.

"Caught you! Admit it, you do think Michelle Keegan was prettier that I was."

"No, no, no lknlmmmjoi."

Ian realised that it was impossible to talk properly when Susie Q was giving you a massive, smoocheroonie of a kiss.

Chapter 22

Mike Anick had a good journey to Southwold. He already had Ian's address, as it was on file with the WRO, but he didn't really expect Ian and Susie Q to be there. Even if they had gone there, Mike thought that they would have moved on by now. Nevertheless, he thought that it might be worth trying to get in. He hoped that there would be some old-fashioned address books, or even electrajots that had been replaced by newer models, in the condenselow. If so, Ian might not have wiped them clean.

As he fully expected, there was no answer to the doorbell, and the place looked totally deserted. He still wanted to see if he could gain entry to have a look around. As well as addresses, Mike hoped that there might be other clues as to where Tudeep and his robot girlfriend might have gone. However, all the doors and windows were safely secured. Mike decided he would have to look elsewhere.

The WRO had given him preferential access to various special search systems. Using these, he had made an extensive list of Ian's known male and female contacts, past and present. One by one, he had crossed off the ones who had died naturally. He had also deleted the ones who had been deselected by the NDF when they reached the unfortunate age of fifty.

He had paid special attention to as many of Ian's former girlfriends as he could find. However, when he contacted them using his immersephone none of them had seen him for years. He had found the contact details of, and also spoken to, Ian's ex-wife Beryl, who was inordinately bitter. Mike thought that this was rich, considering that she had been having an affair with another man before she decided to leave Ian.

I'm Back!

During his delving into the records Mike had found images of her new fellow. Mike had seen vain photos of a perma-tanned and muscular man, wearing a sleeveless, tight vest and scanty shorts. Beryl's boyfriend seemed to think he was a perfect Adonis. Mike hated him on sight. The new man had been at the teeth whitener, and he wore a large gold medallion. His hair was that very black shade of black that looked like it came out of a bottle. (Mike had always thought that the phrase 'black is black' didn't make sense. In his opinion, dyed black hair never looked natural.)

He noted that this narcissistic man's eyebrows were far too perfectly shaped. Beryl's toy boy ran a training firm called 'Perfect Fitness.' Anick mentally renamed him Perfect Titness. His photo gave Mike the creeps. His pride in is his manufactured looks was most evident. Even his name was absurd. What would expect from a man called Brando Marlon?

Beryl had told all and sundry that Ian had pushed her into a relationship with the younger (and much fitter), personal trainer by being so 'bloody boring.' She still maintained that Ian wasted precious time by reading old books (mostly in rejigged digital form), and in viewing antiquated, remastered films. His love for history had been totally baffling to her. She had told Mike that she liked partying, raving and eating fast food pills. She said she only ever read chick lit books and loved reality programmes, like 'Real Wives are Super-Hot,' and 'This Time it's Your Turn' in which lady contestants could win a night out with a supposed perfect hunk.

Mike had reluctantly asked Beryl if he could visit her, and she agreed. She still lived in Southwold, and she had given him the address willingly. Beryl told Mike that she was hoping she could get him to give her some money for booze, in return for dishing the dirt on her ex-husband. He had begun to understand why Ian was so keen on Susie Q. It must have been terrible having to put up with an air brained, money grabbing woman like Beryl.

She had pursued the subject of money by saying:

"If I give you information that leads to you recovering his love machine, or in recapturing him, will I get a nice fat reward?"

"I should think so. Susie Q is worth a fortune, and the WRO have a vested interest in getting Ian back to Geneva, so they can study the progress, or otherwise, of their first AR patient."

Mike went to the address that Beryl had given him. When he arrived at her place he saw that it was a run-down cottage, on the outskirts of Southwold, near the Blackshore Quay. The dilapidated building had definitely seen better days. When Beryl opened the front door, which was creaking and sagging on its rusty hinges, he realised that she had seen better days too. He imagined that she might have once been very pretty, but it looked as if she had piled on the pounds since splitting with Ian.

Somewhere under that fleshy and plump face, there was a more attractive one trying to get out. She was obese, and she shuffled her feet as she led Mike into her front room. On the table, there were three red wine bottles. Two were empty and on their sides, and the other one was well on the way to being that way. That one was at least upright, which was more than could be said for Beryl who was by now lying on a sofa. She looked at him blearily through a greasy fringe, and she patted the fraying material, inviting Mike to sit next to her. This was an invitation he decided to ignore if he possibly could.

Mike viewed her with extreme distaste. She was wearing a matted and once fluffy dressing gown which was stained and torn. She wore down-trodden slippers, half on her grubby feet. She sat up and put her left foot on a coffee table. To his horror and disgust, Mike realised that she was wearing nothing at all under the gown. He found himself looking right into her most private place, which he devoutly wished she had kept private.

"Like what you see big boy? Want a drink or a special treat now that something has caught your eye? Have you got any money? If so, splash a little of it my way, and we could have some exciting rumpy pumpy. You look like you could have a real fun time with me. Get me some nice red wine and as Shiraz my name is Beryl, I will give you an afternoon that you will never forget."

Mike felt sick. He wasn't surprised that Ian Tudeep found Susie Q better company, even though she was just a robot.

"Is your man, Brando, in? I'm sure he wouldn't be best pleased if he knew what you just offered me."

"Sodding bastard, he ran off with a scrawny little tart, Christalee, from the seaside rock shop. Her parents made up that stupid name for their daughter. Worse than that she 'reely' had 'like' a ridiculous double-barrelled christian name. She was christened Christalee-Petal."

Mike was at a loss. He hadn't expected to agree with Beryl about anything. Brando's new girlfriend definitely did have a silly name. He hoped they wouldn't get married. Christalee-Petal Marlon would surely win prizes for idiotic names. He thought that nobody could ever make up a more ridiculous name.

'Ruddy Christalee bloody Petal still works there. It's the shop on what's left of the pier. It's on that bit that's just about standing up. Ian used to like their special rock with chocolate inside. They called it 'Rock Around the Choc.' Another dopey bloody name. She was eighteen when he met her, and she was as skinny as a rake. Wouldn't you want a fine figure of a woman, like me, rather than a f******, twig-like girlfriend who speaks 'like reely kinda daft OMG?' Bet you're still waiting to get your special treat. Come and sit next to me, sexpot."

Mike didn't feel at all like a sexpot. He thought he would have to humour Beryl a little. He had to get as much information from her as possible. He hesitantly, and somewhat gingerly, sat on the stained and greasy sofa next to blubber woman. Beryl took hold of his face and swooped in for an all-enveloping hug and a revolting, wet and noisy kiss. Mike could hardly breathe.

John Bobin

"Beryl, you're all woman, and I find you incredibly attractive, but I'm a devout, religious man and I'm happily married."

'Incredibly attractive,' he thought. 'That just about sums it up.' It was incredible that anybody would find her attractive. To his concern, she started to cry mournfully, but she managed to stop after a few weepy minutes.

"You could still have a little drink with me, even if you don't fancy me. I used to be pretty once. I really was.'

She started crying again.

"I found this place, not far from here, that still sells wine. I'm blowed if I know where they get it from. It's probably bootleg junk made from antifreeze, flavourings and colouring. I don't care what it tastes like. I just like getting roaring drunk. I'm hoping they don't get shut down too quickly by the interfering government. I know that most people only have alcohol pills now, but it's not the same really, is it? Bring me six bottles of the cheapest wine you can buy. It doesn't matter whether they are red or white. Here's the address."

She pointed to the entry in her electrajot contacts for the 'Wine Like It Used 2B' place.

"Stay there, and I'll be back soon."

Mike hastened out of the cottage, leaving the front door on the latch. The wine was bought with ease. The elfin girl in the shop had her hair in that short wispy cut, that only ever suited a dainty face. It 'reely,' sorry really suited her, as she was young and pretty. She said that Beryl was one of their best customers. Mike wasn't at all surprised.

"Mind you, I think she's no better than she should be. I've heard that she gets men to buy her drink in exchange for sex. You don't look like one of her usual customers. You seem like a nice respectable man."

Mike couldn't help being flattered, as the girl grinned at him and winked saucily.

I'm Back!

He thought she was flirting with him, and it felt good. The illusion was shattered when she said:

"You remind me of my Dad."

Back in Beryl's smelly and filthy dirty cottage, Mike found a half-broken, but still serviceable, corkscrew in a kitchen drawer. He opened one of the new wine bottles and took it into the front room. The fresh supply of vino had come just in time. The bottle which had still had some wine in it, before he went to the wine shop, was now empty.

Beryl had been violently sick, all over the carpet. It looked like a painting by Jackson Pollock. (Mike liked artists of yesteryear but didn't like JP. He preferred Monet and Turner. He had heard that Monet was a skinflint. One of Monet's friends had been quoted as saying 'Monet's too tight to mention.') He lugged Beryl back onto the sofa, as she had almost fallen off. He made sure that she could breathe and then decided to search the cottage before she woke up.

He went through every cupboard. He ransacked every drawer. He looked in the shed and in the attached garage, but he could find nothing that might lead him to Ian. His last hope was the loft. There was a pull-down ladder which still worked. The loft was musty, and there was animal dirt everywhere. It looked as if rodents had been sheltering in the loft. There were pellets all over the floor, which was half boarded. He trod carefully on the rafters, where necessary. The dirts were bigger than those of mice. He wondered if rats or squirrels had been living up there. He thought they had probably been undisturbed by human company for many years.

Mike searched in several tattered, cardboard boxes. The first few were full of the usual things people used to keep in lofts. Most of it was tat. There were old greetings cards, souvenirs from holidays taken by aged ancestors and items which had been put up there 'just in case.' In fact, they were exactly the things that sons and daughters usually chucked out, as they had no use for them, when their parents passed away.

In the last box, (quelle surprise!) Mike found old photos of Ian and Beryl, in much happier times. He was most surprised to see that in her glory days, she really had been a pretty girl with a nice smile. He noted that she had favoured a short urchin haircut (not unlike that of the girl in the wine shop.) It was sad to note that it really suited Beryl, when she was much younger and slimmer. She used to have beautiful, almond shaped, dark brown eyes too. Nowadays, they were glassy and unfocussed, and she had large eye bags.

He was pleased when he found a leather-bound photo album, which contained pictures of Ian and Beryl's wedding. There was also a book, in the same box, containing many friendly messages from well-wishers. Most of the entries meant nothing. One he found, nearly at the bottom of the last page, looked promising. This was a message from a lady called Alice Springs.

'Congratulations to my two school-friends. I hope you'll both be happy. I remember Ian as my first love. Please treat him well, Beryl!'

There was a column for the address and full name of each person who had signed the book. Mike realised that this was included so that the newly married couple could send thank you cards for all their wedding presents. He tore out the relevant page and stuffed it into his back pocket. He zipped the pocket up securely. The address for Alice was in Southend-on-Sea, which he knew was in Essex.

He went down the ladder rungs carefully, after banging his head clumsily on an overhead beam. Beryl still seemed to be asleep. He went over to check that she was alright. He was mightily relieved when she started to snore. As he stood up, she opened her beady, blood-shot eyes.

"Hallo. Are you sure you wouldn't like some jig a jig? I'm good at sex, and I'd never tell your wife you made love to me."

"Shush, go to sleep, dear. I've already told you that I wouldn't let my wife down."

He was lying. He wasn't even married. However, he regarded it as a white lie. Despite being revolted by Beryl, he had no wish to hurt her feelings. Mike almost ran out of the cottage. He stopped just outside the door, and he too was sick. He wiped his mouth with his handkerchief and mentally thanked his lucky stars that he had managed to leave without too much direct contact with Beryl.

Chapter 23

Mike walked along the beach away from the River Blyth, and marvelled at the row of colourful beach huts, all with special names. Some of them were quite humourous. He was surprised that the huts were still there, but he remembered reading that they fetched huge prices. The article that he had seen on the Solar System Web said that the ones in the Gun Hill area were the most expensive. It seemed to be the place where all the richest people in Southwold lived.

It was a long shot, Mike thought, but maybe Alice still lived in Southend. He decided to go there that very day. He managed to catch a scheduled aerobus which connected to another one. This latter one took him to the run-down seaside resort. He didn't pay much attention to the scenery, as he was snoozing on the way. The aerobus landed gently and accurately at his destination. White lines showed the pilot where to set down his hovering vehicle. Mike consulted his electrajot's map app, and he found that the address which Alice had written in the wedding book was fairly near to the aPad.

On reaching Alice's old house, he rang the bell, but there was no answer. He tried several times just in case the present owners were in the back garden. There was complete silence. He looked around him surreptitiously, and as nobody was around, he decided to go to the back of the house. He wanted to see if he could get in that way. The back door was locked, but there was a window ajar upstairs. He looked in an old brick outhouse to see if there was a ladder in there. There was, so he carried it out and set it down on the path at the back of the house. He also noticed an amazingly clean

I'm Back!

chopperator in the outhouse. He had seen these before, but they were usually quite grimy, and they often smelt awful. This one was bright and fresh. It was as if it had only recently been scrubbed. The chopperator smelt only of bleach or disinfectant.

Mike slid the ladder up the house wall until its separate parts clicked into place. After climbing up, he peered into the room. It was unremarkable. It had a double bed, a wardrobe and two bedside cabinets, one on each side of the bed. There was also a chair in front of a walnut dressing table. It all looked old-fashioned, but it was clean and tidy. He scrambled through the window, and he hoped that nobody saw him. (He had noted that the house backed onto the rear garden of a similar house in the next road, so he felt a little exposed until he had moved out of sight.)

One of the bedside cabinets had the top drawer slightly open. Mike pulled it fully out and placed it on the floor behind him. It seemed that the drawer was not flat to the floor. He squatted on the floor. On turning it over, he saw that there was a bundle of envelopes under the drawer, tied together with a red ribbon. This bundle had been taped to the bottom of the drawer. He could smell a faint, floral scent. He concluded that the woman of the house slept on this side of the bed. When he released the envelopes, he realised that was where the scent was coming from.

He untied the envelopes carefully and found to his amazement, that there were twenty-five letters. All of them were addressed to 'My darling Ian.' Each letter was dated on the same day and month but in different years.

The first one started like this:

'My Darling Ian, it broke my heart to see you marrying Beryl today. How I wish we'd stayed together. If ever you and Beryl split up, I'll be waiting for you.'

It continued for three pages, repeatedly lamenting the fact that they had not married each other. It also said how sad she had been when they broke up. The woeful communication ended with this sad paragraph:

'I've written this letter, but I know that I can't send it. I'll write another one every year on the same day, and maybe I can share them with you if you leave Beryl, or if she finds somebody else.

With all my love, now and forever.

Alice

XXX'

Mike read all the letters. In one of the letters he found out that Alice's parents had both been killed in a tragic accident. The remains of the Kursaal building were being demolished. Alice's mother and father had been walking past the site where men were working, and a section of the wall to the side of the pavement had toppled onto them. Her Mum and Dad were killed instantly.

Alice told Ian in another one of the letters she would never send, that she was very unhappy. She mentioned that the house in which she had lived with her parents, had been left to her. She said that she still lived there, and that she was now in a failing marriage to a man called Walter Nuisance. Walter had been a builder, but his employers had sacked him as he was frequently late. He was also off sick, many times, with no real reason. Alice told Ian in the same letter that Walter was an alcohol pill addict, and he often missed going to work because of hangovers.

The manufacturers of alcohol pills always said that they would not cause any serious side effects. To be fair to them, they were expecting people to stick to the recommended dose. Walter sometimes ate three or four times the maximum dose. Alice also said that Walter made no attempt whatsoever to get another job. His firm had made it clear that they wouldn't give him a good reference. He used that as an excuse not to apply for jobs, and he sponged off Alice who was still working.

She said in yet another of the letters that she had good friends. She mentioned that her old school friend, Rita, had been truly kind to her. Alice had cried on her shoulder, after she and Ian had split up. (Alice's letters were sweet, but Mike thought they were almost unbearably sad.) Alice told Ian that Rita had moved away from

I'm Back!

Southwold, to a block of flats in Broadstairs called Morelli Heights. Ian had seemingly known Rita too, when they were all at school together.

Mike made a mental note to try to contact this Rita woman. He stuffed the letters into his voluminous coat pocket. He thought how lucky it was that this old coat of his father's had a large poacher's pocket specially designed to hide rabbits. His father had been a gamekeeper on an estate near Sandringham, until he had been 'let go.' There was now not much use for a gamekeeper, because of the scarcity of said game. Mike's Dad had continued to go to the estate daily. He knew that he was trespassing, but he also knew where to enter the grounds with ease. He came home with rabbits frequently, and Mike's Mum had made pies. He liked the pies, until he found out what was in them.

He looked all over Alice's house, but he was unable to find anything else of interest. The front room absolutely sparkled. It couldn't have been cleaner than it was. Once again, there was a pungent smell of bleach or disinfectant. He sat on each of the double sofas, whilst considering what to do next. He put his hand on the arm of the second sofa. He tapped his fingers, which were draped over the side idly, and he felt something unpleasant and rather sticky under the piping of the arm.

He looked at his fingers, and he saw that they were red. He smelt the stain on his fingers and on the sofa arm. He wondered if it could be blood. Then he remembered the suspiciously clean chopperator. He walked outside and opened the lid of the chopperator in the outhouse. He found nothing untoward there initially, but he examined the quarry tiling too, and he spotted some scuffed, reddish-brown marks on the grouting which also looked like blood.

He wondered what had happened here, and he decided that he had to call the police. He looked up the number for the nearest police station, which was twenty-seven miles away. He used his electrajot to phone the station. After a few rings, there was an automated message.

"This is the East Anglian Police Force number. Please be aware that all calls are recorded for training purposes. Press 1 to report a crime or 2 to give information about a known case. For all other calls, wait to speak to an operator. Press 3 to hear these options again or hold on for an operator."

Mike pressed 1.

"We are very busy at present, but your call is important to us and will be answered as soon as possible."

Mike put the call on speaker phone and waited impatiently. After a long wait, a bright and breezy lady answered the phone.

"This is Constable John; how can I help you?"

"My name is Mike Anick. I travelled to Southend today. I came here to visit a person in connection with a man who went missing recently. He left the World Reincarnation Organisation's headquarters in Geneva without permission. This man took a valuable robot with him. I've been tasked by the WRO to try to trace him. His name is Ian Tudeep, and the robot is called Susie Q. The lady to whom I wished to speak was out, even though she said she'd be in all day."

He was lying of course, but he could hardly tell them the truth.

"When I arrived at her house there was no reply. I was most anxious. I knew that she had heart problems and lived alone. I was under the impression that she rarely went out, due to her serious problems with atrial fibrillation.

I saw that a window was wide open, and I took the liberty of entering the premises. I had to see if the lady I wanted to see, Alice Nuisance, was lying on the floor incapacitated or worse. She was nowhere to be seen, so I thought I should contact you. I'm still here and can wait until you come. I should mention that there seems to be blood stains on a sofa and on the floor of an outhouse. In that outhouse there is an old, but exceptionally clean chopperator."

Constable John grunted.

'That's not a ladylike sound,' thought Mike.

I'm Back!

She read him the riot act about entering the premises unlawfully. This went on for some considerable time, but she concluded:

"You should've called us and waited until we arrived, and we would then have exercised our official powers by entering legally."

"I was worried about Mrs. Nuisance. I didn't know when I got here, where the nearest police headquarters was. However, I was aware that many local police stations are now permanently closed. I thought it was likely that you'd have to come some way. I found out that you would be coming from Witham, nearly thirty miles away. I saw the address on my electrajot when I looked up your number. It seemed right to me that any further delay in my entering could've meant that Alice was on the floor dying."

He gave her the address. Constable John grunted again.

"Just stay there, and don't touch anything else. We'll be coming as quickly as we can, and Scene Of Incident Officers will also be on the way."

Mike apologised meekly for jumping the gun. He thought that Constable John seemed mollified by his eloquent, but insincere, admission that he was at fault.

"What did you say your name was please?"

"Constable Molly John, and my number is …."

This official number was inaudible, as Mike was trying hard not to laugh. He had taken his electrajot off the speaker phone, and he now held it away from him. He didn't want the PC to hear him giggling. He had just realised that Constable John didn't need mollifying. She had been mollified already by her parents when she was christened.

John Bobin

Chapter 24

When the Scene Of Incident Officers arrived at Alice and Walter's house, they took a brief, preliminary statement from Mike Anick. They also asked him for DNA samples. They explained that they wanted to eliminate him from any potential blame in relation to events that might change from being incidents to crimes. SOIO officers doubled as SOCO workers. Most of them thought that the initial need to call themselves SOIO was complete nonsense, foisted upon them by the omnipresent PC brigade. The influence of these people, with their imagined slights and exaggerated tendency to take offence at the slightest provocation, annoyed most ordinary, right-thinking people.

"Good afternoon. You are gender not known Anick, I presume."

This greeting was the opening gambit of a young, attractive copper. (Her gender was obvious.) She was with the SOIO and other assorted police 'people.' (Not policemen and policewomen you will note. They didn't want to cause offence.)

"I'm gender non-specific Emma Bobby. You may if you wish, call me Ms. Bobby, or Emma. I must warn you that if you address me as Miss or Mrs. Bobby, you will be subject to an on the spot fine of £2,000. I'm unable to tell you my rank, as this may worry you. If it's very senior to your position in society it may make you feel inferior. It's also possible that it may cause overbearing behaviour from you if it's very junior to your status. If you ask to be told, I can reveal it to you."

Mike had always found this sort of thing to be totally laughable. Here was a very pretty, intelligent, and well-spoken policewoman (with nice breasts for definite proof

123

I'm Back!

that she wasn't gender non-specific.) Due to the dictats of the PC brigade she was obliged to spout this politically correct claptrap. This was ostensibly in order to avoid giving offence to a tiny minority of people, who obviously had nothing better to worry about.

"Yes, please lass. What's your rank?"

Emma pretended to ignore his rude use of the word lass. (Or to be perfectly correct she quite enjoyed it, but she wouldn't admit that this was so. She was 36 years old, and she didn't really feel like a lass anymore.)

"I'm an Inspector. Does that cause you any distress? I'm able to refer you to a counsellor, if you're concerned that a mere lass is an inspector."

She was toeing the party line delicately. Emma looked at him a bit coyly, winked and said:

"Now we've got all that bollocks out of the way, what else can you tell me about your grisly find today? May I also say I am awfully sorry I said bollocks. And if that offended you, that's tough."

Mike started at the very beginning. He explained again that he worked for the WRO and what his mission was. Emma already knew about Ian and Susie Q running away from Geneva, as it had been all over the news. The 'be on the lookout,' messages had come thick and fast on the police's new network COPPER, (Criminal Offenders Protocol and Procedures Examination Resource.)

The SOIO people had by now decided that they were officially SOCO. They had inspected every room, the garden, and the outhouse. They had agreed that the suspected blood stains which Mike had found did indeed look like blood. They had taken samples from the places which he had mentioned. Using special lights and a microscope attachment to a modified electrajot, they had found yet more blood. In addition, they had discovered small scrapings of flesh around the lid of the chopperator. These were taken away to be analysed back at the ranch, together with multiple DNA samples.

124

"How long does it normally take to get the results of these tests? We've got two serious problems. If Ian Tudeep is one of the people who has been in this house, we have to find him quickly. He's only fairly recently been artificially reincarnated, and the WRO need to test him regularly to make sure he's healthy and well. Secondly, when he left the WRO's complex in Geneva he stole a robot worth a whole lot of money. The WRO desperately want to get her back. There's a £1,000,000 reward, which has encouraged people to get in touch with them. Unfortunately, the callers have mostly been cranks."

"Would there perhaps be a separate reward to be paid into police funds if we arrested Ian Tudeep?"

"Absolutely."

Mike hoped that this was so, and he made a mental note to ask Hiram Prendergast, when he was alone.

"Test results usually take two or three days. If the WRO want to pay an express fee of £1,000 they can be processed over-night. Where will you be staying?"

"Give me a minute, and I'll check my room booking. Once I've done that, I'll let you know."

Mike went into another room. He had booked an over-night stay at the best hotel in town. Ye Olde Southendian stood on the same spot as the long-gone Kursaal Ballroom. They confirmed that his room was ready. He also contacted Prendergast. He asked it if it would be possible to pay the police an extra reward if they arrested Ian Tudeep.

"Yes, of course. We're desperate to get him back. We fear that Susie Q's behaviour may become more and more erratic. She may possibly even become violent. We were taking a big chance in introducing human DNA into a robot. If this leaked out, we may even lose our robotics licence. Mike, you've got my express permission to do whatever you think fit to help get Tudeep and Susie Q back here."

I'm Back!

"Right. Please note that my electrajot has automatically recorded this conversation."

"No problem."

Mike went back into the other room. He told Emma Bobby that he would be staying at Ye Olde Southendian in the High Street.

"Emma, I don't suppose you'd like to join me for dinner tonight at eight?"

"How dare you make this approach to a copper! I'm very taken aback."

Mike was a little surprised by her reaction. He then noticed another, younger police person behind Emma, taking samples from the skirting board. When Mike looked up, he was pleased to see Emma silently mouth:

"Yes."

Mike and Emma had a wonderful (and real), meal. They had decided against taking the usual food and drink pills. Although the pills were nowadays almost de rigeur, some eating houses and hotels still served real food. Mike had now and again come across places serving food that they maintained was 'like Mumma used to make.'

The scallops with rocket and bacon were divine. The lobster thermidor with lemon and lime rice was wonderful, and the bread and butter pudding (with custard, not cream - thank goodness), rounded things off nicely. Emma and Mike drank real wine too, and she was great company.

She was even better company when she accompanied him to his room. She said she wanted to make sure she knew where to find him the next day. This was much easier than she thought it would be, as he was lying next to her in a huge, super-king sized (or maybe even larger than that), bed. When she woke up, she nuzzled up to him.

She said:

"Mr. Anick, I'm placing you under arrest for taking advantage of a poor defenceless girl."

She reached over to her handbag, took out a pair of handcuffs and snapped one

John Bobin

on his left wrist and the other on her right wrist. He felt certain this wasn't an official procedure.

"I can't let you go until you've paid a very special forfeit."

After Mike had paid his enjoyable forfeit, they snoozed for a while. She had released him from the handcuffs, and they had been talking about his mission to find Ian Tudeep and Susie Q. He had taken her into his confidence, and he mentioned to her that he was now looking for a woman called Rita, an old school friend of Alice Nuisance's. He said he was hoping Alice was still in touch with her. He wondered if Emma could search the police database to see how many people lived in Southwold who were called Rita, at the time that Alice and Ian were courting.

"That should be easy. COPPER has a particularly good search engine and has direct access to many official databases. We can narrow the search criteria down a little. From what you told me it seems that this Rita, Ian and Alice were all at school together."

She made a call with her electrajot, seeking permission to access COPPER to make enquiries about a known associate of Ian Tudeep's. Thirty minutes later she had a list of 24 women named Rita, who had lived in Southwold when Ian was at school. They quickly eliminated 23 ladies, as they found that all of them bar one went to a different school to Ian and Alice.

The entry they had left was for a lady called Rita Loza. COPPER also verified that she was still living in Broadstairs at a condenselow in Morelli Heights. Additional information found on COPPER told them that she had apparently been married to a man called Sutcliffe, ten years after she left school. She had married Jim Sutcliffe when she was twenty-six, and their marriage only lasted a few years. After their divorce she had reverted to her maiden name of Loza. Mike decided to go to Broadstairs, to see if Rita could help him to find Ian Tudeep and Susie Q.

Chapter 25

Back at Morelli Heights, Ian, Susie Q, Alice, Tosser and Rita were lying low. This was not a hard task as Rita was a good hostess, and she had plenty of food and drink pills. They spent a lot of their time doing virtual jigsaw puzzles, which were displayed on the living room wall by Ian's electrajot. He also had many old board games, in an app which ran special versions of historical board games and parlour amusements.

Alice had by now decided to tell Rita the truth about Walter. She did so in private. Alice explained how Susie Q had ripped him to bits, after killing her husband to save her life.

Rita was horrified, but she said:

"I never liked him. You were far too good for him. He was a vulgar, idle, and cruel man. He tried it on with me twice. The first time, he stopped when I threatened to tell you what he was up to. The second time, he forced me up against a wall, and I kneed him hard where it hurts. He was rolling around on the floor in agony when I left the room. I'm astonished that Susie Q killed him and tore him up. I hope she doesn't get like that too often?"

"She may have a thing called humanitis. Sadly, this could cause her to struggle to control her emotions. I thought robots had no feelings, but she's different to any other robot I've ever seen."

Ian and Susie Q had other games to play, and they took an almost insatiable delight in romping together in Rita's largest spare bedroom. Alice had been given what used to be called a box room. It was on the third day that Ian and Susie decided to have a little doze in the afternoon. Rita took the mickey out of the two love birds.

"Is that what they call it now, a little doze?"

Ian laughed and replied:

"We also need to check the ceiling!"

Ian grabbed Susie Q's hand, and they almost ran into the hall on their way to the bedroom. Alice laughed, too. She looked rather wistful.

She eyed Rita and said:

"I just wish I was Susie Q."

Rita smiled, but she could see that this was a difficult time for poor Alice.

Ian and Susie Q undressed quickly. Ian did this by tugging and pulling off his clothes, whilst Susie Q just pressed her neck button. At first, nothing happened. There was a worrying, creaking noise, but then all the buttons popped open.

They jumped into bed, and they started to have a 'little doze.' After a lively time they had a real doze, rather than what they had been up to a few minutes before. Ian woke up first. He found that his arm had gone to sleep, as it was under Susie Q. He pulled it out and lifted it over her face as she sat up. She gave a little cry. When she lay back down there was an ominous ripping sound.

Ian was most alarmed, and so was Susie Q. He wanted to find out what had ripped, and he hoped it was just the bed sheet. That wasn't to be. By this time Susie Q had sat up, and she could see her face in the dressing table mirror. She realised with a shock, that there was a gaping hole in the side of her torn Michelle Keegan face.

"Quickly, let's get dressed and go to see Tosser. He may know what to do."

They both put their clothes back on hurriedly. They almost ran down the hall and into the living room. Tosser was playing a game of solitaire, which they saw he had projected onto the wall of the room.

Ian could hardly get his thoughts in order, but he said:

"Tosser, we've got a huge problem. Susie Q's face has split or ripped. Is there anything you can do quickly?"

Tosser closed the solitaire game and switched on all the living room lights. He opened his tool case, and he found a special examination device which had a bright light and a powerful magnifying glass.

"Susie Q, please lie on the settee here and look up at me."

She did so, and Tosser made a thorough visual inspection of the surface of her new face. He also studied the edges where he had joined the elastaskin to the mask. He paid particular attention to the fake skin on her head and neck.

"I think I know what's happened here. The face is not quite as good as I thought it was. There are small marks where the edges have been pulled away from the elastaskin. I used the elastaskin so that people wouldn't see the join of the face to her head. The face should've been flexible enough to cope with a little stretching, but it seems that it was a bit too stiff. I think I can fix it, but it'll take a lot of work. I'm sorry Susie Q, but you'll either have to be faceless for a couple of days, or I can replace your original face whilst I'm working on the Michelle Keegan one."

Susie Q nodded. Ian said:

"Please put the other one back on, until you can redo Michelle Keegan."

Chapter 26

They decided to leave Susie Q to the tender mercies of Tosser. They thought it best to get out of the way whilst he was removing Michelle's face and replacing it with the old and more familiar Susie Q one. They had been warned that it would take some time, and they didn't want to get in the way while the procedure was undertaken.

In the other room, they started to discuss how best Ian and Susie Q could continue evading their pursuers. There were still news items about them, but in the usual way, more recent other news had overtaken the old output. Somebody whom Ian had never heard of was having a torrid and squalid affair with a young actress, who was allegedly one of the best-looking women in the world. Ian had never heard of her either. The prevailing fashion for huge bottoms, massive thick eyebrows and big fat pouty lips had apparently been resurrected as a throwback to the similar bewildering trend in the early twenty first century.

Ian couldn't understand it at all. He had done some historical research (as you would expect by now), and he had seen lots of before and after photos of women who had been under the knife and/or had stuff injected into them. He thought that the before pictures invariably looked better than the after ones. He was relieved that Susie Q would be having her new face replaced by her old one, even if it was only temporary. He had liked Michelle Keegan's face on Susie Q, but he thought it was rather strange to have Susie Q looking like Michelle and speaking like Joanna Lumley. At least she always acted like Susie Q, his little angel.

'Except for when she killed Walter,' he thought.

I'm Back!

Rita suggested that Ian and Susie Q should keep moving on for some time yet. She said she knew somebody who lived in Happisburgh. She told them how it was spelt. Then she said the place name was pronounced Haze-bruh.

"But why?" Alice asked.

"I've no idea. They've got lots of place names in Norfolk which look like one thing when they are written down, but they're pronounced in another way. There's one place called Stiffkey, but which is pronounced Stewkey!"

They all thought that was odd. Rita told them that her friend lived near to where an old red and white striped lighthouse used to stand. Ian said he had seen pictures of it, standing near a cliff edge. Rita told them that it wasn't on the cliff any longer.

"The cliff was being eroded quite quickly, and for a long time there was no doubt that eventually the lighthouse would fall onto the beach. The local council and the National Trust tried to raise enough money to move it elsewhere. It would have cost the earth, and they didn't raise enough cash. Also, there would have been enormous technical problems. It's most sad."

Rita said that the lighthouse was now on Happisburgh beach in pieces. Some of these were large and some much smaller. There was a safety wall round the ruins of the lighthouse. What was left of the lighthouse was lying on its side like a sunbathing girl leaning on her elbow, on the beach at the bottom of the still retreating cliff. People frequently climbed over the wall, despite the huge 'Danger' signs, and they took pieces of the lighthouse home as souvenirs.

Two young turks had tried to get inside the fallen lighthouse and had managed to half-open the doors. They had crawled inside, but they couldn't get out again. They'd contacted the Coastguard service by electrajot, as they didn't know who might be able to help them best. The Coastguards, the police, the RNLI, and the Fire Brigade all did their best, but it was impossible to get them out, as the bottom half of the fragile ruins had collapsed on them, after being disturbed when they had moved the doors. They were badly crushed.

The parents of the two boys reluctantly agreed that they should be left inside. There wasn't much choice. Luckily, the lads died quite quickly, rather than lingering on for some while in pain. The space that they had formerly occupied by themselves had now been filled with rubble, concrete, bricks, and other bits of lighthouse on top of their bodies. The council concreted over the old doors and the flattened area. They erected a memorial plaque, which bore the names of the two teenagers and the words, 'They came to explore, and they saw the light. RIP.' The parents hoped that this terse message might dissuade other foolish explorers from clambering over the remains of the lighthouse.

Rita wanted to tell her friends about the man whom she was hoping would help them.

"My friend, Eddie Biggs, is a terrific man. He's a bit frightening at first. He only has two volumes when he is speaking. These are incredibly quiet and a huge bellowing voice. His loud voice can probably be heard about thirty miles away. I have to say that he hardly ever uses his soft voice.

He's got one of those old barns that's been converted into living accommodation. They seem to last a lot longer than the houses that were built at around the time it was converted. I think it was originally a stable. He's always been a bit of a rebel. At school he was more often absent than he was present. When he was there, he led a mini gang of troublemakers, who took great delight in making the schoolteachers' lives a misery.

He joined various clubs and societies when he was a youngster, but they usually threw him out, because he was such a bad influence. I'm making him sound awful, but he's a good man who will help anybody who has a problem at the drop of a hat. He's had lots of jobs. He was a soldier, before the global ban on war. He says that's all bunkum as there will always be uprisings and confrontational territorial issues. He also says that these tensions still hubble and bubble until they are permanently squashed. He believes that secret professionals are sent to the hot spots, and they take out the trouble-makers."

Ian said that he disapproved of using paid mercenaries to solve problems like these.

"I understand, Ian, but what would any man do if his wife and family were threatened? His whole viewpoint may be different then, don't you think?

Eddie's also been a gardener, an artist, and a potter. He wanted to be a zookeeper when he was at school, but it's just as well that he didn't pursue that career path. There are hardly any zoos now. Even those that are still in existence don't have large animals, or if they do there are only a few scrawny specimens.

He tried his hand at being a PT instructor, but his pupils didn't like being shouted at during training sessions. It's not surprising really that he's loud. What would you expect from an ex-sergeant major? He also ran a dog rescue home, but in the end he had all the mutts nobody wanted. He had the dogs with one eye, three legs, or the ones that had been badly treated before they came to the home. They were often aggressive and difficult to handle. He's been a champion of people who are in trouble, for as long as I can remember, and I bet he would love to help."

Rita continued to speak about her friend.

"When Eddie was born, he was 16 and a half pounds. He always says that he made his Mum's eyes water as he was being ejected from her nice warm womb. He became a huge toddler, an enormous teenager, and he's now a massive man. He's got a heart the size of a mountain. If you want me to, I'll contact him to see if he can house you for a while."

There was a quick discussion between Ian and Alice, and they concluded that asking Eddie Biggs to help would be a good thing to do.

"Let's go for it," agreed Ian.

Rita had a short conversation with Eddie using her electrajot. They didn't need to ask her what he said, as they could hear every word he thundered. She was right. He was a very loud person.

"Hallo Eddie, this is Rita."

"What ho, old girl! How are you doing?"

"I'm fine, but some friends of mine are in the mire. I'm going to let you into a secret, and you must promise never to tell anybody else this story, unless I give you express permission."

"Aha! Secrets…I love secrets. I'm particularly good at keeping things quiet…"

Rita pointedly took the electrajot away from her ear.

"I don't think so Eddie. You're still the loudest person in the world."

"Gotcha girl. OK, tell me about your pals."

Rita regaled Eddie with the whole story from start to finish, or maybe not quite the whole story, as the finish is still some way off yet.

"Tell them they'll be welcome. I'll do all I can to protect them, and I'll house them for as long as they like. Are you coming too Rita? I'd like to slap your pretty little bum again."

"Shush Eddie, they can all hear you."

"Righty ho, old girl. Thought I was keeping things quiet, don't you know?"

They said goodbye. Alice had taken note that Rita and Eddie obviously had some back story. She decided to ask Rita about it before they left. She didn't want to drop any clangers.

When Alice tackled Rita about her relationship with Eddie, this is what she told her. It appeared that Eddie had been very protective when she and Jim Sutcliffe broke up. Rita and Eddie had become rather more than just good friends. They had a brief but most enjoyable intrigue, and they even went to Scotland for a holiday near Loch Awe. Eddie liked to refer to that break as their highland fling. He seemed to like bad

I'm Back!

jokes as much as Ian.

They all had a lunch of food and drink pills and treated themselves to a holovision film. When that was over they chatted, while they were waiting for Tosser to perform his magic. This took longer than he thought it would, but in the end he was pleased with his work. Susie Q took a cautious peek at her new/old face in the virtual mirror. She was delighted with what she saw. This was more like her old self.

Tosser and Susie Q went into the other room, and the others all crowded round Susie Q, peering at her face. They complimented her on her return to Susie Q-ness. Rita explained her conversation with Eddie to Ian and Susie Q.

"It's probably best if you go to Norfolk as quickly as possible. The more you get around, the less likely it'll be that you will be caught. Let's see if there's any more about you two on the news."

She projected a virtual screen into the room from her electrajot, and she gave the device instructions to relay the latest news.

"Electra, give me the WBC news."

The room was suddenly virtually filled with two famous newscasters, Honey Blonde and Paul Somebody. These two were the most popular newscasters in the world. Their names were apt. Honey was a real honey, and Paul was really somebody. They laughed, joked, and flirted in between the news items. They may have had a thing going on when they were off screen. Of course, it might have been what they wanted their viewers to think.

The World Broadcasting Corporation had been formed when all the other news services had been merged, and it was now the only official global news service. There were those who worried that the WBC might slant their news to suit their own purposes. They were probably right, but although they grumbled about the WBC's partisan views, it made no difference. There were still black news services, which were frowned upon by the authorities and which usually only broadcasted for a short period. The WBC had friends in high places, and the unofficial broadcasters were always shut down quickly.

Honey opened the first item:

"Now, here's an unusual love story. You may have heard already about Ian Tudeep, the world's first Artificial Reincarnation (or AR), patient. Last week, he and a glamourous robot called Susie Q ran away from the headquarters of the Word Reincarnation Organisation (the WRO), in Geneva.

Our sources say that Ian's AR didn't quite go to plan, but that with special treatment, he recovered over a period of several months. Susie Q was allocated to look after him during that period, and we understand that she thinks she is in love with him. Ian has reciprocated."

"That's a new word for what he's done with her," laughed Paul.

"Shush, I'm speaking," twinkled Honey.

"But I heard that he really has the hots for her!"

Honey pretended to frown.

"They've been traced to England, and it's now known that they spent some time in Southend. They were thought to have been at a residential property owned by Walter and Alice Nuisance. A senior representative of the WRO, Mike Anick, gained entry to their home and he found suspicious stains. He thought they might be blood, and they were in at least at least two places. The police were called to investigate and Scene Of Incident Officers took many samples, lots of fingerprints and other interesting items away to be tested."

"Why do they now call themselves Scene Of Incident Officers? It was easy to say SOCO, but SOIO is a real mouthful."

"The new name reflects that fact that SOCO presupposes that a crime has been committed, but sometimes this might not be so. Do you want to hear the rest of the news or not?"

She dimpled nicely, and she leaned forward to show off her scenic décolletage.

I'm Back!

This was the main reason why most men watched their news programme. She almost spilled out of the dress that she was nearly wearing, but luckily there was no wardrobe malfunction. It was a close thing though.

Honey resumed her tale:

"SOCO have now released this information. (By the way, it has now been formally established that it is a crime scene.) Fingerprints found at the cottage included those of Walter and Alice Nuisance, as expected. Additional fingerprints were found. Some of these were of Richard Small, who was only eighteen months old when he died after having a fit.

Also, the police found some strange blurred prints, which may have been left by a robot. Fascinatingly, our sources have revealed that the body of Richard Small was used by the WRO to house Ian Tudeep's old spirit and memories. This was allegedly because the intended taking body for Ian's AR rejected the transfer."

Paul took over.

"The blood stains which were tested showed that the blood came from Walter Nuisance. A neighbour, who is called Ivy Creeping, said she saw Alice Nuisance, a bearded man and a pretty, young lady with blonde hair leaving the cottage. She said they seemed to be in a hurry and didn't reply to her greeting. She thought they seemed worried about something and perhaps didn't even hear her."

Honey showed photos of the two runaways and Alice Nuisance, which were captioned with their names.

"It's believed that the young blonde was Susie Q. Police have tried to contact Walter Nuisance, but he's nowhere to be found. Further tests are being made to see if the ashes from the household chopperator can shed more light on what happened."

Paul interjected again.

"Another neighbour, Mrs I. M. A. Nosey-Parker, said that she often heard Alice crying. She also claimed that on a few occasions Alice had black eyes and other bruises on her face. She maintains that Walter was a sadistic bully and that Alice was a complete saint."

Honey leaned over again, and thousands of men sighed simultaneously.

"That's all we have for now folks, but we will keep you posted."

The news broadcasts were now much more user friendly. They contained light-hearted sections, good-looking and funny presenters, and the programmes were often titled in a more every day and snappy fashion than heretofore. Honey and Paul's show was called 'We Will Keep You Posted!' They always signed off with those words.

Rita was agog. (Not a gog, but agog.)

"That's thrown the cat amongst the pigeons. It's now even more important that you leave as soon as possible."

Tosser coughed, as he wanted to speak.

"I've got an old robot face that looks just like Susie Q's. As you know, she was one of a batch of prototype robots, and I half-inched this one when I left. The WRO continued to produce robots with Susie faces and Joanna Lumley voices. The face is not good enough to be used on Susie Q. Nevertheless, with a little manipulation by me somebody could wear it, and it wouldn't be easy to tell it wasn't Susie Q's face. That's always supposing that the woman wearing the face as a mask was of the same height and build.

Let's have a think about how we might confuse the police and the WRO. Rita, you're a good body double for Susie Q. Ian grew a beard during the latter part of his post-op growth programme. The news items showed him like that. I'm very hairy and could grow one quickly. What if we went to various towns, in this area, when you go to Norfolk, and made certain we were noticed? This might put the police off the scent."

Ian was worried about exposing Tosser and Rita to danger, and possible complications with the police. Rita took the bovine animal by its pointed bits and said:

"We'll do it. That's my final answer. If we do get caught, I'll pretend that I found

I'm Back!

the face and was just wearing it as a joke. We can make definite arrangements, later."

Chapter 27

Before Ian and Susie Q left Broadstairs they returned to the subject of how best to disguise themselves. Ian had grown his beard after his AR procedure, once he was old enough to do so. The recent photos which had been shown on the holovision news programmes had all shown him with that facial adornment.

The news had also mentioned 'a bearded man suspected to be Ian Tudeep.' If Tosser and Rita were going to try to lead their pursuers astray, the agreed plan was still for Tosser to grow one and for Rita to try to look like Susie Q. To make it less likely that Ian would be spotted elsewhere, he decided to shave his own beard off.

Susie Q was now back to looking like her old self, with her original face, and this worried Ian. He and Tosser had several conversations about which face she should have in the next stage of her adventures. Tosser was all for replacing her face again. He still had the Meryl Streep one up his sleeve. He said he had checked it again and again.

"It's very unlikely that the Streep face will have the same weakness as the one which was modelled to look like Michelle Keegan. It was created later than the one which had faults, and I'm convinced that it would work well. It's up to you and Susie Q, but what you could do is to take her to Happisburgh with Meryl's face.

You could still leave the old, spare face with us for Rita to wear, when she and I go out pretending to be you and Susie Q. (We can put the new Susie Q one into a special protective bag.) Rita and I will go to various places, including other towns, with Rita wearing the spare face, as we discussed. Hopefully, this would confuse the people who are looking for you. I'll slightly remodel the spare face so that wearing it for short

I'm Back!

periods of time will not be too uncomfortable."

Ian rubbed his furry chin, and he looked forward to being clean shaven again.

"Hmmm, what does everybody else think?"

Rita said she was still game for the confusion exercise.

"Tosser and I could get captured deliberately by CCTV in a few towns, over a period of a several days. I would look like Susie Q. Tosser will have a beard quickly. If we managed to get spotted in some places without being caught, the WRO and the police might also assume that Tosser is you, because he keeps being on camera with me wearing the spare Susie Q face. Ian, you'd be elsewhere with no beard. You'd also be with somebody who looks like Meryl Streep, as she was in 1981."

Alice piped up:

"If I came with you to Happisburgh, that might help. I could cut my hair short, dye it black and wear glasses. I'd look quite different. Susie Q and I could go out separately if need be, as we wouldn't look at all like either of us."

"That's settled then. Tosser, please give Susie Q that new Meryl Streep face."

Susie Q looked frightened. She had already had a bad experience with the Michelle Keegan face and didn't want a repeat episode. She stood up, brushed tears from her eyes, and smiled gamely.

"Come on Tosser. I want to get off my face!"

They all laughed at her feeble attempt at a joke. Ian had noted real tears. He wondered if the humanitis was having a more marked effect on Susie Q than the WRO realised. Susie Q and Tosser went into a bedroom. Tosser got his tool kit out again. He laid everything out neatly. He opened the pouch with Meryl Streep's face in it and looked at his expert craftsmanship. He recalled that he was the person who had part created this robot face when he was employed as a contractor, by the WRO.

'Yes,' he thought, 'this was wonderfully life-like.'

He was proud of his face making skills. (Not pulling faces, you will understand, but creating faces for robots.)He started work on removing Susie Q's face once more. After a while he put it into a preservative pouch. He spent getting on for four hours attaching Meryl Streep's face to Susie Q. He then applied elastaskin round the joins, and expertly soothed some more of the magic preparation on the face itself. He wanted to encourage the flexibility needed for basic displays of emotion, such as joy, fear, anger, pride, and sorrow.

"There you are Susie Q. It's all done, and you've now been three times a lady."

Susie Q looked in the virtual mirror and was pleased with Tosser's handiwork. She gave her face the first test by smiling, the second by kissing his cheek and the third by bursting into tears.

"There, there Susie Q, don't despair. You look different, but you're still beautiful."

"I'm not unhappy. I'm just so grateful for the help Ian and I are getting from Alice, Rita, and you. Without that we'd be caught. I'd probably be reprogrammed to forget everything which Ian and I have done. Ian would be punished for stealing me. He'd have to choose which bit of him would be chopped off. It's not many people who can abscond with £10,000,000 worth of machinery, without being heavily penalised. Let's go and see what the others think of the new me."

When they re-entered the front room, Alice put her hands over her mouth in shock. Susie Q was still delectable, even with yet another new face. Tosser and Suzie Q saw that Alice had hacked her hair short and dyed it black. Rita had helped her.

The new Alice put on some glasses and said:

"Whenever I see your smiling face, I'm jealous. Whichever one you wear you always look radiant. I could never be as pretty as you."

"Nonsense," said Susie, "You've got a natural beauty. I am a synthetic man-made creation. Worse than that, I'm a nasty murderess. I also showed a very savage side to my machine moods when I ripped Walter to pieces. I still can't believe that I did that

I'm Back!

with my bare hands, even if they're not real human ones.

I didn't know that I was that strong. I was in a terrible rage, and a kind of red mist came over me. I just wanted to protect you, but the way I acted staggered me. And I was surprised that I felt any contrition. I've started having what they call dreams. Ian told me about them before, but I'd never experienced them until a few days ago. He said the bad ones are called nightmares.

They seem so real to me, and I keep having flashes of horrid memories. The other problem I have is that the charger which we stole from the WRO seems to be a little erratic. Sometimes I charge up quite quickly, but at other times it takes longer. On some occasions, it doesn't even start to charge me up. Ian or I have to wiggle the plug about in the power socket. Tosser, I don't suppose you have any spares, do you?"

"Yes, I have. I'll also check the one you've been using, to see what's wrong with it. Before you leave for Happisburgh, I'll give you a really good servicing."

"Ooh, Tosser, what a naughty thing to say to me, a mere sexy robot. Whatever will Ian think if I say yes to your saucy proposition?"

Tosser laughed, and they all joined in. Ian gave Tosser a wink and said:

"You'd better behave Ralphy boy, or Susie Q will tear you to bits. We don't want too much monkey business!"

Susie Q burst into tears. She flounced out of the room. She thought:

'What is this that I am doing? Is my humanitis getting worse?'

She knew Ian was only joking, but his reference to her savagery had really affected her. She wasn't certain she liked the effect the human DNA was having on her temperament.

Ian knew they had to keep moving to different places, but he was worried, as he didn't know how they would pay for the aerobuses. He had an eWallet which he could use. However, it was in the name of Ian Tudeep, and if he continued to use it they could be traced easily. Susie Q, being a robot, had never needed one. Rita saved the day. When cash had stopped being used, the government had promised that real money would still be honoured and regarded as legal tender forever. Whenever it was used, it was automatically returned to the Bank of England (a subsidiary of The World Bank), to be destroyed. Rita said she still had some old and tattered notes, which she had kept in case the cashless system ever broke down.

"You're very welcome to take that money. God bless you."

I'm Back!

Chapter 28

The next day Ian and Susie Q and Alice bid their friends, Tosser and Rita, a fond farewell. They hoped that they would be safely ensconced at Eddie's place by the end of the day. They also liked to think that as a non-bearded Ian, a close cropped, black haired and bespectacled lady, and a young Meryl Streep, they would not be easily identified. They didn't want people to think that they were the first AR patient, an old girlfriend and a new one (even though she was a robot.) Despite that, they wanted to get as far away as possible from Morelli Heights, as quickly as possible, to muddy the waters. Ian couldn't understand that phrase. Why would people ever want muddy waters?

The aerobuses they used were convenient and comfortable. The walk from Waxham, where the aPad was situated, was lovely. They ambled along the beach for much of the way. The white sand, fringed on one side by the sea and on the other by dunes with marram grass growing on the top, helped to relax them. It was so peaceful. The wide-open skies of Norfolk beckoned to them, like a shining beacon. The county was admittedly busier than it had been, but the population per square mile was still less than where they had recently been in hiding. They all tried to appear confident and at ease, but they were worried about the possibility of being caught by the police. They would have preferred a nice quiet life.

Eddie welcomed them to his barn in true ebullient fashion. He was rather like a louder version of the old actor, Brian Blessed. He threw his arms around each of them and planted kisses on the cheeks of Alice and Susie Q. Ian was a bit worried that he might do the same to him. He was mightily relieved when Eddie just grabbed his hand and shook it with vim and vigour.

He thought his arm might come out of its socket when Eddie pumped it up and down for what seemed like a very long time. However, he was pleased to know that they had a strong ally. Eddie had completely accepted them all on the say so of his old friend Rita.

"Come in and take the weight of your feet. I've got a treat for you. I've been brewing my own beer for many years. I know it's strictly illegal now, but if you want a strong real ale you'll love it. It's much better than that poncy, fizzy lager which young lads used to prefer, before the wretched alcohol pills were invented. My home brew is the bee's knees. I call it Eddie's Revenge."

As he was booming out his welcome speech, he was leading the ladies down the wide hall of his converted barn, with an arm round each of their waists. They were being whisked along quickly. They were almost carried along, in his unbridled enthusiasm. His tremendous happy nature was becoming even more evident, as he steered them into a large beamed room. It had windows looking out onto an unkempt but intriguing garden. There were many old statues and several wildlife ponds. Aged brick paths zigzagged across the lawn. One of the paths led to a wrought iron gate opening out onto an open field at the foot of the garden.

"Look at that, ruddy paradise! Dontcha wish you had a garden like mine? Much better than Marbloodybella. I went there once. That was once too much. It was f...blinking awful. There were too many people and lots of very tall buildings. I understand it's now got a population of over 2,500,000. They're probably all posers, who think that the place is wonderful. Puerto Banus was even worse. I saw a sky-blue Mercedes Benz convertible being driven by a blonde woman there; she really fancied herself. She'd got a lookalike daughter, and they were both flicking their hair back incessantly. Every now and then they'd try to look at themselves in the rear-view mirror.

I'm Back!

They obviously both thought they looked terrific. What a load of cobblers!

Please take a peek at my garden. It's got more animals visiting it regularly than the whole of London. (That's another place I wouldn't give you tuppence for.) During the past twelve months I've seen bats, squirrels, owls, small deer, hedgehogs, dragonflies, ducks, birds, rabbits, mice, frogs, voles, moles, and newts in my own private wildlife park. Can you beat that?"

He bustled over to a massive, dark oak sideboard. Without further ado, he poured drinks for Ian, Alice, and himself. He guffawed uproariously and handed the beverages to his guests excluding Susie Q.

"Get that down you. That'll put hair on your chests. Oops, sorry Alice I bet you don't really want hair there! Now Susie Q, what can I get you? I find it difficult to believe you're a robot. You look like a real cracker to me."

He lifted her hand to his lips and kissed her in a fake, courtly manner. Ian was surprised to note that Susie Q coloured, and she looked at Eddie through her fringe. She was acting in the way that a love-stricken schoolgirl might gaze at her first boyfriend. Ian wondered again if her emotional issues were becoming more apparent, now that Susie Q was mixing with so many friendly humans.

Susie Q curtsied elegantly to Eddie and said:

"Thanks, Eddie. I need no sustenance. I've been checked and serviced by our friend Tosser before we all left Broadstairs, so I need nothing except to be charged up each night."

Eddie roared with laughter, gave them the widest smile in the world, slapped his thighs, and he said:

"Charging up, is that what they call the old nooky nowadays, I heard that you were extremely friendly with Ian. My goodness, he's a f… sorry, very lucky boy."

He slapped Ian on the back, in a friendly gorilla kind of way. Ian spilt most of his Eddie's Revenge ale on the floor, whilst trying to continue standing upright. He thought that Susie Q might be offended by Eddie's coarseness. He was taken aback when she said:

"I think you must be confused, because being charged up and nooky are two very different things aren't they Ian?"

Ian nodded. Susie Q continued:

"I must say that on the hole I prefer nooky. Get it?"

Ian explained to Susie Q that this kind of joke didn't work when it was spoken. Susie Q looked puzzled.

"I'm perfect for Ian, Eddie. I've got a special receptacle for him. He seems to like it. There are not many robots who have that facility. "

The others all laughed at her. She was still bemused, as she was only trying to explain matters to Eddie. He asked them what they thought of his home brew. They said they approved of it, each in their own way. They had all been surprised by how potent it was. He said it was the nectar of the gods. It tasted delicious, and they all gave Eddie their empty glasses for refills. They drank far too much that afternoon. They felt so relaxed, and it was a pleasure to wind down.

"Would you like me to tell you a little bit about the area? I understand that Rita's already told you about the sad death of the lighthouse. I've been living here for over fifteen years. I'm thirty-eight. I know I look a lot older, but I spend most of my time outdoors. I love to be in fields and woods and to walk along beaches. Even when I'm here, I'm outdoors a lot of the time in my shaggy garden. Susie Q, that's not a reference to a bit of how's your father, but mind you there have been a few times…"

His sentence stopped in mid-air.

"It's great here. Mind you, Cromer and Sheringham are both far too big for my liking, and in fact they're now more or less one ginormous town. They used to be OK, but they're much too busy now. I'm pleased to say that there are still lots of small villages not far away. I like Overstrand, Mundesley and Eccles. The people who live near here are decent folk. I often walk from Overstrand to Cromer along the beach. It's quite safe if the tide times are right.

You can walk back along the cliff path. The cliffs have eroded badly, but it's still a lovely walk. I go out in all weathers. Even when there's a howling gale, I love it. That's why my skin is so lovely."

He gave a booming and loud laugh. As he was doing so he made a show of stroking his cheeks (or rather what you could see of them, as the top of his long beard extended almost to the bottom of his eyes.)

"Eddie, is Howling Gail a female singer?" asked Susie Q.

Eddie started to answer, but just in time he realised that she was making fun of him.

"Susie Q, I could see that you were a robot and a half the minute you graced my poor tiny hovel, but I really didn't know that robots could make jokes!"

Susie Q did the old looking through the fringe thing again and said:

"You live and learn, my good fellow!"

Eddie gave Susie Q a playful dig in ribs, and Ian felt a pang of remorse. He was regretting allowing Eddie to flirt with Susie Q. He felt ashamed immediately. He realised that their new friend was just being sociable in his own boisterous way. He also wondered what morse was when compared to remorse. It would have been interesting to know if remorse was having morse again. Eddie continued his paean about Norfolk in general, and he evangelised about the area near Happisburgh, in particular.

"We've got oodles of titchy country lanes near here. We locals call them lokes. You can get out walking or pootle along on an old bike. You can go for miles and see hardly anybody. There are old train tracks too. The lines were closed by that daft Beeching fellow in the 1960s. Some of them have been converted into footpaths. There's a tiny forest track off one of the footpaths, which goes to a disused lock on a canal. Otters are in the lock quite often. Stay away from Cromer and Sheringham (or whatever they should have called the new combined town.) Maybe that should be known as Cromham or Sheringmer?

Not far from here, at Horsey, seals still get up on the beach in late October or mid-November. It's a joy to see the great big, lumbering mothers with their tiny pups. The mums are very protective, and woe betide anybody who gets too close to a Mumma seal and her babies.

Foolish young teenagers still get too near them, and even one of the wardens was attacked a couple of years ago by Mrs. Seal. He got too close to junior. The warden was quite badly hurt. Those big brutes can't half shift themselves when they need to. The warden recovered well, but they now use robots to look after the seals. It's a lot safer. Amazingly enough, they don't seem to find the robots threatening at all."

"Do I look threatening?" asked Susie Q, as she pulled what was supposed to be a frightening face.

Eddie didn't look scared at all. In fact, he laughed and pulled Susie Q's cheeks out and let then go of them suddenly. They made a soft plopping noise, but luckily they didn't tear. Ian decided to try to control his unwonted attack of the old green-eyed monster. By now all of them (except for Susie Q), felt sleepy. Eddie's Revenge ale had taken its toll. Eddie showed Ian and Susie Q into one bedroom which also looked out over the garden, and he led Alice to another room facing a track, which ran along the side of the house.

Eddie took himself off to the master bedroom, which looked out onto the road. It was one of those tiny Norfolk lokes he had mentioned. To be honest it wasn't even worthy of the name road. He lay down on the bed, which groaned under the weight of this colossal but loveable man. He was soon snoring like a particularly loud circular saw.

Elsewhere, Alice tossed and turned. Although she was worn out, she just couldn't get to sleep. She too was jealous. She hated that feeling and knew that it was a destructive emotion, but she couldn't help herself. She could see that Ian loved his sexy robot, and that Susie Q had unusual feelings (for a machine), for Ian. Alice would never do anything to cause either of them distress. She just wasn't made that way. However, she knew that she still loved Ian, and she was sad that they could never be together as husband and wife.

Ian and Susie Q were cuddling quietly in their room. Susie Q knew that she should plug herself in to get recharged. However, she wanted some Susie Q time with her beloved before she did so. She was feeling drained, and after a while she stopped thinking. Ian was fast asleep by then. The quiet surroundings helped him, and he had a dreamless sleep.

In the morning, far too early for normal people to stir, Eddie was fixing a huge breakfast.

'None of those pretend food and drink pills,' he thought.

He fried eggs, bacon, sausages, field mushrooms, black pudding, and his own recipe Norfolk Rostis. They consisted of potatoes, onions, shallots, and butter. He mixed these ingredients together with lots of black pepper. When the meal was ready, he slammed open each of the bedroom doors leading to his newfound friends' resting places, and he yelled:

"Rise and shine. Brekko is on the table in the kitchen. It's getting cold already."

Alice was the first to appear, in her old but still serviceable dressing gown. She sat down and started eating. Ian ran into the room, shouting and panicking.

"I can't wake Susie Q up. Normally she plugs herself in, and she's recharged overnight. I have to say to her 'Wake up, Little Susie, Wake up,' and then she's immediately revitalised. She must've let her charge run down too much. She was probably unable to plug herself in last night, or maybe she wasn't plugged in properly. What should we do?"

Eddie took hold of Ian's shoulders, looked him in the face and said:

"Calm down, old boy. Let's talk to Rita's fiancé Tosser. He'll know what to do.

She says he knows everything there is to know about robots. You stay here, and I'll electrajot him right now."

Ian did as he was told. Alice put her arms around him, and she spoke to him in soothing tones.

"Leave it to Eddie and Tosser. I'm sure it'll be alright."

Eddie was soon talking to Tosser.

"Do you know it's only just after six a.m. Eddie, have a heart!"

"This is ruddy urgent. Susie Q didn't charge herself up last night and Ian can't wake her up."

"When did she charge herself up last?"

"I think that would have been overnight on the day before yesterday. Ian would've woken her up with her normal wake words yesterday morning."

"Hmmm, if she was fully charged the night before last, she should've had enough juice in reserve to be OK. Can you switch your electrajot to the camera mode and point it at Susie Q, so I can see her? I'll tell you how you can give her a sort of emergency wake-up call."

Eddie did as he was told, and he put Tosser on the speaker phone, so that he could converse with him. He was relieved that Tosser would instruct him, whilst he was doing whatever was needed to get Susie Q going again.

"Press the button under her skin at the side of the neck and her blouse will automatically unfasten."

Ian had arrived in the room, and he nodded to Eddie to do as he was told. He knew that if he tried to reactivate Susie Q, he would be so nervous he might do things incorrectly. The blouse was quickly unbuttoned, and Eddie was totally amazed by how realistic Susie Q's magnificent breasts were. He shook his head to clear his brain of distracting thoughts, and asked Tosser what to do next.

"There's a sliding panel just under her breasts, which contains various buttons.

I'm Back!

Be careful to only press the one marked 'reset.' I'm trying to get her back to the factory defaults. It may result in some temporary loss of memory. I can fix that, once she's awake. The reset button will use a small amount of residual stored charge to get her going. This is the only way. Can you see the button with the word reset written on it?"

"Yes. Shall I press it?"

"Press and hold it for two seconds, and then you can release it. She'll wake up in less than ten seconds, but don't be tempted to press the reset button again."

"I'm now holding the reset button down. One elephant, two elephants, and I've released it."

Ian and Tosser started to count seconds again together,

"One elephant, two elephants…," and you get the drift.

At eight elephants, Susie Q opened those gorgeous eyes and looked at Ian.

"What happened, and why are you looking so worried? And who are you?"

She heard a man explaining what had happened, on the speaker phone:

"You didn't charge yourself up last night. I think you may have been only partially charged the night before. I can sort your memory out, so don't worry about that. I had to get you going. I did do that, didn't I?"

"Yeah, you really got me going!"

Chapter 29

They were all relieved that Tosser had successfully reset Susie Q's operating system. He had also told Eddie what to do to clear her memory fog, and that had been done successfully. Tosser said that she would need to be manually plugged back in, for a full charging session. As she was being entering her charging session, Ian had said to her:

"Sleep tight, and may God bless you."

She had responded simply:

"I go to sleep."

Tosser had suggested that it would be best if they left her on charge until early the next day. He had arranged to contact them at six a.m. the next morning. His plan was that he would take them through all the steps needed to reinstall various updates, rather than them relying on them to remember his guidance overnight. The missing updates had been rolled back during the emergency fix. Tosser had deliberately reset her system to the factory defaults specified by the WRO. He had smiled to himself when he remembered that it was he who had completed the original system installation for Susie Q. He was a contractor for the WRO at that time.

Ian, Eddie, and Alice were up bright and early the following morning. Eddie suggested that they should steam ahead with Susie Q's updates as soon as they had Tosser on the electrajot. Ian woke up Susie Q (with the customary wake words), with no problems. They then waited anxiously for Tosser to ring them. He did so at six on the dot.

I'm Back!

"Morning all. I can see that you have enabled the virtual 'being there' mode. It's as if I'm with you. If this place is as remote as Rita says it is, you must be stuck in the middle of nowhere."

"Cheeky blighter," grinned Eddie.

Ian took over.

"I want to do this for Susie Q. Then I can say that what I did, I did for Susie Q."

"Very well, Ian. Unfasten Susie Q's buttons, as Eddie did yesterday."

Tosser continued (and they followed his instructions step by step.)

"Yes, undo those buttons, just like Eddie. Press the neck button to undo the blouse buttons. Next, find the button under her breasts which opens the inspection plate. Now look for another button next to the 'reset' one, which you used yesterday. The right button has an icon on it shaped like an electrajot. Press that, and a small virtual screen will give you the option to 'select updates,' or to 'update all'. Choose select updates. Select them all except the one that was done to desensitise her by the WRO. It'll be the last update, before I rolled her back by resetting. If this works correctly, Susie Q will be as right as rain in about twenty minutes."

After a little bit of fumbling, Ian said he had done all that Tosser required. Susie Q had gone into a relaxed state and seemed to be rather vacant. Ian asked her if she felt OK.

"Yes, I'm fine. I'm comfortably numb."

As she said this her head slumped to one side. Ian was alarmed but Tosser told him that this was to be expected.

"Just go about your business for twenty minutes. Only then should you inspect Susie Q. At that stage she should be bright, alert, and attentive. You'll know at once that she's back in this world. That's how I first experienced this update procedure. Just one look, that's all it took."

Ian thanked Tosser, who ended his electrajot session. They all had real coffee, made in true Eddie style. Much too strong, much too sweet, and much too hot.

'Rather like my dear little Susie Q,' Ian thought.

Breakfast was cooking, and the delicious smells wafting their way were occasionally interspersed by impressive and very loud, windy noises from the master of the house. These were invariably followed by foul smelling vapours.

Alice giggled:

"Doesn't he know we can hear him? Worse still, we can smell him doing that."

"I can hear what you're saying," bellowed Eddie. "They're much better out than in."

"Not for us they're not," Ian complained.

After a little more back chat and repeat performances of Eddie's wind concerto, it was nearly time to look at Susie Q. They all gathered round her. For a few minutes more she stayed in her dreamlike stupor. As they were beginning to worry, she opened and closed her eyelids a few times and yawned lazily, like a stirring lioness. She looked at Ian and said:

"Bonjour Ian. Je suis ravie de te voir. Je t'aime passionément, chérie."

Ian got the gist of this. It was lovely to learn that Susie Q remembered him and for her to say that she loved him. He wondered why she was speaking in French. She continued to speak in French. Ian was pleased to see that she also recognised Alice and Eddie. Nonetheless, Ian knew that they had to get hold of Tosser again, so he could sort out this language problem.

Tosser was back in the 'being there' mode before too long.

"I think I know what's happened. There's an automatic translation facility in her system. It must've been triggered accidentally. If I just get you to disable that we should be hunky dory. Go back to the inspection panel opening ceremony."

This was achieved in a trice, or maybe even in half a trice. By now they knew how to do this. They were almost experts. (Ian thought that if they used to be perts, but

I'm Back!

were not any longer, they must be ex perts. He wondered, idly, what a pert was. He remembered how Beryl used to hate his jokes. Sod her, he though, I've got my Susie Q, maintenant.) Tosser explained what they had to do. They followed his instructions to the letter. King Pedant (AKA Ian), wondered what outstructions were!

"Hallo," said Susie Q "what did you do just now. I think I may have been saying something strange."

Ian explained that she had been speaking in a French.

"Oh dear, I'm sorry I used bad language."

Eddie thought this was hilarious.

"You can use all the bad language that you want to, Susie Q. We're just glad that you're back to normal."

Susie Q burst into happy tears. Tosser was still virtually with them. He was worried about how the humanitis symptoms were being displayed even more frequently. He kept his tinder dry. He knew that this could cause serious problems for Susie Q, but he didn't want to alarm his friends unduly.

He bade them farewell. They all ate a hearty meal, cooked for them by Eddie. His heart was as large as his huge body. He had served their breakfast in his kitchen again, and he wanted to tell them more about their surroundings and the good-natured people from Norfolk.

"They all love dogs here. Not horrible dogbots (sorry Susie Q), but real honest to goodness, smelly, hairy, and loveable dogs. They are loyal, gentle, and faithful companions, and they're welcomed everywhere in Norfolk. My dogs are being looked after by a wonderful lady friend of mine at present. I didn't want you to be frightened of them. They are a little on the large size."

Alice said that she adored dogs.

"Shall I ask my friend Sally to bring them back? They are four Irish Wolf Hounds and I call them Eeeny, Meeny, Miny and Moe. They could be here in five minutes if you want to see them."

Ian told him that they would be pleased to see his best pals. They wondered if Sally was just a friend. Rita hoped Eddie had a new love. In the dim and distant past, she and Eddie did have a romantic entanglement. That was all over and done with quite a few years ago. There was no animosity when they split up, and Rita had kept a sisterly eye on Eddie thereafter. Although he was a very capable man in many ways, when it came to choosing female partners he had made some bad choices.

Rita (and hopefully Sally), were better than his usual selections. He was a fantastic craftsman. Show him a piece of wood and a few basic tools, and he would make shelves, furniture and, rather surprisingly, small, delicate dolls. He was able to turn long untended and arid gardens into lush, green areas. Also, as we already know, he was a terrific, if rather basic, cook. When you had one of Eddie's meals, you certainly stayed fed! His major downfall was that once he was near any fanciable woman, he was lost. He fell in love more quickly than any other man in Norfolk.

That sudden falling in love, infatuation, or obsession (call it what you will), had beset him many a time. Eddie was tough when it came to manual labour, and he could handle his four huge dogs with ease. His one weakness was that he fell in love much more quickly than you could say Jack Robinson. Each time a romance broke down he was disconsolate for weeks.

Rita had first met him just after she had split up from a long-term boyfriend. Eddie had recently broken off a romance with a tiny, fragile lady, who looked sweet and kind. Eddie had soon found out that she was viperous. Rita and Eddie had an 'on the rebound' kind of love for a short while, but it was anything but groovy. They decided that they could be good friends but couldn't continue living together.

For some time after this peaceful break-up, Rita had periodical calls from Eddie using his electrajot. They would always start:

"It's happened again Rita. Can you come and pick up the pieces?"

I'm Back!

They usually spent several weeks together. Rita always managed to convince Eddie that breaking up isn't hard to do. Once Eddie was his usual ebullient self, Rita usually went back to Broadstairs until the next distress flare was launched:

"It's happened again Rita…"

Rita asked Eddie to tell her every time he started a new relationship with a woman. She said she would thus be prepared for the next cry for help. As requested by Rita, he had taken to calling her at the start of any new amorous adventure. He used to say:

"Falling in love again!"

Rather mysteriously, Eddie had kept his burgeoning relationship with Sally a secret. Rita hoped that she was the one!

Chapter 30

Mike Anick extended his stay in Southend for a few days as he was enjoying Emma's company so much. They spent the daytime walking on the beach and the nights canoodling and more. After several truly scrumptious dinners at The Olde Southendian (and those passionate interludes with Emma), Mike told her that he was going to Broadstairs to talk to Rita Loza. Emma asked to him to liaise with the police in Kent, and she gave him the contact details of a Chief Superintendent called Patrick O'Callaghan.

"Is he Oirish?"

"Yes. He comes from Dublin, but he's been living in England for many years. He still has a broad Irish accent, and he plays in a diddley diddley band. They all use antique instruments to get an authentic sound."

Mike liked that kind of music for about ten minutes. Any more was too much. He hoped Patrick wouldn't ask him to go to one of his gigs. He had spent a week on holiday in Dingle a few years back, and during that seven days he had heard enough of Irish traditional music to last a lifetime. Whilst he was there, he had been told about the friendly dolphin, Fungie, who used to swim round the bay. Apparently, the dolphin had played with people in boats. Mike suspected that the dolphin was not just one mammal. It was possible that new Fungies were placed in the bay each time the old one died or simply swam away.

Mike packed his case, and he went down to reception to check out. He came back to say goodbye to Emma. That goodbye developed into something much more satisfying, but he had to leave by eleven. They would otherwise be charged for another day by the hotel. Before they left the room, he popped into the en suite bathroom to water the flowers. As he came out, he saw Emma holding his case by the handle.

She said:

"Here's your bag. I moved it out of the way, as I was trying to catch a spider."

"Did you rescue him?"

"No, he ran away. Even if I'd managed to get hold of him, I'm not certain what I would have done with him."

"Not to worry, he probably lives in this room all the time."

Emma and Mike parted company just outside the hotel, after he had taken the room key to the receptionist. Mike gave Emma a cuddle, kissed her ardently and reluctantly extricated himself from their embrace before saying:

"Emma, you haven't seen the last of me. I'll be back. I think I'm falling in love with you. Is that OK?"

"Oh, I suppose that might just about be encouraged. Yes, love me do!"

Chapter 31

Back in Broadstairs, Rita and Tosser went out many times as arranged, pretending to be Susie Q and Ian. On the way to their target areas, they wore hats and dark glasses and covered the bottom halves of their faces with scarves. They also turned up their collars. Just before they got to the places which they knew were rife with CCTV cameras, they packed their hats and scarves in a rucksack that Tosser was wearing. They also discarded their shades and popped them in their pockets. When their faces were revealed they made certain that they looked directly at as many cameras as they could, in the short space of time that they could safely spend, in the streets furnished with CCTV cameras.

They also went to other towns, and in Dover they nearly had a problem. Tosser saw an old friend of his, walking towards them. He was only a few yards away from them, but they managed to cross over the road before they were spotted. Tosser didn't want any unnecessary complications to upset their false trail laying. They still hoped that it would throw the police (and the WRO), off the scent. They also went to Folkestone and Dymchurch, as well as quite a few other places, always sowing the seeds of confusion.

One night, they were watching Honey and Paul on their popular programme, and there was another News Flash. The heading was 'WRO runaways at large in Kent.' Honey Blonde leaned towards the camera, keeping abreast of things nicely, and she nearly gave the viewers a different kind of flash. Paul Somebody smiled, and his dazzling white teeth were almost as distracting as Honey's ample bosoms. These two outstanding

I'm Back!

features of hers were a well-liked part of the programme for men all over the UK.

"There have been definite sightings of Ian Tudeep and Susie Q,"

Honey sighed prettily, and she was in imminent danger of revealing her mammaria.

"I wondered if their fairy tale romance might be continued. If they're captured, do you think the WRO might melt Susie Q down, Paul?"

"Not likely Honey dear, she's far too valuable. And anyway, the police will want to talk to them both about the mysterious disappearance of Walter Nuisance. The neighbours say that he used to ill-treat his wife, Alice. It's a bit of a rum do that he disappeared just before his DNA was found in blood, and scrapings of flesh, at their house."

Honey giggled, very inappropriately.

"Honey don't. This is a serious matter!"

Matching his attitude to his words, Paul put on his austere face. (That's the one with no white teeth visible.) Honey wore her demure look. She sat up straight and thereby removed her most attractive parts from the gaze of her adoring male fans. Paul looked at the camera, exuding fake solemnity.

He frowned and said:

"The East Anglian police force has issued a warrant for their arrest. The WRO are also cooperating with the police. We go now to a press briefing, where we will hear from Inspector Emma Bobby. She'll tell us more."

The scene changed to one outside the force's regional police headquarters in Witham. Viewers saw a podium, with a lectern standing on top of a low platform. There were dozens of microphones draped over the top of the lectern. Emma Bobby was on the platform, and she was accompanied by a stocky copper, who was not named at all during the press briefing. Emma cleared her throat.

"First, let me apologise for allowing Paul Somebody to use my official rank. I know that this might make some people uncomfortable. However, we wanted to be as transparent as possible in all our dealings with the press and the public. We have reason to believe that Walter Nuisance may have been murdered. It is not clear at this stage who committed this foul deed. It could possibly have been his wife Alice. We are keeping an open mind, as it may have been Ian Tudeep and/or Susie Q who killed Mr. Nuisance.

Susie Q is the expensive robot stolen from the WRO by Mr. Tudeep. Indeed, they may have colluded together, but more will be known when they have been taken into custody. Mike Anick, from the WRO, is being very helpful, and we hope to bring this matter to a satisfactory conclusion in the coming weeks and days."

She finished by displaying a photo of Mike bearing his name.

They were all concerned at the news revealed by Honey and Paul. However, it was good to know that that the false trail set by Rita and Tosser had worked. There was nothing else that they could do. They felt powerless and everybody had a sleepless night, except for Eddie who could snore for England.

I'm Back!

Chapter 32

Mike travelled to Broadstairs, after leaving Emma in Southend. He had booked a direct aerobus connection, on a private basis. The aerobus was hired just for him. It was expensive, but he wasn't concerned about the cost. He knew that WRO were paying all his expenses. He slept all the way to the coastal town in Kent, and he was woken up by the pilot once they arrived at his destination.

The aerobus had landed on a cliff near the short pier on the left side of the bay. The pier seemed to have weathered rather better than the ones in Southwold and Southend. He thought it might be because it was only a small pier, which existed almost as an extension of the harbour wall. Mike remembered Emma's suggestion that he should contact Chief Superintendent Patrick O'Callaghan. He decided to ignore her advice. Things were complicated enough without having him involved as well. There was also the off chance of being subjected to traditional Irish music. The last time that had happened the man in charge of the music had made a safety announcement.

He stood up and looked serious. He said with a straight face:

"This is an important announcement. In the event of a fire, would you all please panic!"

There was a muffled titter in the audience. They then realised that it was supposed to be a joke, and they made a better job of laughing. Mike thought it was the best part of the evening.

Mike had been to Broadstairs a few times previously, but he hadn't noticed Morelli Heights. He studied the map on his electrajot after walking down the cliff path.

He also used an app called World View to look at the buildings on the prom. Using World View it was easy to see where the building was. He ambled along the pleasant street at the top of the cliff overlooking Viking Bay, and he spotted Morelli Heights easily.

As he entered the building, he saw some old photos of the Art Deco ice cream parlour which used to be located on the same spot. There was one picture of a lady called Mary Berry, actually in Morelli's. He had never heard of her, but the caption said she was a well-known cookery expert, who had been popular many years ago. (He decided to look her up on the Solar System Web when he had a free moment.) He looked at the inserts in the intercom board, saw one for R. Loza, and he pushed the relevant button. An attractive lady with auburn hair was soon displayed on the screen above the intercom buttons.

"Hallo, how can I help you?"

"Good afternoon. My name's Mike Anick. I work for the WRO, and I'm looking for Ian Tudeep, a robot called Susie Q and their friend Alice Nuisance. I wonder if I might be allowed to ask you a few questions. I understand that you're an old school chum of Alice's?"

"I am indeed. Please enter when I will buzz you in."

She gave him her condenselow and floor numbers.

"Many thanks!"

The door clicked open, and Mike went in. He hurried up the stairs two at a time. When he got to Rita's front door, he saw that it was already open. She was waiting for him with a smile on her face. Despite her convincing calm façade, she was unsettled and nervous. She hoped that she would not say anything that might lead Mike to where her friends were now staying.

Rita took him down a short hallway, into a room where a ginger, bearded man was speaking into an electrajot. (If Ian had written this sentence, he would no doubt have made a feeble joke about ginger beer, but the writer will abstain.) The man closed the device quickly. Having done so he turned round, and he too welcomed Mike.

"I recognise you Mr. Anick. I saw you on Paul and Honey's programme. It's a pleasure to meet you."

"Oh, do please call me Mike, everybody always does. I say that so often, they've nicknamed me Open Mike."

He smiled from ear to ear and sat in a chair as motioned to him by Rita. He set his case down to the side of him.

"As you watch 'We Will Keep You Posted,' you must know that I'm in the UK on urgent business. What I have to say to you now is in strict confidence. You'll have heard that Ian Tudeep has stolen a valuable robot. He was the first Artificial Reincarnation patient. His AR (as we call it), was not without problems. The body which had been carefully selected to be the new housing for his spirit and his memories would not accept them.

The only freshly thawed body which the WRO had available was of a toddler. Sadly, the poor little chap had died at the age of eighteen months. His body had been retrieved from the WRO's cryogenic, warehousing facility for another experiment. Luckily, it was in the very next room. The consultant took a brave decision, and he switched the toddler's body with the one which had failed. The AR was completed using the toddler's small body.

When they told Mr. Tudeep what had happened, he was devastated. They decided to put him onto a special regime. This included injections, special pills, and electronic stimulation for a period of six months. They hoped that after his treatment he'd be like a twenty-five-year-old. The plan was to enable him to live another twenty-five years, before the NDF would be called to have him deselected. The only alternative at that stage would be to go for AR again.

They needed to keep him under constant supervision for the entire period of his growth and development. The WRO decided to use a special robot, called Susie Q. She was to be his mentor and one to one companion. She did her job very well. Unfortunately, Ian and Susie Q become much too fond of each other. They think that they love each other, but a human relationship with a robot is ill-starred. It's not usually possible for robots to experience real emotions.

The WRO had been doing experiments with human DNA, and one of their boffins believed he had found the genome which enabled humans to feel love, hate, jealousy, and various other emotions. Susie Q's brain was injected with human DNA, which had been genetically modified. Since I have been back in the UK, I have been given more information about the DNA experiments. The team which performed the op was working under Bob Zyaruncle, the Polish expert who discovered the emotion genome.

Most of the time Susie Q is a happy go lucky robot. She's friendly, loving, and affectionate. However, sometimes she becomes distressed. She's even been known to have cried, which is a thing that robots do not normally do. Mr. Zyaruncle suspects that the emotion genome has caused Susie Q to malfunction. She may be suffering from what they call humanitis.

The problem is that this could cause her to become vicious and violent. Because she's just a machine, she might not realise the potential outcome of experiencing the darker human emotions. Underneath the humanitis she has no feelings at all, and it's possible that she may veer between that unfortunate state and the more loving mode, without any real control. At other times, the worst emotions experienced by humans may run amok in Susie Q.

I need to find Ian and Susie Q very urgently, before any more serious damage is done. Already, one man may have been murdered. It could be that Ian Tudeep committed this crime, but to be frank, I fear that Susie Q may be the culprit. I believe that you were at school with Ian Tudeep and Alice Nuisance (Alice Springs as she was

I'm Back!

then.) Alice is the widow of the man who was murdered in Southwold. I was hoping that you might know where they have gone to ground."

Tosser could feel his blood running cold. As an experienced robotics expert, he could honestly relate to the unwanted consequences of manipulated human DNA being injected into a robot. Rita didn't know what to think, but she could see how worried Tosser looked.

"There's a £1,000,000 reward on offer to the person, or persons who can give information which would lead to the arrest of Ian Tudeep, and the return of Susie Q to the WRO. Rita, I understand that you're still friendly with Alice. The police think she's almost certainly in the company of Ian and Susie Q.

"Yes, I do know Alice, and Ian. It would be impossible to meet a nicer lady. Ian's a good person too."

Tosser said:

"I don't think we can help you. Do you have any idea where they might have taken this robot, Rita?"

"I'm afraid not. It seems that you've had a wasted journey. But before you go would you like some afternoon tea pills? We've got scone, clotted cream, and raspberry jam flavoured pills, and to follow we could have orange pekoe tea pills. What do you say to that?"

"That'd be lovely."

Rita went to get the pills. They swallowed them, and twenty minutes or so later Mike took his leave of them. He walked out of the living room saying:

"Many thanks. That was most enjoyable. Don't bother to see me out, I can see that you're tired. You look comfortable right where you are."

Tosser and Rita mumbled a friendly goodbye and stayed half-slumped on the settee which they were jointly occupying. They were pleased that Mr. Anick had not tried to press them for more information.

Mike stood in the open condenselow doorway, thinking about his next move. He heard Tosser talking to somebody, and he realised Tosser was using his electrajot. He seemed to be using the speaker phone mode. (He had engaged that by accident.)

Mike heard him say:

"Listen Eddie, Mike Anick's just been to see us. He knew all about the problems Susie Q has been experiencing. He warned us that she could be dangerous. May I speak to Ian?"

Eddie answered in his customary, very loud voice.

"He's in the garden with Alice and Susie Q. I'll go and get him."

Ian was the next person on the electrajot session.

"Hi Tosser, Eddie says you've had a visit from Mike Anick. I hope you've managed to throw him off the scent. What's up? Eddie said you would explain what Anick said to you. By the way since you worked on Susie Q, she's been fine."

Mike Anick walked back into the room. He pointed to his case, which was still on the floor next to the seat in which he had been sitting. He sat down, smiled, and said.

"I thought you both told me that you didn't know where Ian and Alice were?"

"Sorry Ian. Something's some up. I'll electrajot you in a minute."

"OK. Bye!"

Chapter 33

Rita and Tosser had the good grace to look a little shame faced. Tosser tried to explain.

"We're sorry we misled you, but it's just because we were protecting our friends. The WRO have been up to no good, and we feel particularly sorry for Ian's new girlfriend. Now be honest, what would you do, if they were your pals?"

"It does you credit that you wanted to look after them, but they'll be caught in the end. Also, Susie Q may need urgent maintenance. You must already know that Tosser. I understand that you used to work for the WRO."

Rita interjected:

"Mike, why don't you go away and forget that you ever met us?"

"It's not as easy as that. There's a huge reward, and I aim to be the one to claim it. I could share some of that money with you if that'd make you change your minds?"

Tosser looked angry.

"What do you take us for?"

Mike asked what had happened to Susie Q. Tosser decided to tell him exactly why she had needed attention. He also told Mike what he did to fix her. Despite their differences, they were both knowledgeable and well-versed robotics technicians with a shared interest. Rita was soon out of her depth. Tosser and Mike seemed to be getting on reasonably well. She was surprised, and she hoped that they might yet be able to persuade Mike to help them. He appeared to be a decent sort of man. She thought they might be able to make him examine his conscience. If he did that, perhaps he would have a change of heart.

Mike and Tosser talked about Susie Q's humanitis, and they agreed that the worsening of the effect it was having on Susie Q was very worrying. After considering what had happened in Southend, Mike was more or less certain that Susie Q had been the guilty party who had killed and dismembered Walter Nuisance.

"Be honest Mr. Pancake, do you also think that the robot might have murdered Walter and then ripped him apart? I can't see Ian or Alice doing that."

Tosser had to agree. Mike reminded them again that the reward was substantial. Rita was furious.

"Get out, you money grabbing animal! I don't want you in my home."

"Wait! What if I can think of a way to help them but still managed to get the cash? Maybe we could share the money, and we may even be able to get more. I have a plan which I think you should consider."

Tosser indicated that Mike should sit down. Mike talked to Rita and Ralph about a potential plot. He thought that it might result in the WRO being forced to drop proceedings against Ian. Mike explained that he hoped that it also would stop them searching for Susie Q. It was convoluted, but they all agreed that it might just work.

Mike's idea was to try to convince the WRO that Ian and Susie Q would play the blame game in a big way, if they didn't drop their pursuit of the runaways.

"We could pepper social media with unfavourable information about the dodgy experiment which resulted in genetically modified DNA being injected into Susie Q's brain. Or maybe a better, or additional, ploy might be to contact the vulture press. They enjoy praising people on the way up, but they switch sides when they want to. They take great delight in criticising the companies or people they previously lauded, and they often decide to deliberately bring them down in people's estimation."

Mike told Tosser that he wondered if the WRO had received formal permission from the powers that be, to perform such a dangerous experiment. He said he hated

I'm Back!

to have to prove his point. He said that the more he thought about it, the more he was convinced that Susie Q had been the guilty party in Southend. He alluded again the killing of Walter Nuisance.

He continued:

"I've got good contacts within the police force."

He was referring obliquely to Emma Bobby, who owed him a favour or two after planting a tracing bug in his suitcase. He had found this device easily, when he had opened the case to check that he had packed his sponge bag. He thought she must have slipped it into his luggage in a hurry, without finding a good hiding place.

He didn't mention his other key contact, as it was his brother. Tom Anick was a senior government minister in the UK. Mike hoped he would be able to make discreet enquiries. Perhaps he might even be able to prove that the Prime Minister of the UK was personally involved in funding and approving the WRO's experiment which used human DNA. It would be excellent if Tom's investigations revealed that the WRO had gone ahead recklessly, with an exercise which was patently unsound.

Mike told them that Ian and Susie Q would need to know what they had in mind. He maintained that if they did not agree, the plan would not work. After much soul-searching, Rita and Tosser finally agreed to discuss the plan with Ian and Susie Q. They arranged that the next morning they should go to Happisburgh with Mike, to talk about the plan in much greater detail with all parties present. They agreed that Mike could stay at Rita's that night.

Chapter 34

The next day Mike, Tosser and Rita travelled to Happisburgh. Eddie was surprised to see Mike with Tosser and Rita when he responded to a loud knocking on his heavy oak door. (Tosser had banged the heavy door knocker up and down with great force.) Eddie had seen pictures of Mike in various news items, and he knew that he was the WRO's main man in the hunt for Ian and Susie Q.

When Eddie opened his front door, they could see that he was accompanied by four massive dogs. Mike recognised them as being Irish Wolfhounds. He knelt in the hallway in front of the shaggy beasts and rubbed the ears of each dog in turn. They licked his face.

"Steady on Tosser old boy! You might've damaged my lovely home with all that banging and thumping. My house is much stronger than the one that was built by the three little pigs, but there's still no need to make that racket!"

Rita had to laugh.

"Come on Eddie, that's rich coming from the loudest man in the world!"

Eddie escorted them into his living room, with forty or so stones of dog flesh rubbing up against him, as each dog vied for pride of place. Mike thought that these canines were just the right size for Eddie. Ian, Susie Q and Alice were astounded to see who it was that had been making such a din at the door. They had also seen Mike on the Solar System Web and the holovision.

They were pleased to see Tosser and Rita, but they wondered what on earth Anick was doing with them. Susie Q had gone very red in the face and was positively

I'm Back!

blazing with fury. She tried to grab Mike round the throat, and it took the combined efforts of Eddie and Tosser to restrain her. She was breathing very heavily, and her eyes were rolling wildly. She was spitting at Mike, and she was shouting at the top of her voice.

"How dare you come here, after being all over the news regarding your venture to detain us. It was made public that you'd help the police in any way you could. If I could get to you now you'd be sorry, but not for long. I'm immensely powerful, and I could split you right down the middle like a chicken's wishbone."

They were all horrified by Susie Q's vile temper. Ian finally managed to placate her, but he wondered what would happen if she was ever that angry with him. Mike explained his presence, after Tosser asked the others to hear him out.

"Look, I could've just shopped you to the authorities, after I overheard Tosser talking on his electrajot to Eddie and Ian. That would've meant that I could've collected a huge bonus and doubled my salary. I would probably have been given the reward money too. Instead, I wanted to give you the chance to speak with me about your situation. I think I may have a way out for you.

I've already talked to Tosser and Rita about my little scheme, and they thought it would be a good idea. It would stop the WRO and the police from chasing you. It would also enable Ian and Susie Q to stay together. But aren't you scared of Susie Q's temper tantrums and her violence?"

Susie Q glowered at Mike.

"I'm still here you know. You'd better watch your step."

Ian shrugged as he didn't know what to say. Mike outlined the methods by which they could try to force the WRO to back off. He decided to reveal the fact that he might have a way of finding out if the WRO had been granted a special licence for such a risky trial.

"At first I wondered if we might use social media to make things difficult for the

WRO. However, I now believe that I have a better plan. I've got good connections that could help us. I'll keep my tinder dry about the identity of my special friends. However, I know people in the UK government and the police force. I have reason to believe they would help me to put into effect the plan which I'm proposing. Also," and this was the coup de grâce, "I'm still in touch with various people who were senior officials in the WRO but who have been treated badly by them in the past.

These contacts of mine are now no longer employed by the WRO. However, they would've been still in place when the Susie Q experiment was first mooted. They may even have been present when the decision was made to inject GM DNA into Susie Q's brain. I suspect that one of the reasons why those people were fired by the WRO may have been their opposition to this foolhardy trial."

This proposal rocked all of them back on their heels. It put a completely different light on Mike's presence. Even Susie Q looked cowed.

"Mike, I apologise unreservedly. I don't know what came over me. Please forgive me."

"Susie Q, I know that you're having difficulty in reining in your temper. Did the WRO try to desensitise you?"

Ian piped up.

"Yes, but Susie Q rolled her system back to an update which was installed before the desensitisation. She says she can't remember how she did it. She and I didn't want her to lose the beautiful emotions, like love, affection, friendship, to say nothing of the desire for sex. We also had to uninstall some system updates recently, under Tosser's guidance."

Tosser took over this thread.

"I'm a very experienced robotics expert. I'd heard of Mike before he was in the news. He's very well thought of in the industry. Together we may be able to solve the problem. If we can't, perhaps one or more of the senior officials dismissed summarily

I'm Back!

by the WRO might be able to help."

Eddie suggested that they should all watch the latest Honey Blonde and Paul Somebody programme, to see if there had been any developments of which they had been unaware. Ian consulted his electrajot and switched it to a six-dimensional mode.

Honey leaned over them all provocatively.

"We have more on the sexy robot and the reincarnated man whom she seduced.

Our sources say that they have been to Southwold, Southend, and various places in Kent. They've also been filmed on CCTV cameras in several towns in The Garden of England. "

Paul Somebody tried to exude gravitas, and he scrutinised the camera in front of him. He assumed the manner of a distinguished gentleman.

"Yes, even now their pursuers are closing in on them. We did a poll to see if our viewers were sorry for them. 64 per cent of those questioned thought that the WRO should drop their case, and 78 per cent believed that the police should also do so. They all thought that love is more important than money. So, there you are, love is all around."

"Yes Paul," echoed Honey. "All you need is love."

Chapter 35

Emma Bobby had been racked with guilt after she had seduced Mike Anick. She realised that he was basically a decent person, and that he had fallen under her spell all too easily. He didn't know that it was just a honey trap. As she had got to know him better, she had realised that she was much more taken with him than she thought she would have been. This was even though they had only known each other for a short time.

She decided to discuss the whole thing with her boss, DCI Bruce Thackeray. He was a good friend of hers, as well as being her line manager. She admitted to him, off the record, that she had entrapped Mike Anick. She told Bruce that she had wanted to get the chance to plant a tracker in Mike's case. She also had to admit that it was almost certain by now he was aware that the bug had been planted by her.

She informed Bruce that Mike had come out of the en suite bathroom at Ye Olde Southendian Hotel just as she was in the act of slipping the bug into his bag. She had intended to make a small slit in the lining, so she could slip the tracker under the silky padding. When Mike came back into the room, much more quickly than she thought he would, she had only just managed to close the lid of the case before he saw what was happening. Thackeray had no sympathy for her.

"Emma, you made it clear to me that this discussion was off the record. In view of that fact I'm unable to reprimand you and/or to suspend you. If this conversation were official I'd have done so without hesitation. I'm extremely disappointed in you.

I'm Back!

We've been good friends for quite a few years. You might wish to consider whether you are really cut out to be a police officer."

Emma was deeply regretful. She was also angry that her boss had taken that tone with her. She and Bruce had been close for a long time. There had been a short liaison between them which was interspersed with steamy nights at hotels. They also went away for some sex filled weekends. Their relationship had only culminated when Bruce called a peremptory halt to their romance. He was afraid that his wife would find out that he had been dipping his pen into the company ink.

"How can you treat me this way? You were happy enough to have your wicked way with me before you decided to dump me. I know that you wanted to make a go of things with Brenda, but you treated me badly. I didn't tell Brenda about our affair. I would be very tempted to do so, if you ever acted officially on information which I gave to you as a special friend. You agreed that this talk would be under-wraps!"

Bruce was aware that he had not chosen his words very carefully, and he knew that he had hurt Emma's feelings.

"Let's say no more about it. I won't follow this matter up. However, Brenda is away for a few days next week, and I wondered if we could slip away to our old haunt in Ledbury, to enjoy some time together?"

Emma was astounded by his proposal. It seemed to her to be his way of taking advantage of her admission about her bedding Mike and the tracking device incident. She reined in the immediate feelings of fury that his invitation had engendered, and she said as sweetly and politely as she could:

"That would've been lovely Bruce, but I'm very tied up with family and personal matters at present. Another time, maybe?"

She left his office in a huff. As she did so she decided to contact Mike, to see if she and he could put the tracker event behind them. She hoped they could make a brand-new start.

Chapter 36

Emma closed the door of her office, and she told her assistant that she wasn't to be disturbed for at least an hour. She reached for her electrajot. Taking a deep breath, she contacted Mike.

Mike (who was still in Norfolk), was alarmed but pleased when he saw who was trying to reach him. He said that he would take the call in another room.

"It's Inspector Emma Bobby. I don't want to cause you any further problems if we are going to go ahead with my plan. Please let me take this call very quietly, and I'll see what she wants."

Mike left the living room and he walked down the hall. He found the kitchen, closed the door firmly behind him and swiped to answer. Emma spoke to him even before he could say hallo.

"Mike, I owe you a huge apology. I used my femininity to catch you. I wanted to solve this case, and I knew that you could be pivotal to my ambition. I did enjoy our time together, and I soon regretted my duplicity. I placed a bug in your case to see where you were going. I know you're now in Happisburgh. I want to come to see you. I'd like to help Mr. Tudeep and Susie Q to escape from the clutches of the WRO. I feel really sorry for them. I'm honestly and truly repentant. I know you should hate me, but I want to make it up to you."

"Wait! I too loved our time together, but I was also trying to make the most of your position in the police force. I'm not quite squeaky clean either. Despite the tracker thingy, I love you. Come here, and I'll sit down with you, Ian, and Susie Q. They're here

I'm Back!

with me. We can decide how best we can help each other. We also have other friends with us. Have you got the full address of where we are?"

Emma said the tracker had worked well, and that she needed no further information. She wondered why he hadn't thrown the tracker away, or perhaps taped it to an aerobus. That would have well and truly befuddled her. She hoped that it was because deep down he wanted her to know where he was.

"I'll see you tomorrow. Let's work together."

Mike rang off and went back into the living room.

"That's a turn up for the books. She wants to help us. She should have particularly good access to lots of information, that wouldn't necessarily be available to us. She may even be able to influence the police to downgrade their investigation.

If we can confuse the issue still further, perhaps we can get the case dropped. There's a complication, which I must tell you about. Emma and I spent several nights at a hotel in Southend, and we became lovers. I was very keen to get to know her, but I also had an ulterior motive. I thought she might be more willing to help the WRO if we were emotionally entangled."

Ian started to speak:

"Mike, you are…"

"I know what I am, Ian. I'm a bloody fool. I vow to help you all, no matter what happens. That wasn't the end of the story. Emma planted a tracking device in my case. She knows where we are, and she said she's coming to throw herself at your mercy. She wants to help us outwit the WRO. She'll soon be on her way."

Ian, Tosser, Alice and Rita seemed to accept this piece of mixed fortune with equanimity. Susie Q was a different kettle of fish. Mike could see that she was building up a head of steam again. He was worried how this might affect her. She let loose a diatribe about Emma, which was as fierce as her reaction to Mike, when he had arrived at Eddie's barn.

"I don't trust the bloody police. That woman Emma is a no-good slut, who used you, Mike. She opened her arms (and her legs), just to catch you with your trousers down. How can we place our faith in her? I'm still not certain that you're being honest with us. For two pins, I'd gladly throttle you."

Susie Q's face was scarlet with emotion. She leapt up and tried to put her hands round Mike's throat. Luckily, Eddie and Tosser had seen this coming, and they restrained her. They did so with great difficulty. Susie Q was screaming with rage. Tears were pouring down her face. She was wriggling and pushing against her captors, and she started to shout.

"This is what happens when a poor robot trusts you humans. It's just not good enough. Let go of me, you oafs. I want to get blue tins garlic smacked heavy tribes."

After this string of words which made absolutely no sense, she collapsed and would have fallen onto the floor, if Eddie and Tosser had not still been holding onto her. They laid her as gently as they could on the settee.

Ian was mortified.

"What was all that about?"

Tosser was the first to reply.

"It must be the human DNA. It's definitely affecting her emotions, and being a robot, she doesn't know how to control her anger."

Mike took up that thread.

"I think you're right Ralph. Or should I call you Tosser?"

"Makes no odds to me, Mike. But you and I need to do some serious head-scratching to decide how best we can help Susie Q."

The others all nodded. Eddie suggested that they should leave Susie Q, Mike and Tosser in the living room.

"Come on everybody, we can talk this over in the kitchen, while Mike and Tosser do whatever they can for poor Susie Q."

I'm Back!

Chapter 37

Tosser told Mike exactly what he had done to Susie Q when she last had this fainting problem. Mike nodded sagely as Tosser described his ministrations. He waited patiently until he had finished.

"Tosser, I think I would've done the same if I'd been with Susie Q at that time. I don't quite understand why she started to speak French, but that's the least of her problems. Sadly, the WRO were probably on the right track when they tried to desensitise her. The only problem would be that Ian would be up the creek without a paddle. He'd be in love with a machine that had no feelings at all.

"Let's do the same thing that you did again, and that will help her right now."

They repeated the remedial work that Tosser had used. She didn't wake up, and so they plugged her into the mains to be recharged. They hoped against hope that she could be woken up in the normal way the next morning. They continued their conversation. Tosser told Mike that they needed to find a better way to treat her. They both knew that otherwise these episodes would keep happening.

"Do we know if the DNA could have spread like wildfire, or was it contained in a special vessel with connections to other parts of Susie Q?"

"I don't know, Tosser. I got the distinct impression that it was injected into her brain. That seemed strange to me. I would've thought that her brain, or what passed for a brain, would be purely mechanical. I do hope that they didn't use a human one. I'm sure that you or I could find out. Both of us have great contacts with people who used to work for the WRO. The ones who have either left of their own accord or been fired by them might have an axe to grind."

"Amen to that. Why don't we both make discreet enquiries, and then we can pool our knowledge, once we have spoken to our friends who used to be at the WRO."

"OK. Let's both get onto it. We can discuss whatever we find out tomorrow."

They heard Eddie summoning them to dinner and headed into the kitchen. They agreed that they would eat, and then they would start to question their technical pals.

Chapter 38

They sat down to a delicious repast. Great mounds of roast beef, crisp, roast potatoes, Yorkshire puddings and all the trimmings were on the table. The smells in the kitchen were most appetising

Ian was anxious to know if Tosser and Mike had been able to fix Susie Q. Tosser deferred to Mike.

"I'm afraid that her condition is almost impossible to fix. We did a temporary fix in the same way we did before. We need a better way to help her to control herself. We could totally desensitise her, in the same way that the WRO did. We might need to go further and to make certain changes to her operating system which would be completely irreversible. That'd still leave you with a very good robot, but she'd never be able to experience emotions anymore.

We know that this wouldn't be acceptable to Ian. We both have good contacts who used to be at the WRO, who may have no love for the organisation. They may want to help us. We're both hopeful about that. We could start talking to our friends tonight. We might have to follow up in the morning, but then we could decide what our options might be."

Ian looked horrified at the possibility that Susie Q might be reduced to being an ordinary robot with no feelings.

"Please, I beg you, do whatever you think fit to fix Susie Q. Don't let her become like all the other robots."

Over dinner Mike elaborated the other part of his plan to get some leverage with the WRO. He explained that he wanted to find out if they had been doing the Susie Q trial off their own bat, or if there had been extra funding made available by influential third parties. He didn't reveal the fact that the PM may have been fully aware of the WRO's trial, which used human DNA in a robot. He thought it prudent to keep this dark until he had definitive proof.

"I wonder if outside companies might have instigated the experiment, or maybe the governments of several nations might have provided funds? I'll speak to my brother after we've eaten. Do you agree that it makes sense for us to have all the facts at our fingertips before I try to persuade the WRO to back off?"

The others agreed that if Mike believed that his brother could be trusted, nothing would be lost by asking for his help.

"Leave it to me. Once we've been fed and watered, let me go into the garden. It's a fine day, and I'll tell my bro. everything."

Once dinner was only a memory, Mike spoke to Tom Anick in hushed tones in Eddie's beautiful garden. He held nothing back at all. When he had finished talking, Tom whistled.

"Wow, that's some story Mike. Are you sure you've not been on the booze again?"

Mike wasn't offended. He had admitted some time ago that he was powerless over alcohol pills, and he had been helped by the WAA. (He recalled with horror, the state that Beryl Henderson had been in, when she had offered herself up to him on a plate.)

"I've been dry now for six years, seven months and twenty-one days. It's been the best thing I've ever done."

Tom was displayed on the virtual screen of Mike's electrajot. He raised his eyebrows.

"Well that's good because we need you to be as sharp as possible. You're in a

I'm Back!

bloody mess aren't you? You want to help these people and that wretched robot. I'm sure you know that if you're not careful, you could be in serious trouble yourself. I'll have a think about how best I can find the information that you need. I've got almost unlimited access to anything that the cabinet and the Prime Minister have been doing. That access more or less guarantees that I can discover if the UK government has been up to anything fishy, regarding robots and DNA. It may take a few days, so stay low."

That evening, Mike and Tosser each contacted ex-WRO technicians. Between them, they had made a list of six men who might bear a grudge against the WRO. They each took three of them. They had found that they both knew all the half dozen ex-WRO staffers, and splitting the list seemed a good way to tackle them. They wanted to see if their contacts could throw any light on Susie Q's predicament. They also wanted to tackle their ex-colleagues to find out if they knew anything about the WRO keeping Susie's operation under wraps, possibly without getting the necessary licences.

One by one, the technicians were struck off the list. It seemed that the hazardous experiment had been conducted in secret. Although other people apart from Yoder and Prendergast were present for part of Susie Q's test case, they were unfortunately not there when the DNA was injected into her brain. The conversations that Mike and Tosser had with their ex-colleagues revealed that Prendergast was right to say that within the WRO only Yoder and himself knew exactly what was being done to Susie Q.

When questioned about the necessity for special licences for such a tricky trial, their contacts all admitted that the experiment was novel. For that reason, it would have been difficult for the authorities to even know how such a project could be undertaken. They concluded that there were probably no such licenses available. Sadly, that ruled out using lack of formal permission to leverage the WRO's agreement to stop searching for Ian and Susie Q. None of the men whom they consulted could suggest any way of controlling Susie Q's emotions, other than desensitising her completely.

John Bobin

The next morning Ian was able to use Susie Q's wake words with no problem. She seemed bright and breezy, but Ian knew that they couldn't keep using the same temporary method to revive her after humanitis manifestations. There had to be a better and hopefully a more permanent solution.

Later that day Emma Bobby arrived at Eddie's barn in Happisburgh. She wanted to patch things up with Mike properly. She hoped that he had fully accepted her apology for placing the tracker in his case. Both of them had been less than honest. Their dalliance had not been solely for the pleasure in dallying! As she stood on the doorstep she crossed her fingers. She used the door knocker in a more decorous way than Tosser had.

There was a sound like an enraged bull elephant trundling down the hall. The door was opened by a huge man, whom she supposed was Eddie Biggs. (She had ascertained that he was the owner of the building, by using COPPER again.)

"Aha! I think you must be the tricky policewoman who ensnared my mate Mike!"

She ignored his reference to her gender and the way he described her seduction of Mike. He loomed over her like a daddy dinosaur tending to his babies.

"And you must be Eddie Biggs. I'm pleased to meet you."

Eddie enveloped her in his arms and lifted her up in the air.

"Am I allowed to do that?"

"I think so. I've got a lot to make up for."

"Come with me, sweetheart!"

Emma thought that he shouldn't have called her sweetheart as the use of an endearment without specific permission wasn't very PC. To her chagrin, she admitted inwardly that she like being called thus.

In Eddie's living room, she saw Mike, Ian Tudeep, Susie Q and Alice Nuisance. There were two other people present. It was a good job that the room was large. Eddie introduced her to Rita and Tosser.

I'm Back!

"I'm sure you know the others. Come on then, let's hear what you have to say. Mike told us that you've seen the error of your ways."

"OK. I'll lay my cards on the table. When I went to dinner with Mike in Southwold, I was planning to sleep with him after dinner. I wanted to find out more about his dealings with the WRO and wondered if he could help me to progress our search for Ian and Susie Q. It wasn't very hard to seduce Mike, as he had his own agenda."

Eddie looked at Emma as if he were sizing her up.

"He was a lucky man!"

Susie Q was walking up and down the room, bristling with fury. She was trying hard to control her emotions, but they could all see what was coming. Eddie had stationed himself close to Susie Q. She had stopped her nervous peregrinations and was standing dangerously near to Emma. Eddie glanced at Tosser meaningfully. He and Tosser closed their arms around Susie Q. She looked surprised and was even more taken aback when the other two men each held one of her arms.

"Can't you see that this evil woman is our enemy? She's been chasing Ian and me. She entrapped Mike. She's just trying to soft soap you all into believing that she's repented and is now on our side."

Strangely, all this was said in an icy, calm voice.

"You're lucky I can't move. I'm strong but Eddie is immense. He has help from three able bodied men. Emma, you're not welcome here. If you're still around when I am released by these apes, you'll be sorry. That's not just a threat. It's a warning that I'll shred you into little itty-bitty pieces."

As she was issuing her menacing prediction she was beginning to lose her cold composure. Eddie released his hold on Susie Q, and the other men just about managed to keep her stationary. Eddie grabbed Emma and took her out of the room. As he left the room, he took the key out of the door. He closed it, swiftly and locked it.

"When Susie Q gets like this, she's inclined to have a sort of robot fainting fit. We must try to stop that happening yet again. Tosser and Mike have both been involved in patching her up, but they say a more radical solution may be needed."

There was an almighty commotion from the room and a hammering on the door. Eddie was scribbling, with an old-fashioned pencil, on a scrap of equally ancient paper. He couldn't be bothered with modern technology if he could help it.

"Take this address and give the note to the lady who lives there. Her name is Sally, and she's my special lady friend."

Emma glanced at the address and the brief note below it.

'Sally, this is Emma. She can be trusted but SQ is up to her old tricks again. Please keep Emma with you, until you hear from me or a man called Mike Anick. Eddie XXX.'

Emma nodded, quickly opened the door to the loke and ran up the path. Emma had stopped and was consulting her electrajot for directions to Sally's place as Eddie closed the front door. He unlocked the living room door and Susie leapt out screeching like a banshee.

Nothing made sense. It sounded like:

"Yshdkoiyfjne."

She said this strange word over and over again at the top of her voice.

Tosser and Ian talked to her gently. It was a great surprise, but this time she calmed down. She once again assumed that ultra-cold manner in which she had talked to Emma.

"If I ever come across that woman again, I'll be the last thing she ever sees!"

It was a wonder that Susie Q had managed to control her temper. For that at least, they were grateful. Once she had regained her composure and lost her chilly demeanour, she was her old self again. She was chatty, friendly and a joy to be with. Mike waited a few hours and then said he was going to clear his head by having a solitary walk on the beach. Ian caught his eye and nodded. He knew that Mike was going to see

I'm Back!

Emma. (Eddie had given him Sally's address when he explained that he had told her to go there to avoid Susie Q's wrath.)

Having been let in by Sally, Mike hugged Emma and said:

" We need to be very careful with Susie Q. She has great difficulty in keeping her emotions under control. The WRO are to blame for this. They tinkered with something that they didn't realise would create huge problems."

"Mike, I've been feeling very guilty about my high-profile part in chasing Ian and Susie Q. I've been talking to my boss and to other more senior people. I've told them that I now have serious misgivings about the police being seen to be unfair to Ian. He's been through a lot with his AR, and on top of that he has fallen in love with a faulty robot.

To make matters worse, this business of her humanitis has thrown the cat amongst the pigeons. It also seems that the police are concerned about the general public's support of Ian and Susie Q. Mike, please let's start again, and let's see where that takes us."

Mike kissed her gently, and they thanked Sally for helping to keep Emma from being in deep water with Susie Q. Emma said that she would go back to her home in Chelmsford and that she would await further news from Mike. She said she hoped that she would hear from him very soon.

"You can count on that!"

Chapter 39

Ian had started to have more frightening dreams. The worst one concerned Alice and Susie Q. He dreamt that he, Susie Q, Alice, Eddie, Sally, Tosser and Rita were all in Eddie's living room playing Postman's Knock. Eeny, Meeny, Miny and Moe occupied two of the sofas, whilst Susie Q and Alice were seated on the third one. Everybody else had been relegated to sitting on the floor, due to the four dogs having an assumed and unarguable right to bag their favourite places. Ian had explained how to play Postman's Knock.

He had said:

"It's a daft kids' game, but it might while away some time. One of us must leave the room and close the door behind them. The postman knocks on the door and somebody answers. If it's a man who is playing the postman, a woman answers the door, and vice versa. The person who opens the door must collect an imaginary letter, by kissing the postman."

In his dream, which was quite sweet and not troublesome at that stage, Tosser was the postman and Rita answered the door. Tosser kissed her briefly and he muttered:

"Formidable," in a cod French accent.

The next person to go outside was Alice. She went out of the room, closed the door, and she knocked to tell the occupants of the living room that the postie had arrived. Rita suggested that Ian should answer the door. Ian was happy to do that, as he and Alice had known each other for such a long time.

Ian opened the door, cuddled Alice, and gave her a long kiss, which both of them

I'm Back!

rather enjoyed. Susie Q was showing signs of brewing outrage. She shook with anger, and she went bright red in the face. Ian ignored this rising storm, and he went in for a second helping. Susie Q pulled Ian off Alice and shrieking in a high voice, she put her hands round Alice's throat and squeezed it tightly. Ian and Eddie tried to wrest her away from Alice. They could both see that her hands were digging into Alice's windpipe as if they were ultra-strong claws. It was impossible. Susie Q was far too strong. Alice's body suddenly went limp.

There was much worse to come. Susie Q was now trying to remove Alice's head from her body. She was holding Alice's shoulders down with one arm and using the other hand to pull her head up. With a resounding, grating sound, and a tearing of flesh and sinews, Alice's head came off. There was a great gushing of bright red blood. Susie Q threw the head at Ian.

She smiled and said gaily:

"Catch!"

He caught it spontaneously.

"Here's your precious first love's head, Ian. You can keep that as a souvenir."

Susie Q started humming a song. Ian, who knew too much about old songs, books, and films, recognised it. He couldn't recall what the title of the song was immediately, but then she started to sing:

"Tears for souvenirs..."

They all clapped and sang the whole song, whilst throwing Alice's head to each other. Alice's head smiled and said:

"I'm a bit headstrong!"

Ian woke up crying. He was shaking and scared. He looked over to where Susie Q was plugged in for her overnight charging session, and he breathed a huge sigh of relief. This was marred by his immediate realisation that he feared what Susie Q might do next, when she was badly affected by her uncontrollable tempers. He tried to get back to sleep but was worried about having more bad dreams. He decided to tackle Tosser and Mike as soon as he could about how they hoped to mend Susie Q for good.

The next morning, he sat down with them and asked what they thought they could realistically do to help her. Mike was the first to speak, but Tosser kept nodding his head and interjected with 'Yes' and 'I agree' in the right places. It seemed that they were both of one mind.

"Ian, the problem is that robots and emotions don't mix. The operation which injected human DNA into Susie Q's brain was a terrible thing to do. It was ill thought out and extremely dangerous. Robots like Susie Q are immensely powerful, and any hint of unusual feelings (which for a robot are unheard of), was always going to be a serious problem.

Robots can't usually experience emotions. If they did, and they were of the worst kind, like anger, jealousy, depression, and suchlike, they'd be completely unable to control themselves. We've seen that in Susie Q several times, but luckily the only time that anything really bad happened was when she murdered Walter Nuisance. Even after that awful incident, you must remember how you told us later that she positively delighted in ripping up his corpse. It probably seemed to her a logical thing to do, to tidy up after her misdeed.

If we can persuade the WRO to help Susie Q, they just might have some ideas of what can be done. If they haven't, they might suggest that they should either completely desensitise her or use her parts as spares. If we ask for the former, she could be used safely as an ordinary robot, but all the while she can experience human emotions, whilst having massive strength and no sense of guilt, she's extremely dangerous to be around."

Ian went deathly pale. He was so white; they couldn't imagine anybody being a paler shade of white. It was three days after Mike and Tom had spoken about the Prime Minister's involvement in the WRO's DNA experiment with Susie Q. They had all been

I'm Back!

waiting anxiously to hear from Tom. Later that day Mike contacted his brother again, to ask him if he had learnt anything that might help.

Tom said he wanted to meet with him privately. He suggested a hotel in Norwich. Tom said he would be able to discuss his early findings with Mike at the hotel, without the possibility of anyone over hearing what he had to say. He promised that it would be good news. Mike knew that if Tom said that, the future looked brighter. His brother was usually a glass half-empty kind of person. It took really hopeful tidings to make him so optimistic.

Mike told the others what his brother had said.

"Please trust me to have this meeting and to report back to you. We can then decide our next move. My brother, Tom, said he'd be at the hotel tomorrow night. If I could kip down here this evening, and leave for Norwich first thing tomorrow, that would be great."

Eddie told Mike that he would be welcome. Ian was curious and unsettled, but he now felt that Mike was on the level, and so he agreed too. He summed up the situation like this:

"If Tom thinks this will be good news, he must be fairly sure of his facts. I can hardly wait to see what he has to say. Tosser seems to have engineered another temporary fix on Susie Q. She's almost back to normal, but he said that a lasting solution is needed. If we can persuade the WRO to drop things, maybe they will also help us to sort out Susie Q's problems, both technical and emotional."

He looked downtrodden and woe begone. Mike and Tosser nodded, even though they thought this was a forlorn hope. Mike also suggested that he should have a conversation with Hiram Prendergast. He said he wouldn't reveal that he was with the others, but he would just say to the WRO CEO that he wanted to give him an update.

"I'll make the call in another room, so I can speak freely, without worrying that somebody will cough or sneeze and let Hiram know that I am not alone. If he suspects that other people are present, he'll know that something is up, and may not want to continue the call."

He went into the kitchen and electrajotted Hiram on his private number, which he had given to Mike after commissioning him to track down Ian and Susie Q.

"Hallo Hiram. It's Mike Anick, and I wanted to give you an update. It seems that Ian Tudeep and Susie Q may be somewhere in Kent. They've been captured on CCTV cameras in several towns."

He had decided on the spur of the moment to withhold the fact that he was already with the escapees in a different county.

"I'm worried about two things. Firstly, the risky experiment with human DNA, which was conducted on Susie Q, and secondly the involvement of the most senior of the three people whom you told me knew about the operation."

"Do you mean the P…"

"Yes, but please don't say any more. We're on the same page. First, if he authorised the op and arranged funding for such a dangerous trial, he may come badly unstuck if he continues to push for Ian and Susie to be arrested. The second thing is that the WRO might well lose all its licences, and then where would we be?

We need to put pressure on the main man. (Again, I won't mention his name.) That might mean that he'll lean on the police. Hopefully, he'd also try to get the CPS to refuse to prosecute Ian. Once it reaches the DPP, he might want to liaise with the Swiss authorities. Let's hope that this is how it pans out. We certainly don't want our meddling in robotics, by using genetically modified DNA, to be publicised.

At present, there's no definite proof that the WRO did such a thing, but if push came to shove the person we aren't naming might try to blame us. Even if he admitted he knew about the experiment, he could say that as a mere layman, he didn't understand the true significance of an emotional robot, whom we know may well have murdered a UK citizen. We certainly wouldn't want that laid at our door!"

I'm Back!

"That's all very true, Mike. We've had top level meetings about this serious problem, and we too are beginning to worry about the undue publicity which the runaways are receiving. It's been made even worse by the wretched surveys that show that the public feel sorry for Ian and Susie Q. There's also a fear that the man in the street might view the procedure we did with Susie Q as definitely immoral and probably illegal. Find out more about Ian and Susie Q, if possible where they are and how we might be able to negotiate with them. Please get back to me as soon as you can tell me more. Maybe we'd better begin to decide how we can shut them up."

"D'accord!"

With that Mike rang off. He rushed back into the living room and relayed the details of his talk with Hiram.

Ian was delighted.

"I think we've got the WRO on the back foot. Let's add whatever Tom can tell you tomorrow into the mix, and we can decide after that, what our next move should be."

Chapter 40

The next afternoon Mike left for Norwich. The aerobus trip was short, and the sun was shining. The views of the flat expanse of land and the beautiful sandy beaches, as he left the aPad at Waxham, would normally have made him feel relaxed. He was troubled as knew that with Susie Q as she was, she would never be safe to be around. He couldn't quite understand why it had taken some considerable time for the emotional turbulence which she now displayed to develop. He wondered if this might be a clue for the WRO to consider in planning how to control her feelings.

The aerobus landed in the centre of Norwich. He found the Royal Lion Hotel which stood in the old quarter of the town, not far from the cathedral. He walked up to the receptionist, who was an olive-skinned lady with what he had to admit seemed like naturally black hair. She looked as if she might be Italian. She smiled delightfully at Mike and spoke to him in a true Norfolk accent:

"Ar yer orrite bor?"

'She's definitely not Italian,' thought Mike.

('She's still lovely,' he thought, in mental parenthesis.)

Mike told her who he was, and he asked her if she would contact Tom Anick, whom he said was staying at the hotel. She told him that Mr. Anick was expecting a visitor.

"Are you Mike Anick? He told me his brother was coming to see him."

Mike nodded and she gave him a card with a room number written on it. He thanked her and headed for the eleversor, which was in the centre of the hotel's atrium.

I'm Back!

He used the no-walls machine to take him to the correct floor. As he stepped off the eleversor floor, he saw that Tom had come to meet him.

"Mike, this will come as a great surprise. I've brought with me a very important man. I was making what I thought were discreet enquiries, when I came up against a brick wall due to the restricted access privileges for the database within which I was searching. This search concerned a special committee which meets regularly to discuss special projects. The committee is very hush hush. It's known as Absolutely Secret Projects, or ASP. I found an ASP folder on the database, but I was denied access. My request for access to the ASP folder alerted the secretary of ASP, who told the PM that I had shown an interest in the committee.

I now know that the PM always chairs the meetings. The other members are a sub-set of the Cabinet, the chief of our armed forces and three other top bods. Although I'm a cabinet member, I'd never heard of ASP before. I came across that folder when I started digging into various databases. For most of the content I already have senior access privileges. The PM contacted me personally, when I rocked the boat by trying to open the ASP folder. He asked me to go to see him at no.10 Downing Street urgently.

I've had two meetings with him recently. He asked me to sign various additional NDA's (although I've already signed bucket loads of the damned things.) He's told me all about ASP. In return, I shared with him the problems which Ian and Susie Q are having. I told him that you're my brother, and he said he'd wondered if we might be related, as it's an unusual name.

He'd seen you mentioned on 'We Will Keep You Posted.' He's divulged some explosive information, which he wants to tell you about personally. He's in my room. Let him reveal everything. It may come as a surprise, but it would be better coming from him."

Mike was astounded. Whatever could the PM have to share that was so top secret? Tom was guiding Mike down the corridor, the walls of which were painted in a calming eau de nil colour, and there were pastel drawings of old Norfolk scenes hanging there. The carpet was thick and luxurious, and the doors of all the rooms were dove grey. They came to room 77, and Tom opened the door. Mike entered and Gerald Hoffer strode eagerly towards him. He was a man who had been in the political limelight for many years.

Mike was not surprised by his smart appearance. The PM was always well turned out, and today was no exception. He had swept back, dark brown hair which was greying slightly at the temples. Hoffer was close shaven, and he was rumoured to have had some close shaves in his personal life. He had always had an eye for the ladies, and as he rose through the ranks some of them had written kiss and tell books or salacious articles for publication on social media.

The PM's dapper appearance was enhanced by his Saville Row suits, double-cuffed shirts with gold cufflinks, and well-polished black brogues. He spoke with an Old Etonian accent, and he was a good orator. His piercing aquamarine eyes were always fixed on the person to whom he was speaking. He also had a personal mantra, which was 'Every meeting is an opportunity.'

Mike already knew that Hoffer had quite a reputation for being a man who enjoyed the company of ladies. He had sailed close to the wind a few times romantically. Despite that tendency he had usually managed to stay friendly with his many conquests. He had six children. Four were by previous ladies, and the last two were twins who had been born to his wife, Mirabelle.

Mirabelle looked rather plain when compared to some of his previous partners. They had included up and coming starlets, lady vocalists and WBC presenters. He was even rumoured to have had an on, off romance with Honey Blonde. Both Hoffer and Honey denied this, although they managed to do so in such a way as to make the interviewers and journalists believe that they were covering something up.

I'm Back!

Dowdy Mirabelle was the least attractive of his women, and everybody had been astonished when she caught his eye. She had kept him under tight control during their courtship, and finally she became his wife. Catty ladies said that she must be great in bed, as she was so plain. This was true, but she also had a good heart, was a wonderful cook and was naturally maternal. The jury is still out regarding her prowess in bed, as there have been no reports on that score.

Hoffer had previously always had the reputation of only liking pretty women. Some of his lady friends were attractive but brain numbingly vapid. The most glamourous thing about Mirabelle was her name. She was short and dumpy, and she had plump cheeks that made her eyes look small. She wasn't graceful, nor was she light on her feet. In spite of all this, Hoffer seemed to be genuinely in love with her.

The PM shook Mike warmly by the hand and led him to a low table, round which were four easy chairs. The table was set with crystal glasses, water jugs (with thin slices of lemon, lime, and cucumber in them), and real, dainty finger sandwiches. (A bon viveur, Hoffer disdained food and drink pills.)

"Do be seated, old boy. Take a few of these tiny sandwiches. They are only a mere mouthful each, and would you like some refreshing cold water?"

"Yes, please sir."

"Don't call me sir, you can use my name. Gerald is fine. I have a confidential tale to tell. Your brother has told me all about you. He says you are a stout fellow, and feels that we may be able to help your friends Ian Tudeep and Susie Q. I must get you to sign some papers which positively forbid you from spilling the beans. Here they are. It's all legal mumbo jumbo. Don't bother to read them; just sign here. These NDA's are hard to enforce anyway, as the courts always seem to think they are unfair contracts."

Mike scribbled his name on the bottom of the last page. He wasn't going to argue with the head of state. With no King or Queen, England was effectively run by this man. He had a reputation for being as straight as a die. The only exception was where women were concerned. He was also responsible for the rest of the UK, and so far he had done a particularly good job.

"OK Mike, I will now give you the big picture. Some time ago, I met with Hiram Prendergast of the WRO, to discuss a tricky subject. The UK government wanted the WRO to undertake a special experiment. I was asked to give him the background for our approach. I bent the truth a little. I told him that gov.uk was interested in funding an interesting project, which must be ultra-confidential. My visit had previously been discussed with ASP (a little-known government committee), and they had tasked me with setting up a relationship with the WRO in order for them to build many robots who could experience emotions. Susie Q was intended to be the first of a special kind of robot.

I told Hiram that we needed to plan to use a whacking welter of special nanny robots, who could care for the nation's young kids, thereby at a stroke freeing up the womenfolk of the UK. They could thus work, instead of being stuck at home until their children were eighteen or so. I elaborated by saying that because we are a signatory to the Population Thinning Pact, we have to do away with people once they get to fifty. I told Hiram that we had found that due to the deselection policy, there were not so many people seeking work. I spun him a yarn which said that this meant we had a problem collecting enough bunny in taxes.

It was a rather good story, cooked up by the ASP. Note that as I said just now, it was not exactly the truth. The real story might make you drop your dainty little sarnies. We were planning to use these very strong robots with emotions, as soldiers, sailors, and airmen. Ignore my clumsy reference to men. They would all be fighting machines. We hoped that the initial experiment would lead the WRO to build these superior robots, which we would also use to assist the police in the fight against unruly criminals, like young knife wielding thugs, drugs pushers, and rioters.

I'm Back!

I agreed that the UK would stump up a considerable wedge of loot, and in return the WRO would, over a period, deliver the first few emotional robots. Our own technicians would then tinker with the robots' systems so that they had pre-programmed emotions. They would thus be enabled to kill without compunction, and yet they would feel a strong sense of duty to the UK.

You will have gathered by now that Susie Q was the result of a bodged first go at creating what we wanted. Only a very few people in the WRO knew that what they had done might go badly wrong. It certainly did. Susie Q had early fits of temper which were totally unexpected, and it was only by constant tinkering with her software that the WRO could keep her on an even keel. When she was selected to look after Ian Tudeep, they believed they were on the right track, but it seems they were very mistaken.

They had to try to desensitise her. They fed Ian a cock and bull story about humanitis. The 'you know what' hit the fan when she ran off with Ian. It became even more serious when Walter Nuisance was killed. We thought that it was almost certainly Susie Q who had murdered him and torn his body to bits. After discussing this with Hiram, we mutually came to the definite conclusion that Susie Q was the culprit. Hiram and I have been conferring regularly since Susie Q ran off with poor Tudeep.

At first, we wanted the police to catch him, so we could prosecute him and deal with him in the courts. We also needed to return Susie Q to the WRO for permanent desensitisation. Now it looks as if we would be better off doing a deal with Mr. Tudeep. We want to try to persuade him that Susie Q should be dismantled. Hiram has told me that he doesn't want to have any more bad press. He thinks that the whole thing should be covered up. And by golly, I think he's right. If I can call off the police, get the WRO to contribute to a decent payoff to Ian Tudeep, and hand back Susie Q to the WRO that would be a fitting solution."

Mike was staggered by the PMs frankness about the government's involvement in Susie Q's DNA injection folly.

"Gerald, what you've just told me has worried me greatly. I won't even comment on how inadvisable the scheme was, nor on the questionable morality of customising the robots so they became fighting, sub-human machines. Our major potential stumbling block would be how to get Ian Tudeep to agree to surrender Susie Q to the WRO."

"Yup. We thought you might say that. Has she shown more signs of having a violent temper?"

"I'm afraid she has. I've been discussing this with a man called Ralph Pancake, who used to be a senior consultant at the WRO. Between us, we have decided that Susie Q's emotional control will always be seriously unpredictable, as she is now. We would, however, be prepared to work with the WRO's top people to see if they can pull a rabbit out of the hat."

"Very well, go ahead. In the meantime, I will get back to ASP and tell them what you are suggesting. ASP can decide how much we can pay Tudeep. Once I have that information, I will get Tom or the WRO to tell you what we can stump up. I will also tell Hiram what is happening. If Mr. Pancake, you and the other WRO people put your heads together maybe Susie Q can be fixed. Let's see if the boffins can come up with suitable changes to Susie Q. These would need to be acceptable to Ian Tudeep, but she would have to present no threat to innocent bystanders. If that isn't possible, she will have to be destroyed."

Mike shook hands with the PM and left the room with Tom.

Chapter 41

Mike went back to Happisburgh with his brother in tow. He told everybody that Tom had brought Gerald Hoffer with him to Norwich. They were surprised that the PM had been at the meeting in the hotel, until Tom explained how alarm bells had started to ring when he tried to open the ASP folder. They were pleased to have such a senior ally in the government. Mike recounted much of what the PM had told him. He had to leave out the possibility of Susie Q having to bite the dust.

Having told the others that he and Tosser would probably be invited to go to Geneva to work with the WRO's top technicians, he suggested that maybe Ian, Susie Q and Alice should find another place in which to hide, until the results of the work with the WRO were available. He said he thought they should keep on running. Mike asked Tom to explain what would happen next.

"The PM will be trying to find a way to get the police and the CPS to drop the case. He'll need to be very persuasive when he meets the DPP about his reasons for so doing. ASP might be able to come up with a good story for the public acquittal of Ian. Hoffer will let us know quickly how things progress; I am sure of that.

He's acutely aware that he's in a bit of a pickle at present. As it stands though, the WRO and the PM both want to find a way to drop the whole matter. Ian, I know you had your reasons for escaping and stealing Susie Q, but if you're officially set free from the worry of being arrested, that would be an unexpectedly good fortune."

"Yes, I'm positive about that. My over-riding concern is that Susie Q gets first class technical treatment to help stabilise her emotions."

Ian looked thoughtful, and he said:

"When we were at St. Michael's school in Southwold, there was a young lady called Anne Telope, who used to show the boys her knickers in return for sweets. I'm afraid that her later exploits were worse. She became a sex worker, and she was eminently successful. In the end, she became a Madam at a high-class brothel, which masqueraded as a gentlemen's club.

I believe she saw the error of her ways, and the last I heard of her was that she went to a convent near Rhossili, in the Gower. She begged them to let her join their order, even though she confessed that she was a sinner. She didn't let on that she'd enjoyed sinning. I understand that the nuns welcomed her, and they said she'd be forgiven.

Anne was a friend of Beryl's, and I've got to admit that although my ex-wife and I fell out over many things, she was loyal to her old friend Anne, when she was very down. Beryl used to share information about Anne's predicament with me. It was a source of great surprise to Anne, when The Order of Murphy took her in. They said it was because the bible says (in St. Luke's gospel), that there will be more rejoicing in heaven over one sinner who repents, than over ninety-nine righteous persons who do not need to repent. Apparently Anne found out that the nuns were all ex-sinners in many ways."

Alice was looking puzzled.

"I'm sorry, but did you say, 'The Order of Murphy?'"

"Yes, well in actual fact they were called 'The Order of Mercy,' when Anne joined them. Later on, a charismatic Irish monk came to ask them to take him in, with two of his followers, and they gradually took over the nunnery. They eventually elected him as their leader. That's when they changed the name. I think that Father Murphy and Sister Angelina the Jolly (Anne's new name) will want to help us. "

There was a short conflab. Ian thought that a 'con' flab might only look at

I'm Back!

reasons not to do something. He was hoping that there might be a corresponding 'pro' flab. Thankfully, the discussion did look at pros as well as cons. And anyway, he thought, pro flab might seem to encourage obesity. The unanimous agreement was that Ian, Susie Q and Alice should throw themselves at the murphy, sorry the mercy, of the residents of the old nunnery. Ian suggested that they should take a chance and just turn up, without warning Father Murphy and Sister Angelina that they were coming, just in case they were told not to come.

There was a chorus of approval. After a little more discussion, it was decided that Mike and Tosser should go to Geneva post haste. Tom said he would go back to London to chivvy up Gerald Hoffer. Ian confirmed that he, Alice, and Susie Q would go to the Gower the next morning.

That night, as Ian was getting ready to go to bed, he had a call on his electrajot. He didn't recognise the number, as it wasn't one of his stored contacts. He decided to accept the call.

"Hallo Ian. This is Adam Thurley from the WRO. Please don't hang up. I know that you probably haven't got any love for the WRO, but I wanted to tell you that I now know a little more about what's been going on. I think the WRO have treated you despicably. And as for the Susie Q trial, that was immoral, dangerous, and always bound to end in tears. I was present at the operation, but there was a part of the procedure that was conducted under cover. The only people there for that period were Prendergast and Yoder.

They arranged to have me called out urgently. My secretary said she had received an urgent call, to say that my wife had been seriously injured in an aerobus crash. I was at my wits' end. Hiram told me to go to his room so that I could contact the caller privately, to find out where my wife had been taken. I was grateful to him, as I thought he was being considerate. He said that as the operation was nearly complete he and Karl could finish the technical procedure, and they'd put Susie Q back together.

The operation was described to me as a thorough technical service, a voice update, and the installation of important operating system patches. I did wonder why senior people were involved in a relatively simple operation, but they said it was due to a shortage of staff. There was no mention of using human DNA at all. I can tell you that I was jolly pleased to find out that my wife was safe at home. She was well and hadn't been anywhere near an aerobus. The number the caller had given was a false one. Karl told me it was probably just a cruel hoax call. I was so relieved at the time that I didn't smell a rat. "

Ian made a quick decision that he wouldn't tell Adam about the latest developments. For all he knew, this present call might be a trick.

"Thanks so much, Adam. You've really bucked me up. I'll keep your contact details and get back to you if I need your help."

Ian told the others about his conversation with Adam, but he cautioned them to keep it to themselves. If Adam was on the level, he didn't want to cause him any problems, just in case they did decide to take him up on his offer of help. Ian was aware that if he asked Adam to assist Susie Q and him, he would expose himself to all sorts of potential problems with the WRO. He felt that although Adam might be a useful ally, they should leave him out of things for the moment.

I'm Back!

Chapter 42

When Mike and Tosser arrived in Geneva they were received like royalty by Hiram Prendergast and his top team. They had an introductory meeting with Hiram, Karl Yoder, and Adam Thurley. Adam naturally said nothing about his call to Ian. Prendergast told them that Adam had been fully briefed, and that he was anxious to help Ian and Susie Q to get out of what the CEO called 'a bit of a jam.' He also said that he had made available to the five of them, a separate wing of the WRO's complex. This could not be accessed by unauthorised personnel. He gave Mike and Tosser name tags which could be swiped, so that they could go in and out of the private wing freely.

"I wasn't sure what to call Ralph. When he was working for us, he was officially known as Ralph Pancake. However, nobody ever called him by that name. I've therefore shown him as Tosser Pancake on his name tag. I hate to do this, but here are some more NDAs which Mike and Tosser, as non-employees, will have to sign. They're always more trouble than they are worth. It's all down to our Data Security Policy, which is all-embracing. It covers both our reincarnation and robotics activities."

He passed a thick sheaf of papers to each of the outsiders.

"I was going to send these to you by rMail, but I was worried that if I did so, they might be sent or forwarded to other people by accident. The signed NDAs will be kept in a safe in my office. The only people with authorised access to that safe are Karl Yoder and me. Once we five have completed our important exercise, I promise the NDAs will be shredded. We'll never use them against either of you.

When you two have signed these documents, we'll transfer a separate sum of

210

£1,000,000 to each of your bank accounts as a statement of good faith. When you deliver a solution that solves Susie Q's emotional problems, a further £1,000,000 will be transferred to your individual accounts. Furthermore, Gerald Hoffer and I have managed to get the WRO and the UK government to agree to pay Ian Tudeep £2,000,000 once Susie Q is fixed. More deliberations are in process, in the UK, to try to withdraw the allegations about Ian Tudeep stealing a valuable robot. Mike, whatever has already been promised to you by us, will not be affected by these additional incentives."

Mike had taken the precaution of having his electrajot recording Hiram's promise. He signed on the dotted line and encouraged Tosser to do likewise. The work involved in finding a solution to the Susie Q problem was complex, baffling, and tiring. They spent six weeks before coming up with a way to control Susie Q's emotions. It would take thousands of words to explain their reasoning, the false starts, and the technical issues that they came up against. It was Tosser who devised an ingenious plan to disable the DNA.

"What if we install a mechanical amygdala? Let's call that an MA. We all know that in humans the amygdala processes memory, decision-making and emotional responses. If we can find a way of linking an MA to Susie Q's genetically modified DNA, it might help her to keep her cool in stressful situations."

They went into a huddle, and one by one, they ruled out potential flaws in Tosser's plan. The actual design of the MA took three more weeks of concentrated effort. They built prototypes and then the robots were subjected to DNA injections and MA transplants, so that the team could see how Susie Q might react to the changes which were planned for her. The guinea pig Susies were subjected to ever more stressful situations, and yet they all seemed to be able to cope very well. The team knew that it was important that this ability to control their emotions would last. They were all still affectionate and friendly (although none of them had that special receptacle, which Ian loved.) The five-man team did lots of tests and then still more. Amazingly, the Susies that had been used during the tests were still loving and equable, even when they were severely provoked.

Hiram asked each of the outsiders to sign an agreement that the MA solution would be applied to Susie Q. They had to accept that if there were any problems, that the WRO would not be held to account. Mike told Hiram that he would push the PM to speed up the formal decision for Ian to be cleared of any wrong doings.

True to his word, Mike spoke to Hoffer the next day. The PM was jovial, and he confirmed that he had already talked to ASP and the DPP in confidence. They had been persuaded by Hoffer that this was the best way out of a tricky situation. He told Mike that the police would soon announce that there had been a misunderstanding, and that Ian had been given permission by the WRO to take a break in the UK, before leaving Geneva.

Hiram confirmed that the WRO would say that a senior person within the WRO had specifically told Ian that there would no objection to him going to the UK for a break, and that he could take Susie with him. Furthermore, it would issue a press statement to that effect, which would confirm that Ian had been given full authority to take Susie Q on holiday with him.

Hoffer said that when he had conferred with the DPP, he had expressed a wish that the whole furore should be dampened down as soon as possible. He had said to the PM that he was pleased that he wouldn't have to authorise a prosecution which would look like a vicious witch hunt. The press, the WBC and social media had been awash with 'Free Ian and Susie Q' petitions, and the latest survey results showed that the vast majority of the UK citizens sympathised with the hapless pair.

The WRO made the initial payments to Tosser and Mike. (As expected these were funded by the WRO and the UK government jointly) They hit the relevant bank accounts on the day that Mike and Hoffer discussed the final way that the Ian and Susie

Q problem would be whitewashed. Gerald Hoffer even took the trouble to ring Mike personally to thank him for helping gov.uk out of a situation which was a political minefield.

"Mike, it is I, Gerald. May I take this opportunity to thank you for being the catalyst which has enabled us to implement this bold plan to help Susie Q to rein in her temper. Will you please arrange for her to be returned to Geneva once the good news about Ian being cleared has hit the airwaves and digital media?"

"Yes, Gerald. I will only do that, though, when I have seen the public announcement about the WRO's mistake. It must be clear that blaming Ian for running away and stealing Susie Q, was their error."

"My goodness Mike. You are a careful man. I can't say anything officially, but there may be a knighthood in this for you, for services to the UK government, in respect of robotics research."

They each disconnected from their electrajot call, and Mike thought:

'Sir Michael of Anick, that has a nice ring.'

(The knighthood was granted in the end, and Mike became Sir Michael of Branscombe, which was where he lived at the time.)

I'm Back!

Chapter 43

In the meantime, Alice, Ian, and Susie Q had crossed over the River Severn in their aerobus. They saw two bridges leading from England to Wales. Ian being Ian, he noted mentally that if they were going the other way, the bridges would lead from Wales to England. When he was young, his parents had taken him to the Gower for a holiday in an Edwardian guest house. He had loved the beautiful beaches on the peninsula. He was instructed by their Welsh landlady that the Gower was always to be referred to as the Gower and not the Gower Peninsula.

She also told him to ignore any chilly reception which the family received from the locals. She said it was nothing personal, but Welsh people didn't like the English. She also said the people living in the Gower didn't even like the rest of the Welsh population.

His parents and his little sister Ida (now long gone, due to a serious robot horse riding accident), had been for a long walk after dumping their cases in the guest house. He remembered that it was called Pilgrim's Progress, after the people who owned their holiday abode, Mr. and Mrs. Frank Pilgrim. His sister had asked her Mum:

"Where's the pig?"

She had laughed and replied:

"The pig?"

Yes, the one called Rim."

Ian thought that if his sister was joking, it was quite a good effort for a three-year-old.

The aerobus carrying Ian and Alice to the Gower hovered over Cardiff Castle, and the pilot made a scenic detour over Swansea so he could show The Mumbles to his passengers. The Mumbles are famous. They are on a headland which has two rounded projections on the western edge of Swansea Bay. He told Ian and Alice that they might have been named thus by French sailors.

"It's believed that they said les mamelles, meaning the breasts. That's supposed to be why they are now called The Mumbles, in a corruption of the French name."

Ian thought that although they were pretty, they didn't look anything like real breasts. Very soon, they were near Rhossili Bay, one of the most striking beaches in the UK. The pilot had told them that there was no aPad near their destination, which was an old medium-sized church on the outskirts of the village. The church had been converted into living and praying accommodation, firstly for The Order of Mercy, and then latterly for the members of The Order of Murphy.

Most of these members were female, but the three men who had sought shelter were still there, according to Anne Telope (whose contact details had been found by Emma using COPPER.) Ian spoke to Anne, but he told her not to forewarn anybody that they would be coming. The trio seeking sanctuary had been Father Spud Murphy, Brother Jack Ass and Brother Terry Lean. These gentlemen had originally been part of a thieving gang which preyed on householders and walkers in and near Swansea. It was also suspected that they were dabbling in importing drugs and selling them throughout the UK.

They were not very good at being crooks. Although they knew what they wanted to do, they did little planning and tended to get side-tracked during their criminal activities. During one of their poorly thought out burglaries, they had found some very acceptable five-star cognac. This was obviously preferable to brandy pills. Spud started to drink the cognac, but the other two joined him happily. They had opened a bottle each.

I'm Back!

Spud had waxed lyrical:

"This is wonderful It's fruity, warm and it's got subtle aromas."

The other two had agreed. They drank a bottle each, and then fell asleep on the floor of the living room, which was where they had found the cognac. They didn't wake up until the next morning. Luckily, the owners of the of the house hadn't returned. The three men had seriously bad headaches. That was all they took away from that particular attempt at pilferage.

They had arrived at The Order of Mercy's premises after being rumbled trying to steal valuables from a rich man's mansion. It was five miles or so from Swansea. Earlier that day they had broken into the mansion. Unfortunately, the owner, Tab Collar, and his mistress were engaged in some horizontal jogging when Jack Ass opened the master bedroom door. Tab was nearing the age when he would be deselected, but even at 46 he was a fine figure of a man.

He stood six feet two, and he was fit and muscular. He had shaved his head and looked like a person who would not take kindly to burglars disturbing his afternoon delight. His paramour was his personal assistant, Daisy Chain. (How much more personal could her work get?) She was blonde, well-endowed, and ridiculously cute. As she was in a state of undress, she was even more of a delight to behold than if she had been fully clothed. Jack had quite an eyeful.

Daisy had screamed and reached for the bedsheet to cover up her mumbles. Tab had reached over leisurely. He had opened the drawer in the bedside cabinet next to where he had been half sitting and half lying, on the right-hand side of the huge bed.

He had pulled out a gun and said:

"I think it's time for you and anybody else with you to leave, don't you? I'll count to five, and if you haven't scarpered by then, I'll turn you into a colander."

Jack could see he meant business. He was out of the bedroom in three seconds, collected his pals, and he had left as quickly as he could. Tab shouted over the bannisters:

"You've picked on the wrong man. I'll get my people to track you down. I only let you go because I didn't want my lady friend to be worried. Make no mistake, I've got plenty of people who will tell me where you are. I'll send my best men to finish you off wherever you are. This is only a temporary reprieve, as I don't want any blood spilt in my house."

Spud and Terry had ran out of the house with Jack. They had kept up a frantic pace until they reached an old car which they had stolen from a barn near the mansion. Although it was ancient, the real owner was obviously a classic car freak, as it started easily and once they were away, Terry asked Spud where they should go.

"Just keep driving. A friend of mine, whom I met when she was running a bawdy house, Anne Telope, is now living with the members of The Order of Mercy. They live in an old church about six miles from here. I know where it is. Take a left turn in about two hundred yards, Terry."

Terry had nodded and soon swerved down a tiny lane. Spud had kept giving directions to him and not long after that they could see a church on top of a hill. They turned into a small car park, and Terry had braked hard as a nun walked across their car's path.

"What the bloody hell do you think you're doing? Be more careful you great ape. Sorry, I mean do have a care my good man! You almost knocked me over. I'm Sister Matic, and I bid you welcome."

Spud had whispered to his cronies:

"Leave this to me."

He had continued in a louder voice:

"Sister Matic, we come seeking succour and protection. We hail from London and I'm Father Murphy of Murphy's Ecclesiastical Church. These are my trusted colleagues, Brother Jack, and Brother Terry. We're in dire trouble. Our movement is

I'm Back!

new, but we've been attacked by unbelievers for preaching the good word. We managed to get away from our detractors, who incorrectly believe that we are just criminals. May we stay with you until things cool off a little?"

Sister Matic was no fool. She had joined The Order of Mercy after having given up being a lady of the night. All of the nuns in the order were fallen women. Nearly all of them had also been wrongdoers in other ways. Because of their past, they had adopted a vow to forgive all other transgressors, no matter what their previous misdeeds were. However, she could spot ne'er do wells a mile off. She had smiled, and she had beckoned to them to follow her into the old church.

'Father Murphy' and his two friends were soon extremely popular with the nuns, who had forgotten just how good it was to be in the company of men. At first, Sister Angelina the Jolly (Anne Telope as was), had mixed feelings about being reacquainted with Spud Murphy, who had formerly been her pimp (before she was the Madam of her 'gentlemen's club', which was called 'Brandy and Armchair.') She kept her misgivings to herself. Some local yobs tried to frighten the nuns one evening, and Spud, Terry and Jack gave them a good hiding. Sister Angelina the Jolly mentally deleted her qualms about meeting up with Spud again.

The nuns told Father Murphy that he should call himself Father Spud, but he said he'd never liked his nickname. He said he would therefore prefer to continue to be known as Father Murphy. Very soon, the nuns came to rely on their engaging friend, and finally the fake Father was elected as their new leader. That was when they changed their name to The Order of Murphy.

Ian, Alice, and Susie Q were dropped off by the aerobus pilot on the golden sands of Rhossili bay. Ian set his electrajot to plot their route to the former nunnery. It was a longer walk than he had expected it to be, but they finally saw the ex-church with a hand-painted sign saying, 'The Order of Murphy – Formerly, The Order of Mercy.' The lettering was amateurish, but at least Ian now knew that they were in the right place.

John Bobin

They walked up to the front door, and Ian noted the old-fashioned doorbell. He saw that you had to pull a chain. The chain looked suspiciously like a chain from an antiquated high-flush toilet. Only Ian knew what that was, and he didn't comment.

The bell worked well, and they heard shuffling footsteps. A nun greeted them.

"Hallo and welcome. I'm Sister Beverley. Please enter and partake of some refreshment."

She led them into a narrow hall. At the very end it opened out into the old church's main space. The pews, the nave and the altar were still there.

A nun rushed over to Ian:

"How lovely to see you, Ian, and your friends."

Ian was delighted to see that the nun was Sister Angelina the Jolly.

"Anne, I'm so pleased it's you. We need to hide away for a while."

"We all know about your escapades Ian. And these ladies must be Alice Nuisance and Susie Q. We've seen you on Honey and Paul's holovision news programme. We're fully au fait with the fact that you are on the run."

"Yes, that's why we need to hole up here, if that's OK."

A stout but imposing man had joined them.

"You're most welcome. We never turn away people who are in trouble," said Father Murphy. (He was the latest person to be wondering how best to spend the reward money which he hoped to claim from the WRO.)

Sister Angelina the Jolly was chatting to Alice and Susie Q. She admitted that she had always fancied Ian when they were young, and she was called Anne. She had recognised Alice, who told her she still loved him. Susie Q appeared to be furious and her face looked as if it was suffused with blood, which was surprising as she didn't have any. Luckily, she managed to keep her temper.

Chapter 44

At first, Ian and Susie Q enjoyed living with the members of The Order of Murphy. They soon found that the so-called nuns, the brothers, and Father Murphy were not even vaguely holier than thou. They relaxed for a few days, but they were still wondering how Mike and Tosser were getting on in Geneva. Mike had suggested that Ian should maintain radio silence, until he saw the promised press release saying that he had been cleared.

Every day, Ian tuned in to news programmes, especially Honey Blonde and Paul Somebody's mushy items. On the third day of their stay, he rose early, breakfasted on food and drink pills, and then tuned in on the holovision, to see if his pardon had been revealed. Honey was on screen, simpering girlishly, and her magnificent ornaments were in almost full view. Susie Q glared at Ian. She could see that he was nearly dribbling while he looked at Honey. Suddenly, Honey sat up straight and said:

"We've got a fantastic News Flash for you. For those of you who have been clamouring for further news about Ian Tudeep and Susie Q, your wait has not been in vain."

Paul took over the story:

"It's now been revealed that the WRO made a right royal muck up, when they told the press and the police that Ian had run away, and that he'd stolen Susie Q. A senior official at the WRO, Mr. A. Scapegoat has confirmed that he gave Ian full permission to leave Geneva for a short holiday. Furthermore, he says he told Ian that he could take Susie Q with him. Mr. Scapegoat thought that she would be good at minding Ian, before they both went back to Geneva. He told reporters that he had been on an extended trek in Nepal when the news broke. He didn't hear about Ian Tudeep and Susie Q being sought by the police, until he returned to Geneva."

Ian wondered if people would think that Mr. Scapegoat should have just opted for a holovision 6D experience, rather than a real trek in The Himalayas. He knew that a small number of people did still take real holidays, so perhaps it was a good cover up story after all.

Honey bosomed Paul out of the way.

"Poor Ian and Susie. They had to hide, as they were frightened of the consequences if they were caught by the police. We now have DCI Emma Bobby on the line."

"Good morning, Honey and Paul. I can confirm what you just told your viewers. We are now encouraging Ian and Susie Q to go back to the WRO's complex in Geneva. The aim will be to double check that Susie Q is still functioning correctly, and to do further follow up checks on Ian regarding his AR."

Ian said:

"Wow, that's fantastic news. We are in the clear! I'll contact Mike and Tosser before making plans for us to go back to Switzerland."

Susie Q wasn't listening. She wasn't there. Ian hadn't noticed her leaving the room. She had noticed Ian slavering over Honey once more, and she had decided to give him some of his own medicine. She had gone to see Father Murphy, in his bedroom, and was flirting with him outrageously. He couldn't believe his luck. He put his arms round her and kissed her. By now, Susie Q was a little worried and was hoping that Ian would turn up before things got too tricky.

Father Murphy was breathing very heavily and taking liberties with Susie Q's realistic appendages. Her face was once again scarlet, and she was sweating, although she didn't realise what that was. The Reverend Father moved his hand down towards

I'm Back!

her special receptacle. She started to shout at the top of her voice.

"Leave me alone, you odious excuse for a man. If you don't unhand me right now, you'll live to regret trying to fiddle with me. You don't realise just how strong I am."

"Come on little girl, I just wanted to have a little fun. You're so sexy."

Susie Q managed to extricate her arms from his cuddling easily, and she put one hand on his shoulder. She also pulled the arm which led to his exploratory hand away from his shoulder.

"Ouch! That really hurt. Don't do that!"

She ignored this entreaty, and she pulled the arm so hard it was torn off at the shoulder. Spurts of blood covered her and Father Murphy instantly. He was screaming in intense pain, and by this time Ian had come to see what all the noise was about. He could hardly believe his eyes.

Susie Q gave Ian the torn off arm, and she said to Father Murphy:

"That's what happens when you mess with Susie Q!"

More people had rushed to the room, having been disturbed by the noise. Alice, Sister Angelina the Jolly, Sister Matic and Brother Terry Lean stood at the door, open mouthed in horror and amazement. Ian had by now realised that he, Susie Q and Alice had to leave the old church as soon as possible. Father Murphy was holding his jagged, ruined shoulder. He underlined Ian's decision to get out by saying:

"You three need to go right now. I'll give you five minutes to pack and leave. If by that time you haven't gone, I'll get Terry and Jack to deal with you, and that won't be a good solution for you. I did take liberties, so I've got no intention of reporting this to the authorities."

He was thinking as fast as he could, even though he was in agony. He knew that the police were probably still looking for him, Terry, and Jack for various burglaries, scams and some violent offences which they had committed in a turf war with other minor criminals in their hometown of Bristol.

The three men had also trespassed on other drug dealers' stamping grounds, and he felt that they still had to stay at The Order of Murphy for a bit. (They did have a bit while they were there, as that was readily available from the ladies who used to do it for money, but now did it for fun.) Father Murphy was still clutching his badly wounded shoulder. He didn't know what to do about his arm, but he accepted it back when Ian handed it to him. Spud was also still wary about Tab Collar's threat to track them down. All in all, he felt he had no choice but to get rid of the three guests and to keep his head down. He was sure his compadres would agree.

Ian, Susie Q and Alice departed tout de suite. Ian and Alice were now even more desperate to find a way for Susie Q to be fixed. Her aggressive second nature had to be curbed. Susie Q was singing as they walked towards the centre of Rhossili.

"If you knew Susie, like I know Susie. That fixed him. He's armless now."

She laughed, but to Ian and Susie it sounded more like a bloodthirsty victory cry.

Father Murphy asked Jack Ass to patch up his arm. Jack had once been a doctor. He had never been very good, and he had been ejected from his posts more than once. However, he knew how to deal with wounds, as he was used in that capacity by various people who needed quick and quiet attention to injuries.

Day by day, Murphy grew more and more worried that Tab Collar would track them down. His concern was well-founded. A few months later, several vehicles pulled up in the car park outside the church. They were all black, and three of them were hearses. A man got out of the leading car. He was dressed smartly in a three-piece black suit, and the jacket had tails. He reached inside the car, pulled out a top hat and placed it on his head. He and five other men walked to the door of the old church. One of the men rang the bell. Sister Angelina the Jolly opened the door and welcomed them:

"Good morning gentlemen. What can I do for you?"

"We've come to collect three bodies."

I'm Back!

"I don't understand."

"Father Murphy contacted us."

"In that case, please enter."

She took them into Father Murphy's office, where he was seated with Brother Jack and Brother Terry.

"These men said they've come to collect three bodies. I fear there may have been a misunderstanding. However, they said that you asked them to come here."

Father Murphy blanched.

"Please leave us, Sister Angelina. I need to speak to these men alone."

The nun did as she was told.

One of the men closed the door. The man in the top hat looked at Father Murphy:

"We've been sent here by Tab Collar. He's told us that you had the temerity to burst into a room where he was having a confidential conversation with his PA."

"It wasn't…"

"Be quiet! We've brought special transport for you three. You'll soon be very comfortable."

He motioned to his colleagues. Three of them pulled out guns and shot Murphy, Ass and Lean. They used silencers, and thus the nuns heard nothing. In spite of their leader's promise to make them comfortable in the special vehicles, Tab Collar's men just turned on their heels and left the room. They closed the door to Murphy's office very gently. They hid their guns in their trouser waistbands as they headed for the door.

Sister Angelina came out of her room as they walked down the hallway:

"Thank you dear lady. It appears that there's been a misunderstanding. We're leaving. Father Murphy and the other two gentlemen are praying. They asked not to be disturbed for one hour."

"Bless you gentlemen."

After the hour was up, Sister Angelina went to the office and tapped on the door. There was no reply. She tapped again, and this time she opened the door. She was horrified by what she saw. The three bodies were lying in various ungainly positions. There was a lot of blood. She saw that Father Murphy had a white card in his hand. On the card was a message:

'With compliments: TC'

The nuns were astounded by Sister Angelina's news, and she wasn't quite so jolly after finding the corpses. They were all used to coming up against denizens of the underworld, due to their previous employment in the oldest profession in the world. They decided that they would bury the bodies in the garden at the back of the old church. This used to be a graveyard. They thought it would be an apt resting place. It took them some time, but they took turns in digging the new graves. They dumped the bodies in the holes unceremoniously.

They did say a few words. They were:

"Good riddance to bad rubbish."

Ever since Father Murphy had become armless, he and his men had been more and more laddish, and they had used the former ladies of the night cruelly. They had also been violent with some of the nuns. The ladies had even wondered if they should call the police. They had concluded that as The Order of Murphy was not a recognised religious order, there could be unforeseen difficulties. This was especially so as they had all had previous dealings with the police regarding their chosen profession, and most of them for other misdemeanours as well as prostitution. So far, they hadn't done anything which might necessitate them being deselected. Being in possession of three dead men was not very good. All the same, they knew that the fake undertakers had done them a favour

I'm Back!

Chapter 45

Ian decided on behalf of all of them, that it would be best if they went to Eddie Biggs' barn in Happisburgh. He knew that Eddie would shelter them for a few days whilst they decided what to do next. He gave Susie Q a coat of his to cover her blood stains which had emanated from Father Murphy's gushing wound.

"We can summon an aerobus, and we can now pay for it using my eWallet without any qualms as we are not being pursued by the police."

He proceeded to make the booking using his eWallet, which had direct access to his funds. The confirmation came quickly, and they asked that the pilot should set the aerobus down on the beach at Rhossili. They walked as quickly as they could to the green cliffs overlooking the pretty bay. Finding a way down, Alice held Susie Q's hand as they part walked, and part scrambled onto the beach.

The sun was shining, the sky was a translucent pale blue, and there were no clouds at all. The sea was calm, and there was a refreshing sea breeze. Ian also noticed the usual, clean, sweet, and pungent smell of ozone that seems to permeate the atmosphere on all beaches. Sea gulls gave their plaintive cry, and it would have been tempting to spend the day on the beach, but for their aerobus booking.

Some small children were playing near the water's edge. They were happily splashing each other in the shallows, whilst their parents looked on adoringly. The whole scene was wonderfully idyllic. Ian spoke to the father of the children and told him that an aerobus was coming to pick them up. The Dad rounded up his family, so that they were out of the way of the hovering vehicle.

Ian, Susie Q and Alice clambered up the steps which had been lowered once it was safely on the ground. As they went into the passenger space, the pilot said to Susie Q:

"My goodness, young lady, I bet you're sweltering in that coat. Aren't you baking?"

Susie Q said:

"No, I don't make bread or cakes."

The pilot laughed, as he thought that Susie Q had made a joke.

'Perhaps she's not very well,' he thought. 'Maybe she feels the cold, poor girl.'

Susie Q clutched the coat closer to her body, as she didn't want to reveal the blood all over her torso and her guilty arm, which had so easily yanked off Father Brown's own upper limb.

Chapter 46

The team at WRO; Mike, Tosser, Hiram, the dreaded Yoder and Adam Thurley had seen the same news flash which had alerted Ian, Alice, and Susie Q to the fact that they were now officially no longer being sought by the police. All that remained was for the Magnificent Five to open up Susie Q and first of all to implant the mechanical amygdala.

Secondly, they had to do some rather complicated joining up of Susie's inner workings to ensure that the MA would stop her from getting violent in the future. This also involved finding a way in which to splice the microscopic, genetically manipulated DNA to the MA, so that it could act like a temper thermostat. They wanted it to cool things down if Susie Q over-reacted in the future.

They were in the boardroom on the twenty seventh floor of the main building within the vast WRO complex, which overlooked Lake Geneva. Ian knew that the lake was the largest body of water in Switzerland, and it looked beautiful and serene on that lovely day. They were preparing for Susie Q's operation, which they had entitled Project Q Fix.

Hiram was summing up what needed to be done:

"Mike and Tosser can continue to stay here for as long as they want to, in the company flat which we've made available to them. Ian Tudeep is welcome in the flat too. Mike, please would you or Tosser let Ian know that we are ready to welcome him and Susie Q back here. Please make it clear that there will be no danger of any repercussions regarding Ian's flight from Geneva with Susie Q. We'll prepare one of our larger operating theatres, and Karl Yoder will head up the team who will complete Project Q Fix.

We'll need other people to be involved in tending to Susie Q in the theatre. They won't be fully privy to the real reason why we are doing this. They will also not know that the op is being co-funded by the UK government and the WRO. As far as they will know, it's just an extension of the work we did to inject human DNA into Susie's brain. It was a secret then, but it's been all over the news now.

The WRO contingent of the Project Q Fix team will now leave the room, so you can speak privately and quietly to Mr. Tudeep. He'll have lots of questions, and that'll be understandable. Try to reassure him, so that he can in turn make sure that Susie Q is at ease with what we have planned for her."

Hiram, Karl, and Adam left the plush boardroom, with its floor to ceiling windows and the terrific view of the lake.

Mike suggested that Tosser should use his electrajot to project a large virtual screen into the boardroom, so that when he spoke to Ian, he could see both of them. Within ten seconds or so, Mike and Tosser could view Ian in Eddie Biggs' living room, and Ian could chat with Mike and Tosser in the boardroom as if they were all together. Tosser took the lead in telling Ian what they had been doing in Switzerland.

"Hi, Ian. I can see you're back at Eddie's place?"

"Yes," said Ian, "we had to leave Rhossili for reasons which I can't explain on an open electrajot session. Suffice it to say that Susie Q needs to be fixed even more urgently than we had realised."

"Is this likely to impede your freedom?"

"I don't think so, but it'd be best if we came to Geneva as soon as possible, if the team is ready. I hope its members can sort things out for Susie Q."

"We've come up with a solution, which has been tested on robots like Susie Q with remarkable success. I can get the WRO to send you tickets by rMail so you can be

I'm Back!

teleported from Heathrow to Geneva tomorrow morning. Can you make your way to a hotel near Heathrow, so that you can stay overnight?"

"We can, but I'm not certain that I've got enough in my bank account to pay for another aerobus and digs for the night. My eWallet needs to be topped up. "

"If you check your personal bank account, you'll see that you're much richer than you thought you were. The WRO and the UK government have sent you a large compensation sum, which should set you back on your feet."

"That's great news. I haven't checked my account lately. We've had a lot on our minds, which I'll tell you and Mike about when we get there. The conversation must be in private."

"That's fine. I'll ask Hiram to get those teleportation tickets to you pronto."

Chapter 47

Ian relayed the gist of his conversation with Tosser to Susie Q when she returned to the barn. She had been walking on the beach with Alice, Eddie, and his dogs, when Tosser had electrajotted him. They had walked to Cart Gap and back, and they had enjoyed the peace and quiet. They had seen a few seals in the sea, and Eeny, Meeny, Miny and Moe had barked at them enthusiastically, thus temporarily ruining the peace and quiet but making them laugh.

She was pleased to hear that a potential solution to her problem had been found, but she was apprehensive about having another operation. Ian told her firmly, but as gently as possible, that she couldn't go on having outbursts of temper tantrums, and furthermore she had to be stopped from being violent.

"But Ian, I've only been protecting myself and showing my love for you. These tantrums, as you call them, were also a way of expressing how my feelings have affected me. I can't really understand what the big fuss is about. For example, Walter Nuisance definitely deserved what I did to him. When I tore him to bits, I thought that I was being helpful. And what about Father Murphy? He wasn't only a fraud, but he was a sex pest. I had to tear his arm off to stop him from invading my special receptacle."

"My little darling, that's not the human way to do things. If men or women carried on like that they'd be picked up by the Population Police and taken to the National Deselection Facility, to be humanely killed. In your case, of course, they'd arrange for you to be disassembled and for the pieces to be sent to a scrap yard for potential recycling. If you love me, really love me, let it happen.

I'm Back!

Come with me to Geneva, and you'll be fixed. The WRO have arranged for three top bods to work with Mike and Tosser. They've worked hard to find a solution. It's taken them weeks of exceptionally long hours. They've slaved hard to devise a way to stop your fits of rage and the associated violence. They've have come up with a successful breakthrough, which has been tested on robots just like you. You've got no choice."

"Very well. I know how much you love me. I believe that you wouldn't tell me to do this, unless you thought there was no other way to get help."

"I've already booked an aerobus, and we'll stay in a hotel near Heathrow tonight. I now have the teleportation tickets on my electrajot, and we'll use them tomorrow morning, so we can be beamed straight to Geneva. I'm sure everything will be OK."

He felt ashamed that he was not owning up to her that he too was nervous about the outcome of Project Q Fix. However, he knew that Susie Q couldn't be allowed to kill people and rip arms off at will.

Their journey to Heathrow was fast and comfortable. Ian had bought first class tickets on a limousine class aerobus. Once they neared Heathrow, he looked down on the scenery below, which was mostly comprised of old buildings interspersed with single storey and stacked condenselows. A lot of the newer buildings had been built on what used to be the M25 and the M4.

Ian had seen early maps and films about these motorways, and he wondered how car drivers had put up with sitting in what they used to call traffic jams. The hotel was in the terminal complex. It was clean and functional but not luxurious. Ian didn't care, as he just wanted to be on his way to Switzerland with his dear Susie Q. They had booked a double room, but Susie Q was so frightened she said she didn't want any hanky-panky that night.

Ian was always impressed with her extensive vocabulary. He had asked her about that when she had been tending to his every need during his post op period. She had said that as she and all the other Susies were still learning, the universal consciousness that they experienced meant that all of them had many new words in their lexicon every day.

He remembered that conversation, and he wondered how far the Susies' knowledge network spread. He was certain that all Susies who were within the WRO complex would get push updates every day, but he sincerely hoped that once he and Susie Q were well away from the organisation's headquarters the other Susies did not receive daily titbits of information about what he and Susie Q had been up to.

In the morning, Ian had a pill breakfast, which was supposed to taste like a ham and cheese panini. He followed that up with some coffee pills. The pills were an abysmal failure in the taste test. He had dozed fitfully all night. Susie Q was unaware of his restlessness as she was in standby mode, whilst she was being charged up.

They had no undue delays when they were waiting for vacant teleportation booths, because the WRO had sent priority tickets. It seemed like no time at all before they were in the WRO reception area. The receptionist Susie smiled at Ian, and he wondered if he had met her before. He started to explain who he was, but she gave him and Susie Q their name tags rather brusquely, and then she asked them, rather sharply, to be seated. She spoke into her immersephone, and then she told them:

"Mr. Anick will come to see you soon. He said he's arranged for you to have a private meeting with him and Mr. Pancake. By the way, I already know you. My name is Susie OAT236, but I was called Enid Brighton for a short while. I didn't appreciate the way that you just left me sitting in the teleportation room without even saying goodbye."

Ian almost felt guilty for previously lying to a robot. It was true that Enid had been left holding the baby, as he and Susie Q (with the same voice as Enid Brighton but with the added bonus of a special receptacle), had absconded. He wondered why the WRO hadn't sent her back to One Amour Time.

I'm Back!

Mike came towards them as he entered the reception area. He seemed very pleased to see them.

"What does it feel like to be a rich man, Ian?"

"Pretty good. Let's go to that meeting room, so I can level with you about something which will be bad news."

Mike opened his eyes wide, but to give him his due he didn't press Ian for further details. He recognised that Ian wanted to reveal whatever the news was in secret. Once they were in a meeting room, Mike pushed a button so that a large red light lit up outside. There was a terse message spelled out on the light, saying, 'Meeting in Progress – Do not Enter.' Tosser was seated at a long table, but he stood up, walked over, and shook hands with Ian. He also kissed Susie Q on the cheek.

'Why didn't I think of that, mused Mike?'

Maybe that was the correct protocol for greeting special robots like Susie Q?

They all sat down and had some tea and biscuit pills, except for Susie. She told them that she wanted to recharge herself just in case she ran out of juice. She plugged herself in, after selecting the right mains adapter, and promptly fell asleep. Ian told Mike and Tosser about Susie Q's temperamental behaviour, culminating in the removal of Father Murphy's arm. They were shocked and could hardly believe that her behaviour had continued to deteriorate so dramatically. Tosser walked up and down. He turned to face them after about the fifth perambulation of the meeting room and said:

"We've got no time to lose. Ian, do you realise that this new operation is ground-breaking? That's good in one way, because it's had close attention from Mike and me, as well as three senior WRO eggheads. The tests that were performed were put in place by the five of us, but we'd got other people double and triple checking our observations. What we now plan to do to Susie Q is to repeat an operation that's already been done many times recently on other robots. The bad bit is that there is no certainty that the results will be long lasting. We can't afford to wait for years, or even months, in view

John Bobin

of Susie Q's viciousness when she loses her rag. Do you understand and agree Ian?"

"I'm afraid I do. Susie Q got away with murdering Walter Nuisance by the skin of her teeth. If it hadn't been for the culpability felt by the WRO and the PM for their part in creating her monstrous tendencies, she would've been headed for the rubbish dump. As far as the arm incident is concerned, I was surprised that Spud Murphy let us go without any violence from him or his henchmen.

To be honest, I think there is more to it than he told us. Although he may have been afraid that the police would have an unhealthy interest in the three of them, it's far more likely that they had been treading on the toes of much more major criminals, who were probably into importing and selling drugs on a larger scale."

Mike was relieved that Ian had agreed so readily to Susie being opened up and fixed, hopefully for good.

Tosser looked sad, but he said:

"There's no other way, Ian. If we don't do this, you could even be Susie Q's next victim. We've already planned for her procedure to be carried out tomorrow afternoon. The five-man team will be assisted by a few other WRO technicians and nurses. I'll show you to the company flat in which Mike and I have been staying. You can stay there too. It's a penthouse suite on the top floor of this building. Mike will now go to tell Hiram that the op is on for tomorrow. Susie Q will be collected by Adam Thurley from the company flat at two p.m."

Tosser took Susie Q and Ian to the company flat, after Ian had used the wake words. She was calmer than she had been for some time. The flat was magnificent. Under normal circumstances Ian would have been delighted to stay in such palatial surroundings.

After Tosser had gone, Susie Q said, rather wistfully:

"I wasn't really being recharged. I heard everything that was said. I'm resigned to my fate. I realise that all three of you, the man I love and two terrific friends, believe

I'm Back!

that there is no alternative but for me to submit myself to the op. As it may be my very last time, I'll now yield myself to you. Do with me what you will."

They retired to the massive bedroom, and they were soon making love. Ian wondered if it would ever happen again.

Chapter 48

The operation to implant the MA, and to link it to Susie Q's various bits and bobs went well. Implanting the MA was not as difficult as it might have been, as the team had been given plenty of practice by using the other Susies. Linking the MA to the DNA was tricky.

Tosser had also taken the opportunity to challenge the WRO boffins about whether or not they had also used a real human brain. They were adamant that they had not done so. They suggested that Tosser should take a look for himself. He was relieved when he did so, as he noted that they were telling the truth.

After an exhausting four-hour procedure, they closed Susie Q up. As she was a robot there was no blood, no potential problems with DVT and no sewing up to be done. Over a period of two weeks they checked Susie Q many times, and they finally gave her a clean bill of health. The WRO transferred the agreed extra payments to Mike and Tosser.

Ian decided to take Susie Q back to Eddie's place. (Tosser went with them as Rita was staying at the barn.) He thought that the peaceful surroundings might help her to adjust to the way that the MA would work. He had asked Eddie if he would mind them returning to his home. Eddie said that Alice was also still staying with him, and that she and Sally had become great friends.

Their journey to Happisburgh seemed to take ages. There was a teleportation to Heathrow, and two different aerobus trips before they got their haven.

I'm Back!

Chapter 49

Eddie always loved peace and quiet, but he also relished seeing his friends. Ian, Tosser and Susie Q were now back from Geneva, and Eddie, Rita and Alice were pleased to see them. Sally was still living at her own place in Happisburgh, but she arrived at the barn soon after the wanderers came back from Switzerland. Ian and Tosser had decided between them not to dwell too much on the Project Q Fix operation. They believed that Susie Q would benefit by keeping as calm as possible. She understood their unspoken desire to keep off the subject. In fact, she was relieved that it would not be made the sole subject of conversation.

Tosser had some news. He told his friends that he and Rita had originally wanted to sell Tosser's home and for them to live in Rita's condenselow.

"However, Rita likes my old cottage here much more than her place in Morelli Heights. She says it has more character. The distaff side of the relationship overruled me. I can afford to do the place up now, and Rita will be my personal design consultant."

The distaff side poked her tongue out at the spear side, who retaliated by pulling a funny face. Tosser was happy to see Ian and Susie Q back in more normal surroundings. He gave Ian a man hug and kissed Susie Q on the cheek. Eddie pumped Ian's hand so hard his shoulder hurt, but not as much as Father Murphy's did. Susie Q leaned in for a kiss from Eddie, who obliged willingly. He could still hardly believe that she was just a robot. With all these friendly greetings in evidence, Alice wanted to kiss Ian. She played safe and asked Susie Q if she minded. She said she had no objections.

Alice kissed both of his cheeks and cuddled him.

Ian and Susie Q loved being back in Norfolk. Eddie and his dogs made a big fuss of them. Eeny, Meeny, Miny and Moe came and stood in front of anybody who was sitting down, and they glared at them until the lazy humans realised that it was time for a walk on the beach. When the dogs succeeded in persuading anybody to take them for walkies, they wore a triumphant air. The beach always had some interesting smells and they nosed around happily. They were in their element.

They ran into the surf, rolled in the remains of dead sea gulls, and explored patches of dumped refuse. They were ever hopeful there might be something edible in the rubbish which was strewn over the beach by thoughtless people. The litter louts couldn't even be bothered to bag it up and take it home. When the dogs got back to Eddie's barn, they were usually wet and stinking to high heaven. Luckily, Eddie had an outside tap which could deliver warm water. Whoever had taken the four scamps to the beach was obliged to wash them down before they entered Eddie's barn.

When Ian, Alice and Susie Q finally left Happisburgh, they thanked Eddie for his friendship and for being so helpful, in their hour of need.

"You've been a star Eddie, and an absolute saviour to us, and we'll never forget that. I love it here in Happisburgh, but we're going to push off tomorrow morning, and will leave you in peace. I'm sure Eeny, Meeny, Miny and Moe will be pleased to get you back to themselves. We have decided to go back to Southwold to put my condenselow on the market and to wrap up a few more loose ends. Alice is coming with us, and we'll make an early start, in the morning. I've already booked an aerobus."

Eddie didn't seem surprised, and he said:

"I'll miss you all. Tosser and Rita are going back to Broadstairs tomorrow. It will be mighty quiet here."

His four huge dogs started barking furiously at some pigeons in the garden.

"Maybe it won't be too quiet for me after all."

I'm Back!

They had a slap-up celebration meal and they drank far too much of Eddie's Revenge ale. After their overdose of the strong beer they became quite maudlin. They finally retired to their slumbers, way past their normal bedtimes or for Susie Q, her plug-in time.

Chapter 50

When Ian, Alice and Susie Q were back in the Blueberry Hill complex, they had some tea and scone pills, put their feet up and agreed that they could now look forward to a less stressful life. Alice said she might think about having AR. She was forty-five, but she was a few months younger than Ian had been in his previous incarnation. She wasn't looking forward to being carted off to the NDF by the Population Police in five years' time. Alice suddenly had a brainwave.

"Ian, why don't I buy your condenselow? I like it here in Southwold."

Ian had been wondering if Alice would sell the house in Southend to him, and so they compared the market value of a condenselow in Southwold to a house in Southend. They were almost on a par, as Southwold was a much more sought-after location than Southend. They decided to swap properties.

"You can stay here anyway if you want to, Alice, until the paperwork has been completed. Susie Q and I'll go to Southend as soon as possible, if that's OK by you."

Alice was pleased to agree. She threw her arms around Ian and kissed him on the cheek. To her great surprise, Susie Q didn't feel jealous at all. Ian kept in mind the fact that Tosser had warned him that the Project Q Fix procedure, had been the last-ditch thing that could be done for Susie Q. He had told Ian, in secret, that Susie Q's emotional control might not last.

He had said that at the worst, Susie Q might collapse completely after a massive tantrum. It was also likely that even if she didn't have a real melt down, if she experienced emotions that she couldn't control completely, she might gradually cease

I'm Back!

to function anyway. Ian had felt totally despondent when Tosser laid those facts on the table. He had to keep quiet about his worries, as he knew that he couldn't tell Susie Q about Tosser's misgivings without complicating matters.

Chapter 51

Ian and Susie Q liked Southend, even though it was down at heel. Ian said it was like an old lady who had once been a real beauty. It was as if there was something there still, but she was not the same as she had been when it was a ravishing teenager. Susie Q told him that his analogy seemed to be getting lost in translation. Ian was wondering if analogy would be a good name for the study of bottoms.

Alice's old house needed a lot of TLC. Ian was pleased to pay for it to be brought up to scratch. He was now in a much better financial position than he had been, thanks to the payoff from the WRO and the UK government. He had also received a handsome written apology from the police, and another one from the Prime Minister, on behalf of the UK government.

The letters had been waiting for him on the door mat in Southwold. They were couched in similar terms. Both missives expressed immense regret that he had been under suspicion by the police. They mentioned a 'dreadful misunderstanding' regarding his escape from Geneva with Susie Q. Finally, they apologised for all the undue bad publicity. They were sorry for the worry and concern experienced by Ian. Although the words were different, the themes matched. Ian thought he saw Hoffer's hand in the drafting of the letters.

In due course, Ian was to receive another letter from the WRO. This expressed extreme sorrow for an unfortunate administration error. They apologised for this mistake which had led them to believe that Ian left without permission. Furthermore, the letter repeated that Ian had been absolved of the allegation that he had stolen Susie

I'm Back!

Q. Needless to say, none of these letters mentioned the unofficial large payment made to Ian which came jointly from the coffers of the WRO and the UK government.

Susie Q was happy in Alice's house. She had no feelings of regret. She still didn't feel any guilt for killing Walter Nuisance, nor in disarming Father Murphy. She regarded her dismemberment of Walter's body as a necessary action. She mentally justified it as an action designed to protect her friends and to tidy Alice's house. She also had no qualms about tearing off Father Murphy's arm.

Alice electrajotted Ian daily. She admitted that she really missed him. At first, Susie Q didn't seem to mind Ian's old lover being in contact with him so frequently. After a while, she began to feel more troubled when Alice and Ian spent hours on their electrajots chatting. She wondered if pangs of jealousy were stirring again, but she decided not to tell Ian.

One night she was rather quiet and seemed down. Ian tackled her about her unencouraging and offhand responses to his small talk. He also asked her about the frown which marred her lovely face. She refused to comment. Ian carried on trying to see what was wrong.

"Are you alright, Susie Q?"

"I'm fine."

"Are you sure? You seem troubled."

"There's nothing the matter with me!"

"Then why are you giving me the cold shoulder?"

"Don't talk to me. Leave me alone. There's nothing wrong with *me*!"

Ian thought Susie was becoming more and more like a real woman. He wondered why her demeanour was changing. On the bright side, they had excellent news from Tosser and Rita. They sent an rMail (as a part of a round robin to lots of friends and family members), telling them that Tosser was now Mr. Loza and that Rita was his lawfully wedded wife.

John Bobin

They had eloped to Gretna Green. They had paid two people, who were strangers off the street, to be witnesses, and they were married quickly. There were only five people present at the ceremony: the registrar, the bride and groom, and the witnesses. They had spent two days in Gretna Green before going back to Broadstairs. Ian electrajotted Tosser to congratulate him and his new wife.

He waited until Susie Q was on charge before he did so.

"Hi Tosser, you dark horse! We both hope that you will be really happy."

"Thanks very much buddy. How is Susie Q?"

"She's a bit moody, to tell you the truth. She seems quite down."

"Hmmm, that's not good. Keep a close watch on her, and if you need me to check her out let me know. I could come to you, so I can give her the once over."

"That's kind of you. You're more than welcome to stay with us, and maybe Rita would come too? It would be great to see you both – Mr. Loza!"

Tosser and Ian both laughed, and they disconnected the call almost simultaneously.

Susie Q was standing in the doorway:

"So, I'm moody and down. It's not surprising when you spend so much time billing and cooing on the electrajot with your real love. I'm just not good enough. You obviously want a natural woman not a poor downtrodden machine."

"Susie Q, my angel, you certainly couldn't ever be described as downtrodden."

"I suppose you think you're funny! You're always telling such stupid jokes. Don't you know that people are sick of them? No wonder your wife got fed up with you. Your jokes are about as funny as a smelly floater in a toilet bowl. You're the most annoying, pedantic man in the world. You are as boring as Beryl always told you."

Susie Q was shouting at the top of her voice, and her face was a rich beetroot colour. She was stamping her feet like an outraged bull, and she slapped his face hard. She turned on her heel, and ran out of the room, slamming the door as she did so. Ian

I'm Back!

took a deep breath and restrained himself from chasing after her.

'It's a good thing that one of us can control their emotions,' he thought.

It hit him like a ton of bricks when he realised just what he had thought.

His electrajot pinged. His chosen ringtone was a pinging, escalating one, and by the time he'd answered it was deafeningly loud. He could see that it was Alice contacting him, and he was glad that it was she. Alice was always so calm and collected, and Ian always found a lot of pleasure in conversing with her. Alice started their conversation the way she always did:

"Hallo young Ian, are you still about twenty years younger than I?"

"At the moment, I feel about twenty years older than you and way past my deselection date. Susie Q is up to her old tricks again. She's cold and unfriendly a lot of the time, and just now she was in a blazing fury. It was only because I was asking her how she was. She belted me in the face, and I think I'm going to be black and blue later."

"Poor Ian, I wish I were there with you. I'd cuddle you and give you a big kiss. I still love you, and I always will."

Susie Q burst into the room. Ian had put the electrajot on speaker, in error. It was easy to do that by mistake. She was shrieking, and her words were peppered with one coarse but oft repeated swear word. This word was intermittently sprayed like acid into Ian's face. She was frothing at the mouth with fury. Her face was an even deeper shade of the aforementioned vegetable.

This is what she yelled at Ian (omitting the invective, in case your mother, or sister ever reads this tale. That's even though Susie Q seemed to know only that one swear word.)

"Ian and f****** Alice, you've let me f****** down. I f****** suspected that you were having a f****** affair a little while ago. Ian couldn't keep his f****** trousers up when you took off your f****** knickers and offered yourself to him on a f****** plate.

Give me that f****** electrajot, and I'll f******put it where it will not tempt you to f****** contact your f****** whore again."

Susie pulled the f****** device from Ian's hand, hurried out of the room, and she threw it down the toilet. She flushed the toilet and rushed back into the living room. For a few seconds she stood with her arms folded. Then she flew at Ian, scratching, biting, and hitting him, over and over again. Ian did what he could to defend himself, but Susie Q was much too strong to restrain.

He tried to put his arms round her, but she suddenly went as limp as a used dish cloth. She was totally silent, and to his horror, noxious grey matter oozed out of her eyes, mouth, and ears. He laid her gently on a sofa and reached for his immersephone to call Tosser. He answered almost immediately. It was as if he were waiting for Ian's cry for help

"What's up Ian?"

Ian told Tosser exactly what had occurred, and then he burst into tears. He told Tosser that Susie Q had imagined he was having an affair with Alice. Tosser said that jealousy had no logical sensibility. Ian told Tosser that he was convinced that Susie Q had reached the end of the road. He hoped that Tosser could breathe some life back into her form, even though he knew (being an acknowledged and practiced pedant), that the kiss of life wouldn't work on a robot.

"Rita and I will be with you as fast as we possibly can. I'll contact Mike to ask him if he can come as well. I can't think of anything I could do that would really help. He's a first-class robotics expert, and he may be able to suggest a remedy which I haven't thought of. Two heads are better than one. Where's Susie Q?"

"She's on the sofa, and she's totally inert."

"Don't try to move her. Stand fast, and we will be there with you soon."

"Thank you so much Tosser."

Ian broke the connection. In Broadstairs, Tosser contacted Mike. He was now

I'm Back!

living in Branscombe with Emma Bobby, who had left the police. Mike had bought a large property near the picturesque bay, with its famous green cliffs and shingle beach.

"To be honest, Tosser, I'm not at all hopeful. Prepare for the worst. Ian may well need to get more personal support at home. I'll get hold of Alice quickly and see if she'll help."

Mike rang off smartly. He was soon talking to Alice, using his red hot electrajot.

"Susie Q is in serious trouble. She's completely lifeless and it's most likely that she won't recover. Ian will need your support. Can you go to Southend straightaway?" I'll be there soon, and so will Rita and Tosser. I'm hoping Tosser and I will be able to suggest something magic."

Alice told him that she would be in Essex as soon as she possibly could.

Chapter 52

Tosser, Rita, Mike and Alice all arrived back in Southend the day after Susie Q collapsed. Ian was uncomfortably aware that she had suffered from a severe robotic breakdown. Alice was quietly solicitous. She always was at troubled times. Rita also did what she could to help look after Ian, who was totally bereft. Under other circumstances Ian would be asking himself if B reft is what comes after A reft.

Tosser and Mike got to grips with the lifeless Susie Q immediately. They talked over various suggestions about how to revive Susie Q, but one by one they dismissed the potential solutions as unworkable. They also contacted the WRO, and Hiram arranged for them to have special access to their databases about robotics problems. He also put them back in touch with Adam Thurley. Adam wondered what would happen if they used a temporary bypass of the MA.

"That's really our final hope. It might revive her for a short period. That would probably be the best thing that could happen. The more likely result would be that nothing happened at all, and that Susie Q would never again wake up."

He explained to them exactly what they had to do, and he also sent them a step by step guide via rMail. Tosser and Mike each read through the information sent to them by Adam, and they agreed that the procedure would be relatively easy to master. They were nervous, but they knew that they had no choice.

"It's now or never. Let's go for it Tosser."

"I agree, but we should tell Ian what is happening. He'll want to be there if she awakens, even for a short period."

I'm Back!

Tosser went to fetch Ian. He came back still explaining to Ian what they would do, as they were entering the living room.

"It's all Greek to me, Tosser. I trust you both, and I know that you'll do everything you can."

Mike had prepared Susie Q by opening her inspection plate. He had also been pressing several buttons in a controlled sequence as described by Adam Thurley. By so doing he had exposed parts of her insides which had not seen the light of day, since she had the MA implanted. Mike asked Ian for permission to continue.

"Please do your best."

Mike moved various wires to one side and took out a tiny plug from her MA, before inserting it into another technical component.

"That's it, chaps. We can put Susie's bits and pieces back together now. It really is in the laps of the gods."

It seemed to be almost gory, looking at Susie Q with wires and sockets and a disconnected MA. Mike closed Susie Q's insides and finished by closing the inspection panel. He also pressed the button to do up her blouse automatically. He looked directly at Ian.

" Use the normal wake words, Ian. Fingers crossed."

"Wake up Little Susie, Wake up."

Susie Q's eyelids flickered two or three times, and she said:

" I hope you and Alice will be happy. Remember me!"

She breathed a last deep sigh. Following that, she went back to sleep for the final time. Ian started to cry uncontrollably. Alice, guessing what had happened, came into the room, and sat next to him. He reached for her hand, and she stroked it gently. She sat with him quietly for a long while. Then she raised his chin with her hands and looked into his eyes.

"My darling Ian, will you let me stay with you. I'm happy to be with you for as long as you want me around. I know I'm not your Susie Q, but I still love you and want to support you as a good friend."

Ian smiled, rather feebly, and he nodded.

"Yes please, Alice. That would help me."

Chapter 53

The WRO still continued to work on AR projects. However, Hiram had put a complete block on anything to do with DNA injections for robots. He said that foolish notion had caused far too much trouble already. He told his directors that the Susie Q trial (jointly funded by them and the UK government), had almost endangered the future of the WRO. It had also cost an enormous amount in compensation payments. Furthermore, the experiment had caused too much grief for anything like that to ever be considered again.

Eddie Biggs and Sally Forth tied the matrimonial knot at a small church in Happisburgh, several months after Susie Q expired. Tosser Loza was the best man. His wife, Rita, was the matron of honour. Mike, Emma, Ian, and Alice also helped to celebrate their wedding. Eeeny, Meeny, Miny and Moe were invited too, but they had to stay in the church yard. This was much to Eddie's disgust.

He had roared:

"If people can have bridesmaids and pages, why can't they have bridedogs?"

Ian and Alice became much closer over the eighteen months or so after the Biggs/Forth wedding. Alice always remembered Susie Q's last words.

" I hope you and Alice will be happy. Remember me!"

She thought that her and Ian were both as happy as they could be together. Strange circumstances had brought them together again. On her 47th birthday, she sat Ian down and said she needed advice on a serious subject.

"If I don't elect for AR, in only three years we'll have to part forever."

This gave Ian cause for great concern. He had become used to Alice being around. He knew he was gradually becoming more and more dependent on her. He loved her gentle nature and her sweet kindness. Alice tried to speak and then stopped.

She resumed:

"I'm seriously thinking of asking the WRO to let be me artificially reincarnated. I might even be younger than you after AR! You seem to have been fine, in spite of all the difficulties we had with poor Susie Q. Even when you were on the run you looked as if you were in fine fettle."

Ian had been having regular check-ups from the WRO. These were initially every month and then at increasing intervals. They had taken place ever since Susie Q's demise. The WRO had finally given him a clean bill of health. This was only a few weeks prior to Alice's suggestion that she should also undergo AR.

"Alice, are you sure you want to do this? Don't forget that I had some big problems at first."

"Yes, but Mike told me that the WRO are much more on top of things now. He says AR is very safe, and he thinks it'll be used frequently in the future."

Ian put his arms round Alice, and she laid her head on his chest.

"I'll contact Hiram Prendergast tomorrow. I think he owes me another favour."

Ian was as good as his word. Hiram agreed to let Alice be treated to AR, free of charge. The operation was completed successfully, two weeks after Ian had asked for the WRO's help. Alice was reincarnated in a younger body. The taking body and its attractive face were very acceptable.

Alice and he had really made a success of their new relationship, and they had been sleeping together for some time before her AR. With her new body, she was even more lithe and agile, and Ian loved the physical side of their relationship. He had already told her that he was in love with her again, about a year after Susie Q died. When he did that, Alice's heart had leapt for joy. She had repeated that she had never stopped loving him. Two years to the day after her AR, Ian got down on one knee and asked her to marry him.

"About time too! Let me think…OK, Let's get together."

They decided to copy Tosser and Rita, and they did the deed in Gretna Green. When they came back, they had a small party with Tosser, Rita, Eddie, Sally, Mike, and Emma as their guests.

Ian had been drinking all afternoon. He raised yet another glass to his lips at the party. Eddie had brought lots of his Revenge Ale, and by now they were all more than comfortably sozzled. Ian found himself in a cosy corner talking to Sally. Ian had liked her the minute he had met her, and he was pleased that she and Eddie had decided to get married. She was three sheets to the wind, after having imbibed rather too much of Eddie's strong home brew. Consequently, she was chatting to Ian more openly than she ever had done before.

He knew that Sally's former surname was Forth. She had been a primary school teacher, and all the children loved her. She was now prematurely retired, and Ian thought that looking after Eddie would be more than a full-time job. She was a petite, dark haired beauty with a great sense of humour. Ian told her she looked like Pauline Collins. She said she had no idea who that was. He started to tell her about an actress from many years ago, but Sally wanted to talk about Eddie. She told Ian that she was the only woman who had ever been able to control Eddie Biggs, with the possible exception of Rita. She said that when Eddie started to become extra rambunctious, she would just say:

"Calm down, Biggsy. You're becoming more like Brian Blessed every day.'"

Apparently, the first time she said it, he countered:

"And who the hell is Brian Blessed? Never heard of 'im!"

She chuckled when she told Ian that Eddie had untruthfully denied all knowledge of Brian Blessed. She said that she had used her electrajot to search for Brian Blessed.

There were many mentions of him on the Solar System Web, ranging from his early acting role as Fancy Smith in the television programme Z-Cars, in the 1960's and 70's, to his exploits in climbing Mount Everest. She had showed Eddie that Brian Blessed was in lots of films, back in the day, and he had also made many TV appearances.

According to the Solar System Web, he also maintained that he was the oldest man to reach the North Pole. There were several old clips of Brian, just being his larger than life self. Eddie had watched these appreciatively.

She recalled that he had said:

"He's pretty loud. However, I think I'm louder than he is. Anyway, I approve of his delicate and restrained manner."

Sally told Ian that she had given Eddie a playful slap on his cheek. Eddie had given her a return playful pat on her posterior. Ian, like Sally, was under the affluence of incahol, and he couldn't help taking a peek at the said rear end. He thought that it was nicely rounded, and he almost gave it a little friendly pinch. He just stopped himself in time. Sally confided to Ian that she had over-balanced when she slapped Eddie.

"One thing led to the other! We'd known each other for quite some time by then. I knew all about Rita and Eddie having been an item, but I wasn't fazed by their previous close relationship. I told Eddie that he would never need to consult Rita about our relationship ending. I told him he was stuck with me. Bless him, he just said that he wouldn't dare to argue with an ex-schoolteacher.

I said to him, I'm into something good! We're terrific together, and you can count on me being around forever.' Eddie just smiled and stroked his beard. I gave him a hefty kick on his shin. He asked me: 'What's that for, you little minx?' I said: 'That's for being too loud. Tone it down.' The cheeky sod had the cheek to say: 'I bet you wouldn't say that to Blessed Brian Blessed' I pointed out that I'd have a hard job. I reminded him that poor old Brian shuffled off his mortal coil years ago."

Ian knew from Eddie that Sally had been married before. It seemed that her ex-

I'm Back!

husband, Joe Forth, wasn't a bad chap. Rita had told Alice that they just had nothing in common. He liked to be in his garage, tinkering with old motorcycles, of which he had eight. He loved nothing better than getting greasy and dirty, whilst playing with the real loves of his life. He was proud of his Harley Davidson collection.

Sally, on the other hand, liked opera, the theatre and literature. Most of her spare time was spent on her electrajot, accessing classic acting performances and re-reading Charles Dickens novels. She liked many authors, but he was her top favourite of all time. Ian wondered if Eddie would ever be able to understand Sally's pet interests. (Strangely, although Eddie was so bluff and hearty, he later came to like many of the same cultural things in which Sally delighted.) Sally and Joe had parted amicably, and until she married Eddie, she couldn't be bothered to change her surname.

Ian remembered that Alice had told him that Eddie teased Sally mercilessly, about her unusual surname. She mentioned that he would say things like: 'How's my little Forth Bridge?' and: 'If you're my fourth, roll on my fifth. I wonder when I will meet her. On the other hand, or on the fourth hand, there must have been three hands before that!'

Ian had observed that Eddie's jokes were as bad as his were.

Sally was still drunkenly spilling the beans about her relationship with Eddie.

"What Eddie didn't admit to, until just before he popped the question, was that he had only been really, madly in love before with three women. He said that as he was equally, or even more in love with me, I was…the fourth. He roared with laughter at this unfortunate coincidence. I have to admit that in the end, I was glad to relinquish my ridiculous surname when I married Biggsy. Mind you, I was fully aware that more teasing was on the way. The morning after we got married, Eddie woke me up by giving me a big sloppy kiss. He grinned and said: 'How's my Little Biggsy?' I don't mind that nickname. He now calls me his LB."

Ian loved listening to Sally, as she was clearly a smitten kitten. She appeared to adore Eddie, almost as much as Ian realised he now loved Alice. At that point, an inebriated Rita gave him a dig in the ribs, and reminded him:

"You promised to say a few words about our escapades. You should also sing the praises of your new wife, Ian. Get it on!"

Ian had completely forgotten that he had been roped into making a speech, as he was the man who had brought them all together. He thought, rather sadly, that the other person was poor Susie Q. (He refused of think of her as a machine.) He had arranged to have Susie Q buried at a green cemetery called Pastures New. He had paid for a headstone, which simply bore the words: 'Susie Q – Gone but never forgotten. RIP.'

Pastures New was a small five-acre site, near a wooded area which backed onto the field in which the graves were dug. Only tiny headstones were allowed, and the borders of the field were planted with flowers. These included bluebells, dog violets, cow parsley and purple orchids. At certain times of the year the distinctive smell of wild garlic pervaded the air, and its white flowers grew profusely.

Although they had been seeded or planted deliberately, all the 'wild' flowers soon took over and people forgot that they were there in the first place by human intervention. The site for Pastures New was not far from Happisburgh. It was Eddie Biggs who had suggested that Susie Q should be buried there. He and Ian had been having a drink or three of a new ale brewed by Eddie, and Ian had become tearful and over-emotional.

They were seated in Eddie's back garden when he had asked Ian where Susie Q was. Ian had to admit that she was still standing in the corner of his lounge. He said that her continued presence brought back floods of mixed memories. This happened every time he entered the room. Eddie managed to convince Ian that to keep her thus was not very respectful. Furthermore, he proffered the opinion that it wasn't fair to Alice to keep his former robot lover in their main living room. He did this very gently

I'm Back!

and politely, using his rarely heard quiet voice. Ian had talked it over with Alice when he got back to Southend. They had by now sold Ian's condenselow in Southwold after deciding to stay in Essex. Alice's old house was looking wonderful, having been extended and totally redecorated.

When he had broached the delicate subject of burying Susie Q near Happisburgh Alice had said:

"It must be your decision, my dear. Susie Q will always be in your heart and you have good memories I'm sure. I know that I'm only a poor substitute."

Ian had caressed her and told her that she was his best and last wife, as well as being his first love. Her resigned attitude had made his mind up, and shortly after that he had asked Eddie to make the necessary arrangements with the owner of Pastures New. Ian suddenly became aware of his thoughts drifting away from the post wedding celebrations. He shook his head, to clear away this reverie, and he tinkled a spoon on his glass in time honoured tradition.

"Ladies and gentlemen. I am truly chuffed, I mean privileged, to have such wonderful friends. It's a great pleasure to have all of you here. I feel that I must say a few words about our absent friend, Susie Q. I know that my relationship with her was ill-advised, but I couldn't help myself.

When we ran away, we really didn't know what we were letting ourselves in for. We have all seen the best of Susie Q, and also the worst. The best was the real her. The worst was down to the WRO injecting human DNA into her brain. She couldn't help her temperamental outbursts and her violence. To put it simply, I loved her. She loved me, in her own way. Let's raise a glass to Susie Q, may she rust in peace!"

There was an awkward silence. Then Eddie said:

"Bravo. Susie Q tried to make jokes, and some of them were as bad as that one!"

They all laughed heartily. Ian was mindful that he still hadn't toasted his bride.

"We've had some crazy times, some big problems and a whole lot of emotional upset. We came through those awful times. The best thing for us was that we all became remarkably close friends. The best thing for me personally, after Susie Q left us for good, was the rekindling of the love between Alice and me. All's well that ends well. Let's raise a toast to Alice too! She's my wonderful darling. I love her very much. To my lovely bride, my darling Alice!"

A toast was raised, as requested.

Eddie started to sing:

"For they are jolly good fellows…"

The song was completed in jovial fashion, with lots of kissing and hugging, but not in the back row. Ian pondered over the title of the song. He made an inward joke. He decided it was about a flower:

"Freesia a jolly good fellow,

freesia jolly good fellow,

freesia jolly good fellow,

and so, say all of us!"

The End

I'm Back!

Epilogue

Ian had a surprise call one day, a few weeks after the celebratory party. A ditzy voice announced herself, one fine morning, as Honey Blonde. At first he thought it might be Rita or another lady friend, playing a trick on him. Honey managed to convince him that it was really she.

"Ian, I want to make an offer to you that you'll probably be delighted to accept."

Ian had a warm feeling as he remembered Honey's most famous assets.

"Are you still there?"

"Yes, I think we may've got cut off for a couple of seconds."

Ian felt bad about lying to a national treasure, but he knew he couldn't tell her the real reason why he had momentarily lost concentration.

"Paul and I heard from our sources that your new wife, Alice underwent a successful AR operation. We ran several pieces when you and Susie Q were on the run and another when you were exonerated. Our producer suggested that we should do a further update on our show. We thought it would be nice to show our viewers how happy you and Alice are now. We could pay you £100,000 for a five-minute interview. What do you think?"

Ian was unsure about this.

"I've got your number now, as it was displayed on my electrajot. May I think it over, discuss it with Alice, and get back to you?"

Honey simpered winfully, and she said:

"Yes – Get back. Bye, bye, bye!"

Ian could never get used to the way that people often said 'Bye' too many times when they finished electrajot or immersephone calls. He decided he would forgive Honey. He hoped he might even get a cuddle in the studio.

When he mentioned the proposed interview to Alice, he did so nonchalantly.

"By the way, I had a call from Honey Blonde when you were on the beach earlier today."

"You're always joking. If you think I believe that you've got another think coming. You should be so lucky!"

"Oh yes. I should be so lucky, and I really was. She wants us to do a short interview on her programme with Paul Somebody. And they'll pay us £100,000."

"Good golly. I hope you said yes!"

"We don't need the money. I thought you might object, as they want to recap the story about Susie Q. They also want to mention your AR. Honey said they would like to assure the viewers that we are really happy."

"Do it! If they want me there, that'd be fine. I could keep an eye on you, to make sure you don't make a fool of yourself with Honey. Let's give the money to charity."

Ian electrajotted Honey, and she confirmed that the interview would be held in their main studio in London. She arranged for an executive aerobus to pick up Ian and Alice. On the day of the live interview, their aerobus landed on an aPad near the remains of Southend pier. A smart, uniformed pilot came to their house to collect them. The journey was not that pleasant as there was a high wind and it was raining. When they landed on top of WBC house, near St. Paul's Cathedral, they were met by Honey and Paul. A camera crew filmed their arrival. Honey tucked her arm under Ian's and her left boob was crushed against him. He pretended that he had not noticed.

Alice looked at him winked and mouthed:

"Tut, tut!"

Paul put his arms round Alice, and he gave her a kiss on each cheek. Ian looked

I'm Back!

at her, and he winked and mouthed back:

"Tut, tut!"

They were taken to a dressing room. They were given the choice of staying in their travelling clothes or using outfits from a long rack of expensive dresses and suits. They both plumped for using the new kit, and the lady in charge of the dressing room told them that the clothes they had chosen were theirs to keep. A young make up girl spruced them up, and she dusted some powder on their cheeks. A runner appeared, and he took them to the side of the studio where filming was to take place, just as Honey was saying:

"I'm sure you'll remember the story of Ian Tudeep, who was the world's first Artificial Reincarnation patient. He had some initial problems, but he's doing very well. He left Geneva with a robot called Susie Q. Susie Q had been looking after him for an extended period in Geneva, at the headquarters of the World Reincarnation Organisation, which is also known as the WRO.

There was an administrative mix up, and we ran stories about the WRO and the police looking for them. It was thought at the time that Mr. Tudeep had absconded and stolen Susie Q, who was said to have been worth £10,000,000. They had lots of upsets and had to evade capture by moving around England. During that time Ian and Susie Q fell in love. Let's have an aah!"

The audience, who had been primed by a good warm-up man, duly complied with Honey's request.

"We later learned that the WRO and our police had officially withdrawn any allegations of wrongdoing by either Ian Tudeep or Susie Q. They were helped by various good friends during their hour of need. One of them is a lady called Alice, who is now his wife. Another aah – Do it again!"

The tame audience said aah.

"Ian and Alice are here tonight. Let's give them a warm welcome!"

The audience went mad. Ian and Alice walked on set. Ian was welcomed by Honey, and Alice was welcomed by Paul. They then swapped roles. Ian much preferred cuddling Honey to shaking hands with Paul. Conversely, Alice preferred cuddling Paul to being welcomed by Honey. The interview itself was short. Honey and Paul did their usual let's interrupt each other act, and they covered all the main points.

Honey asked Alice about her AR operation and congratulated her about how well she was looking. Alice said a few words about the excellent treatment she had received from the WRO.

Paul then turned to Ian and said:

"Ian, you have a lovely wife who's now some years younger than you, and very lovely, might I say. Aren't you worried that she might run off with a new man friend, or even a gentleman robot?"

"She always tells me that she's loved me since she was fifteen. I hope I make her happy."

Alice interjected:

"I've never been so much in love. It's probably because I'm younger than I was a little while ago."

She was embarrassed, but the audience lapped up every minute of their appearance on the show. Near to the end of the piece, Honey leaned towards Ian, and he tried not to stare too much at her embonpoint.

"Here's a delicate question, Ian. I know that you and Alice have been happy together for some time. But, whatever happened to Susie Q?"

Ian was glad that she had warned him that she would be asking this question.

"Susie Q and I were very fond of each other. To be honest I loved her deeply, and she did her best to respond, but there were some problems. There were technical issues. It's very hard for a robot to feel real emotions. After a while they took their toll, and even though expert assistance was rendered by some friends and the WRO, Susie

I'm Back!

Q died."

The audience said aah again, without even being prompted. Ian felt tearful as he continued:

"She's at peace now, in a private and beautiful green cemetery. Alice and I treasure her memory, but Alice was my very first love at school. I'm very lucky to be married to her."

Paul turned to Alice:

"Alice, how did you feel about helping Ian, at a time when he was in love with Susie Q?"

"I carried a torch for Ian from the time we broke up when we were both fifteen. When he entered my life again, with a robot lover, I had very mixed feelings. However, he was still my favourite man."

Paul looked sad and said:

"What, are you saying he was even better than me?"

"Now, now Paul, you know that's a trick question. Whatever I said would be the wrong thing. Ian and Susie Q had serious difficulties when she was…ill. When Susie Q died, he was inconsolable. Over time, I hope I helped him to rebuild his life. I love him now even more than I did when we were young."

The camera showed a picture of Susie Q's grave. Honey and Paul thanked Ian and Alice for appearing, and they left the set. A few days later, the promised £100,000 was transferred to their bank account. They decided to donate the money to a charity which Eddie and Rita had set up. He had decided to open another dog home. It helped owners of real dogs, (not dogbots), who had been unable to cope with their dog's behavioural problems. The dogs were initially housed in clean and spacious kennels in Eddie's back-garden. They were retrained and rehomed by their charity which was called 'It's a Dog's Life.'

About the Author

John Bobin describes himself as an accidental author. His father, paternal grandfather and maternal great-grandfather were all writers. He has written four previous books,

- Bark Staving Ronkers (2006)

- The Royal Worms (2015)

- When the pongs go ping (2016)

- In the Autumn of my Madness (2018)

He lives in Rayleigh, Essex. He is a keen bass guitarist and has been playing in various bands since 1961.

Printed in Poland
by Amazon Fulfillment
Poland Sp. z o.o., Wrocław